Taken by the Night

A.P. Jennings

ISBN: 9781095476819

DEDICATION

To my friends and family, thank you for believing in
me.

PROLOGUE

To Whom It May Concern,

Remember when you were young and had your parents check under your bed for monsters? I remember. Believe it or not, I wish I could go back to that time! Our imaginations ran wild at that age. My immature mind misinterpreted shadows of my dollhouse with a tower of books teetering at the top as a hideous monster just waiting for me to pull the blanket from my head. The accumulation of junk under my bed only added to the fear that I'd see two bulging red eyes and sharp teeth. I always called my dad in to verify that I was safe to sleep. In our little town, the monsters are real. We aren't dreaming. It isn't just paranoia. It isn't something we've seen out of the corner of our eyes, either. Those shadows we think follow us in the forest are real. The sharp teeth we see in the darkness patiently wait for us to lower our guard. There's no one checking under our beds for us, though. This is our story. I hope

A.P. JENNINGS

you remember when you consider telling your young sibling a

spooky tale just to get your giggles in. Ask yourself: what's behind

it all?

Welcome to our worst nightmare.

Best Wishes,

Molly Martin

.

Chapter One

"Titan Fake Pass Right, on one, on one! Ready--"

"Break!" The eleven boys' collective voice rang out above the crowd as they broke from the gathering. Leading them was Wyatt Richards, a junior quarterback that no one in the small town of Lyonside knew, apart from his own parents and a few friends. He shot the other team's nose guard a cocky grin accompanied by a wink as he kissed the air in front of him provocatively. Wyatt couldn't hear over the booming crowd surrounding them, but he could read the lips of the player as he responded cruelly. Wyatt didn't particularly care what people thought of him, especially the

5

other teams. He played the sport to prove to himself that he could do it. The trash talk was a bonus, and it was his personal favorite part about game day. It was fun to elevate people's blood pressure, and in the game of football, it held a strategic advantage. If you get the opposing team mad enough, they can't focus. He recalled attempting to explain this to one of his coaches who didn't take too kindly to Wyatt's constant barrage of insults towards linebackers who could easily take his head off if they tried.

The fans among the bleachers let out an eruption of cheers as banners flew above their heads, painted in black and decorated in red glitter forming the words: *Go Lions!*

"The Lyonside Lions," Wyatt once bantered to his head coach at a particularly hot practice. "Kind of redundant, huh? Surely they could have come up with something better than that!"

Twenty push-ups and two sets of sprints later, he learned it was better not to point out the trivial things.

"Hike!"

The game was on, even as the fierce thunder heard minutes earlier finally delivered a soaking and steady rain from the dark skies. Wyatt had to yell over the constant pelting of the rain drops on helmets to signal his center to snap the ball to him. As soon as his hands met the wet leather, Wyatt turned and dug his cleat into the soft muck and grass as the sound of pads and helmets colliding roared through the cold November night air. He faked a toss to number twenty-four, Carlos Rodriguez, the team's tailback. Nicknamed "Eight-Ball" for his ability to bounce tacklers like a billiards ball gliding for the corner pocket, his hands were much safer than Wyatt's when it came to who could get the ball out farther. However, the other team had locked in on Carlos all night.

Time slowed as Wyatt backed up into the pocket his blockers had made. Wyatt was more of a scrambler. His ability to weave in and out of narrow gaps far surpassed his skill in throwing. He sidestepped a fallen blur of yellow, a defensive lineman who had dove at his feet, forcing Wyatt to scurry over to the right side to find an open receiver in the end zone. The inside linebacker was relentless, chasing him in and out of the pocket, clearly motivated by Wyatt's fat joke about his mother in the first half.

Wyatt struggled to lock in on a target. Every moment his eyes would settle on the red and black uniform of his teammates, another player covered in yellow and white would intervene in a rather unorthodox manner that clearly qualified as pass interference and deserved a flag. The referees were as useless as they'd come to expect. A trip to the championship was something that he was not going to lose because of missed calls, so Wyatt was determined to put some dirt in the other team's eyes.

He bounded backwards; his footwork was as graceful as a ballerina to avoid the blitzing linebackers. They pounced towards him, the bright yellow uniform and helmet resembling a swarm of bees, and Wyatt had just kicked the nest. He nimbly tucked the ball underneath his left arm, allowing himself to grasp one of his opponent's face masks with his right hand and yank him downwards as he spun and rushed along the left side of the field.

There was Wyatt's target. The barely six-foot-tall backup receiver, sophomore Porter Bancroft Jenkins, or P. B. n' J. as everyone called him. He was wide open in the far-right corner of the end zone with his hands poised in front of his eye slot. This was it. If Wyatt successfully threw this pass into his clutches, the town would move on in the playoffs, then win the State Championship.

Wyatt knew he had to get the ball out quickly. His blockers were already holding off the defense for much longer than was usually expected, especially in the slippery conditions that they were playing in. However, Wyatt couldn't concentrate. He had caught sight of something in the woods, just beyond his receiver on the other side of a chain-linked fence that separated the field from the forest beyond. Just a glimpse of something that caused him to double back in shock. He was only on the ten-yard line, which meant he was a mere twenty yards from the fence. He couldn't pull his gaze away, as the eyes of what he saw hypnotized him.

Just two red dots painted onto a silhouette. They lacked an iris or a pupil as they glowed in the darkness. The form of whatever owned these eyes seemed an inky black, its skin darker than the night surrounding it. Below it stretched the most hideously eerie grin he had ever seen, piled with rows of what seemed to be sharp, unclean teeth. It created an otherworldly grin. There was something about the pouring rain that blurred his vision just enough to make him hesitate and consider if what he saw was real.

The defensive lineman blind-sided him, sending Wyatt flying backwards, his back splashing against the cold, muddy ground. His mind began spiraling back to reality. His helmet flew off his head and hit the ground with a hollow *thunk*. Grass and dirt made its way into his mouthpiece as the collision knocked the ball out of his hands. Cheers erupted from the opposing team's sideline and cleats trampled passed him like a thunderous herd of wild horses. On his hands and knees, out of breath, he could do nothing but think. He knew the game was over, but his mind refused to acknowledge the feeling of loss and regret. He was instead antagonized by one question.

What just happened?

****

Robbie Burnett cursed as he ran through the storm, his lungs on fire and a sick feeling in his stomach. There was an ache in his side that wouldn't cease as his chest pumped out air. He turned down an alley between the doughnut shop and a small inn, his sneakers skidding across the wet gravel as the cold wind and harsh rain stung his face. His left ankle turned awkwardly as he splashed in a puddle, sending him tumbling forward with a sickening smack as he face-planted into the concrete. His nose dripped blood down onto the brim of his mouth. He sat up, breathing heavily as he spit crimson from his lips.

"Gross, Robbie." Jesse Davis said with a look of aversion as he slowed his pace and strolled up to the young man. He clenched the back of the scrawny boy's neck and threw him back down on the cold wet ground. Robbie scooted backwards until he met the outer brick wall of the ice cream shop. Jesse's right foot connected with

Robbie's ankle, resulting in a screech of agony from Robbie. On any other night, this would have brought attention to the boys in the alley, but the entire town was at a high school football game. Robbie was on his own.

"How ya doing, Scarecrow?"

The nickname Scarecrow was earned by being the only teenager in Lyonside that weighed less than a buck-fifty. He was skinny and extremely introverted, keeping his thoughts to himself as others, such as Jesse, expressed themselves. Jesse outweighed him two to one, which made sense that he would be captain of their high school wrestling team. Robbie had been attempting to make friends at the football game that night, and that's when he bumped into Jesse's girlfriend, Betty Mulburrow. She was pretty and way out of his league. He didn't care, though. He took his shot at a date with her. She hadn't had the chance to answer him before he saw the behemoth of a boy steaming towards him. Robbie fled into town, and that's when he entered the alley.

"Jesse, I swear…" He slurred through his bloody mouth. "I didn't touch Betty…"

Robbie smiled wickedly.

"…but I'm sure she would rather me than you."

The giant of a teenager grew red in the face. "She's too good for you!"

Robbie stared into the bully's eyes, wanting him to see the cocky grin he sported. Jesse kicked him again, sending Robbie sprawling to the ground.

As he sat up again, he caught a glimpse of someone standing at the end of the alleyway. From what Robbie's watering eyes could make out, the figure was a male around his age with tall brown hair. He was in a t-shirt, jeans, and a pair of clean, bright red sneakers. The person seemed anxious as their eyes locked. Robbie was screaming inside, wanting whoever it was to help him take Jesse down. He almost yelled out to him, but the boy sprinted away.

Who would leave a person being beaten in an alleyway?!?
Coward!

Robbie couldn't get the boys expression out of his mind, though. He looked terrified, like he was being chased by someone.

His thought process was interrupted by a vicious kick to the lower abdomen from Jesse, causing Robbie to fall over on his side in pain. Jesse's big boot splashing in the puddle only added insult to injury. Robbie laid there, his legs curled up and his arms wrapped around his stomach as a protective mechanism. He was still and silent as he noticed a crow landing on the big blue dumpster on the other side of the alleyway. He wasn't afraid, though. He just wanted the big loser to think he was.

"You got anything to say, freak?"

Robbie kicked his leg out towards Jesse's knee, sending the kid stumbling backwards. The crow on the dumpster cawed, singing a nerve-wracking melody as Robbie gained the upper hand.

Robbie shot up like a rocket, his slender limbs reaching out and grabbing Jesse's hair. He slammed the boy's head into the brick wall, accompanied by another shriek from the black bird that meshed with Jesse's agonizing yell.

"Better watch that bum knee, Jess!"

He kicked Jesse behind his leg as the boy cried out in pain. Robbie heard the bird call once again.

Robbie began laughing, finding humor in the animal cawing. It felt almost as if it was rooting him on.

He felt his foot impact Jesse's side, over and over until he ran out of breath. He looked up for the bird's approval again, but the crow was gone.

The bird cawed once more from down the alleyway. Robbie snapped his head around as a crooked smile began to form in the left corner of his mouth, but it stopped as his eyes caught a glimpse of something horrifying.

A black figure stood at the other end of the alley. It appeared to be the shadow of a tall man, but it was illuminated by the light of a streetlamp behind it. Its beady, red, soulless eyes burrowed into Robbie's. Its smile was repulsive, much too large for its face and filled with grimy, crooked needles for teeth.

Robbie felt a shiver creep down his spine as he blinked.

The figure was gone.

Robbie cocked his head to the side curiously, unsure of what he had seen. He crept forward until he reached the end of the alleyway. He searched the area, but no one was within sight.

He heard Jesse groan from deep within the alley. He knew the boy was hurt, but it hadn't dawned on him that it was his doing.

It was self-defense. He told himself repeatedly. *I had to do it to protect myself!*

It had felt as if he had lost control for those few moments when he was attacking Jesse. He didn't think he had it in himself to do such a thing.

14

TAKEN BY THE NIGHT

Robbie kept repeating the same excuses to himself as he sprinted home, away from Jesse, the bird, and the figure he had seen.

****

Alexandria Egan whispered the poem to herself as she processed the words and the deeper meaning behind the written lines. Edgar Allan Poe, though morbid, was easily her favorite poet. That wasn't really saying much, since he was one of the only poets whose material she had ever read. She wasn't one for symbolic poetry, besides the occasional couplet written in modern English.

She repeated the lines of *"A Dream Within A Dream"* in her mind, searching for its deeper meaning.

She set her book down and looked over the room. Nothing. Not a soul in sight. Of course not. *Why would there be? Who in their right mind would be in a bookstore when there was a football game?*
Oh, yeah. I would. After all, she had volunteered to help the sweet old lady who ran the place. She was nearing seventy, but even age would not stop that woman from seeing the town football team fight its way to the championship. Alex sighed and tucked a strand of her brunette hair behind her left ear. She took a sip of her soda

and looked at the front of the store, which was neatly framed by stacks of used biographies. She blinked. Alex nearly fell out of her chair from what she saw in the store window.

A silhouette pressed against the glass, its red eyes burrowing into hers. As if it could sense her fear and smell the adrenaline that pumped through her veins with each heartbeat, a sickly smile grew on its face from ear-to-ear. Its teeth weren't human. They weren't square or diverse in any way like a human being. They were like a thousand rusty needles aligned chaotically between two thin lips. Alex, still shocked, screamed at the top of her lungs. Her soda slipped from her hand and spewed onto the desk and in her face. She didn't care though, as the adrenaline in her body did its job and caused a fight-or-flight response.

Alexandria climbed under the desk. After smacking her head against the wood top, she quickly huddled into the back corner. She was horrified by those eyes and that smile. She stayed silent until the soda seeped through the cracks in the wood top of the desk and steadily dripped near her crossed legs.

Oh my God! Oh my God!

TAKEN BY THE NIGHT

She began muttering the Lord's prayer frantically to herself, stuttering through and occasionally skipping a few words. She fumbled with her pockets to find her phone and call for help.

Where was it? Where was it? Dear God, the door to the building was unlocked!

The only sound left in the room was her frantic breathing and uncontrolled heartbeat as she listened for the fateful ringing of the front door opening.

Where was it?!?

****

Desmond Martin rushed through the front door, slamming it behind him with his foot as he slung around bags of food and drink from the clearance section of the town's supermarket in his hands. He bumped passed his sister, who was trotting down the hallway, her headphones in and a cup of microwave noodles in her hands.

"Jeez! Where's the fire, moron?" Marcella Martin, who also went by Molly, yelled at her older brother in frustration as she wiped broth from her chin that had spilled. She had dark yellow eyes like him, black curly hair, and full cheeks. She had a reputation around town for a hot temper and a better-than-everyone

17

attitude she sported often and liberally. All were inherited from their mother.

He ignored her as he rushed to his bedroom and pushed the door closed with his back. He had so much weight in his hands, his fingers felt as if they were being cut off by the plastic handles of the bag.

It was coming. Bad things and evil stalked their small community. Things that would rock the sanity of every mind in the town of Lyonside, and he could do nothing to stop it. He didn't know what would happen. He just knew it would be the end of life as he knew it. That's why he was rushing to stockpile as many supplies as possible, just in case he had to book it with his family and get away.

A can of cheap market brand orange-flavored soda dropped from one of the bags, thumping on the carpet. Dez leaned over and picked it up. As he stood, his eyes caught something staring at him through his bedroom window. He knew what it was before his mind could even process what he saw.

The silhouette stared back, its glowing red eyes burrowing into him. The smile stretched wide, as he could only imagine the horrible thoughts that ran through its mind.

TAKEN BY THE NIGHT

He tried to study the figure the best he could, but it's rather difficult to analyze nothing but a shadow, two blood-red eyes, and a repulsively creepy grin. The intensity of his gaze was intended to match that of the creature. They were rivaling animals, challenging one another to look away in a competition of dominance. Dez dared not to blink, for fear of what the --whatever it was-- might do. His eyes watered, causing his vision to go blurry. Despite his best efforts, Dez had to blink to chase the burning sensation away.

In an instant, the creature was gone, leaving nothing but a bewildered Desmond in the cold silence of his bedroom.

****

Derek Hoff watched Wyatt call the play.

He watched him snap the ball.

He watched him scramble for his life.

Then, he watched him fail.

The thud of his helmet hitting the ground could be heard all the way to the sideline, announcing the backup quarterback's failure to those who did not witness it firsthand. The silence of the Lyonside bleachers signified the end of their season. He cupped his face in his hands while still propped up on his crutch. *That screw-up just lost the game!*

In what felt like a blink of the eye, reality set in as the final whistle declared Lyonside had been bested by its rival. As the winning team prepared to leave with far more than it arrived with, the Lions made their way back to the locker room. Heads dropped, hearts dropped even lower, those four points would haunt the small town. It was almost as though their wet cleats were marching in tune with the inescapable truth: "it was four points, it was four points, it was four points".

Even the coach's guidance to remain motivated fell woefully short. After a severe lecture from the coach over keeping their heads held high, Derek had to listen to his teammates' apologies for losing the game. He was the starting quarterback, and he was their leader. After he had broken his leg earlier that season due to an overly ambitious flip on a skateboard, his team had promised they would win the title for him. After a grief-filled hug with a lineman, he went searching for Wyatt, who he found walking in the school parking lot through what had become a light drizzle.

Wyatt had changed from his football uniform into a white t-shirt that had the words SAVE FERRIS in large bold letters, a clear reference to the 1980's film *Ferris Bueller's Day Off*. He wore jeans as well as his signature cherry red high-top sneakers.

20

TAKEN BY THE NIGHT

He had his red headphones on and was holding his muddy pads above his head to ward off the now sprinkling rain from ruining them as best as possible, though he seemed too tired to hurry. His other hand grasped at his wild brown hair that stuck up in the air. After some hobbling, Derek had gotten himself and the cast on his broken leg next to his colleague. They trotted side-by-side through the parking lot for a minute in silence, until Wyatt pushed his headphones around his neck and Derek wondered if he was revving up to have one of his signature moments where he rants about irrelevant topics to avoid his problems.

"Joey told me before the game that Nickelback has just as many good songs as Led Zeppelin. I laughed in his face!" He pointed his finger at the asphalt below them accusingly. "How dare he even compare the two! That's blasphemy! I-it's sacrilege!"

"Wy!" Derek interrupted, calling him by his shortened nickname, as the two finally made it to where Derek's shiny red truck was parked. He could tell his best friend was trying to avoid the responsibility of his failures. Wyatt could be difficult at times. He had been known by the few friends he had to be impulsive, immature, insensitive, and a few other words Derek had been forbidden by his mother to ever say. However, he knew Wyatt better than most. He had been around the guy every day at practice. Derek saw how much harder Wyatt worked for what he wanted; he gave more blood, sweat, and tears than anyone else on the team. He saw how much morality meant to him when he broke up a fight between two of the largest players. Wyatt stressed the role of teamwork, all the while doing so without proving once again the jerk he could be. Derek had long since decided that Wyatt Richards was one of the craziest, yet most logical people he had ever met.

"What?" Wyatt spoke as he turned around and fell back into his monologue about comparing the two rock bands. "Alright, I admit Nickelback is severely underrated, but they are nowhere near the great and almighty Led Zeppelin!"

By then, Derek was frustrated. Finally, with a raised voice, he exploded.

"Oh, for all that is good and holy, please shut up! What happened out there?!? You hit another gear that I've never seen! It was like Michael Vick was out there wearing that number four jersey! Then you froze!"

Wyatt's expression turned blank as he set his bag in the back of the truck. He unzipped it and pulled out a retro style skateboard.

"I'd rather not talk about that. I already won't hear the end of it at school until the day I gradua--"

He stopped and stared over Derek's shoulder. Derek was about to make a cruel yet harmless joke about him not being able to graduate, until he saw his friend's tan face go pale. A gulping noise arose from his throat as his Adam's apple floated then dropped, his eyebrows rose, and his emerald eyes widened. Wyatt was frozen in place, afraid to look away, afraid to talk and too terrified to even move. He suddenly grabbed Derek's crutch and heaved it into the back of the truck. Derek began to fall over but caught himself on the tall back left tire.

"Wy, what the--"

"Shut up Derek, and look!" He grabbed Derek's shoulders, which were a good two inches above his own, and turned him completely around. Derek sat on the tire, most likely putting a dirt smudge on the back of his white shorts. His eyes scanned the lot behind him and into the unlit forest a good football field's length away.

That's when he saw it. A dark silhouette, with nothing but two red dots for eyes and a smile that would haunt his nightmares lay near where the light faded. He couldn't tell...but it seemed like....

It was moving towards them.

It moved slowly, like a wounded person, but he soon realized that this thing was anything but human. It weaved in-between parked cars with intent, its beady, nightmarish eyes locked on the two boys as it scurried closer.

"Good God! What is that?!?" Derek let out, terrified out of his wits and at a complete loss as to what to do.

Wyatt grabbed his arm and swung it around his neck, letting Derek lean on his shoulder for support. Both boys' adrenaline was pumping as Wyatt helped Derek into his truck. He had forgotten in the moment that Derek had restricted motion in his leg, so he just slung his friend's upper body onto the leather seat and into a bag of drive-thru trash. He was shaking in terror as he turned to look where the thing was. He let out an expletive when he saw just how much distance the creature had covered over the short amount of time.

The thing was straight out of a nightmare, that much was evident with its hideous eyes and jagged teeth. It also seemed as if it stood at least ten feet tall, towering over all the cars it past. Still, as it closed the space between it and the two friends, it occurred to them that it was sprinting, its legs pumping in a way similar to a man. It covered half the distance between them in a matter of seconds. As it neared, Wyatt realized its speed was due to its long and slender limbs. It scurried like a spider, its two legs stretching and bending to gain the most distance possible with each movement. This terrorized him even more than before as his nerves began firing off, screaming at him to hurry. He slammed the door and ran around the truck to the passenger side in a panic. He jostled the door handle in a desperate attempt to get inside and escape.

Locked.

"Oh h-holy crap! I don't want to die!" Wyatt let out with a shaky voice. He could hear the thing's quick yet heavy footsteps approaching. Terrifying thoughts raced through his head, detailing what would happen if it caught him.

Derek fumbled with the locking system, his sweaty fingers pressing the button frantically to let his friend inside. He turned to the passenger window.

Wyatt was gone.

For a split second, Derek worried the thing had caught him and dragged the teenage boy away. He peered through the rain of the night and could see that Wyatt was in a sprint down the road into

25

town. The creature followed in pursuit, completely ignoring Derek
and the truck. Derek turned the key, letting the engine roar to life
and igniting the music from the radio. An oldies station that Wyatt
had set it on during the ride to the game was blaring the chorus of
"Stand by Me". He couldn't concentrate with the tune rattling his
speakers, so he slammed his wrist against the button and peered
back up again, only to lose sight of Wyatt and the monster all
together in the distance.

What was that idiot doing?!?

Chapter Two

While his running was originally an effort to escape the horrid creature of the night himself, Wyatt realized that in doing so, he had led it away from the crippled Derek.

How noble and selfless of me, he thought.

His inner boasting was interrupted by the sound of raspy breathing over his shoulder. He dared not turn around. He was still a good distance away from the town's center. Even then, he knew he wouldn't be safe. It was almost 11:00 p.m., well after his little community's bedtime. No one would be out roaming the streets besides maybe the occasional drunk trying to get home from the bar, but they wouldn't be very much help.

His legs were shaking as he ran, already weakened by the football game he had just played not even an hour before. His tight jeans squeezed his legs and groin, restricting his movements exponentially. He didn't think he could go any faster, but he pushed. His thighs were numb, and his lungs felt as if they had burst into flames. He could hear something behind him, even over the sound of his own breathing and the heartbeat that thumped in his ears.

Laughter.

The thing was laughing at him! Like it was some sick game!

He yelled over his shoulder at the nightmare. "I swear if this is a prank, I'm going to kill you! You hear me?!?"

The only response he received was the threatening, ice cold breaths of the creature.

He arrived in civilization, making it to the town's center faster than he ever thought he could run. His chest rose and fell at lightning speed as he glanced around him. His eyes scanned the storefronts for anywhere to hide. Something caught his eye.

A boy around his age lay in an alleyway to his right with Jesse Davis standing over him. Even through the sprinkling rain and dimness of the light in the alley, Wyatt could see the blood dripping from the boy's lips. It was obvious Jesse was giving the boy a beating.

His eyes locked with the boy's, and Wyatt wanted to do something, to intervene and help the kid out.

The laughter had returned. It echoed from around the corner on the road he was recently on. It was getting closer. It was sickening, like an overgrown hyena after it had heard the greatest joke ever told.

Wyatt had decided that his own preservation was best as he fled from the alleyway and continued searching for any sort of sanctuary.

"C'mon, c'mon!" He desperately pleaded with himself in a growl of frustration.

A ray of light beamed from the window of the town bookstore. *Salvation!*

He praised God for the little lonesome town as he sprinted to the building that was sandwiched in between a small family-run clothing store and the parking lot to a grocery mart. For reasons unknown, the town's mayor refused to let chain businesses in. He was an eccentric old man who didn't take to the Richards family's liking.

He grabbed the handle of the glass door and violently swung it open as he ran inside. He heard glass shattering as he stumbled into the building, and a sharp, blood-curdling scream followed. His leg smashed into a stack of books, knocking piles over like giant dominos. As soon as he heard the crash, Wyatt immediately assumed the worst. The creature had shattered the window and was coming after him, no matter where he was. He dove, out of what he thought were the reaches of the charging creature, slid across the clerk's desk, and landed on his back on the other side. His shirt felt sticky with something, and he prayed that it wasn't blood.

All that could be heard was breathing. However, he realized it wasn't his own, as he struggled to regain the ability to inhale. Wyatt leaned up and looked underneath the desk.

A girl sat under the desk with her head in her arms, clearly terrified. He could see her peek through her arms at him after a moment.

"Hey, how you doing?" He spoke, trying to re-inflate his lungs.

She looked at him for a moment, her head picked up, revealing a pair of dark brown eyes.

"Eh," He let out. "Not my type."

TAKEN BY THE NIGHT

She was taken aback by what he said, with a disgusted look on her face. "Excuse me?!?"

"You're excused." Wyatt stood and looked at the aftermath. It looked as if a tornado blew through the store. Books were scattered everywhere, and the door was standing open, its glass shattered.

The girl let out a huff as she crawled from under the wood desk. Wyatt helped her to her feet, then offered her his hand to shake. She recognized Wyatt's tall brown hair and wild eyes from one of her classes. Everyone thought he was crazy.

"My name's Wyatt. Nice to meet you." The boy spoke with a cocky grin, as if he didn't just come crashing in like a bat out of Hell.

"Uh...what?" The girl babbled in genuine confusion.

The sound of a car engine rose just outside, then halted. A few moments later, someone came hobbling through the doorway, his one shoe crunching against the glass particles on the ground. She recognized him as the Lyonside quarterback.

"Wyatt!" Derek blurted out.

Wyatt looked at the girl, then back at Derek. He nonchalantly held out a fist to bump. Derek slapped it away in frustration.

Alex started to grow aggravated. "Can someone *please* explain to me what is going on?!?"

Derek turned to Wyatt. "Did you lose it?!? Is it gone?!?"

The girl threw her hands in the air with a violent scoff. "Lose what?!?"

"The monster!" He couldn't believe the words that came out of his mouth. Wyatt had wandered over to the window in search for the hideous freak of nature as they kept talking.

"You guys saw that thing, too?!?" She asked. "Was it a...monster? Monsters aren't real, though!"

"No, but I'm pretty sure the wiz running down my leg is real." Wyatt commented.

Derek turned to the girl, whose pale skin was glimmering underneath the light of the store. He cleared his throat before speaking. "So, what's your name?"

She eyed him for a second, then smiled slightly. "Alex."

Derek told her the story from the beginning. About how after his friend had spotted the thing, they both attempted to flee. How Wyatt had unintentionally committed a heroic act by distracting it. Derek had driven his truck after them, but the only light he had were his headlights on the dark road. He couldn't find them, until he checked the town center and saw the broken window.

When he finished, she looked astonished. "Are you serious? I saw something like that, too! In that window!" She pointed.

"So *that's* why you were hiding underneath the desk!" Wyatt put his hands on his hips.

She turned her head around, flipping her brunette hair in Derek's face. "Yeah. It was some kind of...shadow...thing." She looked at the ground with a confused expression.

Derek grasped his short black hair, attempting to make sense of the situation before them. "Look, as far as we know, we're the only people to have seen this thing. Maybe...I don't know. We have to go to the police! We can't just keep this thing to ourselves, can we?"

"We have to," Wyatt said. "No one will believe it. As a matter of fact, they may just check all three of us into that mental institution outside of town!" Wyatt leaned against the wall and crossed his legs. "No, can't tell a soul. It'll make a killer campfire story, though!"

The trio stood in silence for what seemed like an eternity. No one wanted to keep talking. It felt unwise to stay on the topic, almost as if discussing the creature would bring it back. Wyatt coughed, breaking the silence as he muttered something about wanting to go home. Derek normally would have teased him in a situation like this. He would have told him not to be a baby. However, Derek felt he was just as shaken. His eyes floated to his friend's face. His skin was still pale, and his hands were shaking. The girl, Alex, shared the same look.

Terror.

Derek turned back towards Alex, pulling out his phone and handing it to her. "Here. Put your contact information in. Maybe we can discuss this further tomorrow if you want."

Wyatt dry-heaved, knowing that Derek had intended to do more with the information than follow up on what had happened that night. He was hitting on her. Derek responded by scratching the back of his head with his middle finger.

Alex handed him back his phone, then the two boys said goodbye and began walking out the door, their shoes crunching on the broken glass. She looked at the glass, wondering how it had shattered. Her eyes focused on the door itself, its frame slightly bent outward. It clearly had smashed against the metal trash can outside when that Wyatt kid had thrown it open. The broken glass shimmered from the moonlight outside.

What am I supposed to do now?

****

The bus bounced along the old dirt road out of town. It moved at a consistent fifty miles an hour as the driver tried not to pop a tire on any random sticks or fallen limbs from the forest along the road. All the while, the football players hollered in victory. The Knights had beaten the Lions, and they were on their way with a straight shot to the championship. The cold, dark night outside the confines of the yellow walls contrasted greatly with the inside. The cab was filled with gossip from cheerleaders and the sounds of disappointed football players being turned down for dates. The air inside the bus was humid and the stench assaulted her nostrils. Chloe Fuller sat alone in the third row on the right side, her short blonde hair falling just above her hazel eyes, her head rested on her hand. She realized how burned out she was and how the frustration grew from one game to the next. She was tired, sore, her feet hurt, and she was sick of smelling sweaty teenagers every Friday night. Chloe decided this would be her first and last year to cheer for the West Side Knights.

"Hey, Chloe," a cheerleader named Amy, whose hair was a beautiful shade of red, spoke, "Come sit over here!"

She was sitting in between two players, neither of who were known for their brilliance. One had stapled his own finger to the teacher's desk in literature class. The other once glued his entire algebra textbook together page-by-page out of boredom.

She turned her head towards them. "There's no room."

One of the boys patted his lap.

"Not on your life, creep." She let out in disgust.

The bus swerved violently, sending a few of the teens out of their seat.

"Sorry kids!" The driver yelled over his shoulder. He turned back to the road and saw it, illuminated by the headlights.

The silhouette.

The eyes.

The smile.

He swerved again, this time with the momentum too strong to control. The bus flipped, then hit the ground violently. The driver's head hit the side window as it completed another turn and was entirely upside down. It skidded along the road with a sickening series of screeches. The teenagers inside were thrown around like rag dolls without their seat belts. Windows shattered as the kids collided with them, the floor, the seats, equipment, and even each other. By the time the bus came to a halt, nearly everyone inside had blacked out, except Chloe, who was still grasping onto a tiny thread of consciousness. She lay on what was once the cold ceiling of the bus, blood trickling down her head and into her ear. She could feel the warmth contrasting against the cold wind of the night air invading the vehicle. Her vision was blurry as she fought against her closing eyelids, but not before she saw something. A black figure reached inside the gaping hole where the windshield had once been, and ripped the driver from the seat, dragging him away into the forest. The cold, dark, unforgiving forest. Just outside the window, Chloe saw a sign.

LYONSIDE CITY LIMITS

Chapter Three

Wyatt's eyelids sprang open as he let out a scream. The sound of it coming from his own mouth in the silence of the night sent a chill down his spine. He must have been sweating buckets, because his shirt was soaked. His eyes felt swollen, like he had been crying in his sleep. He tried to lean up to catch his breath. That thing...that freaking thing was in his dreams! In his nightmares. He ran his fingers through his messy brown hair. His fingers intertwined as they slid to the back of his head. He let out a sigh and stared at the digital alarm clock on his desk.

12:01 A.M.

He rubbed his eyes as he reminisced on what had awakened him from his slumber. The nightmare to end all nightmares. He remembered hearing glass shattering, vicious snarls, and blood-curdling screams. His mother's screams. His father's screams had accompanied hers as Wyatt tried to cover his ears. Even with the nightmare over, the image of the creature returned to his mind. He could see the sharp teeth, the eyes, and the never-ending limbs vividly.

His phone buzzed atop the nightstand. Wondering who would text him at that time, he picked it up, unplugged the charger cord, and turned the screen on as he wiped the sweat off his forehead with his already soaked shirt. The brightness caused Wyatt to reel back and let out a curse under his breath.

DEREK: Hey. You awake?

What's he doing up at this hour? Wyatt thought.

WYATT: Ya

He stood, set his phone down on his bed, then proceeded to his restroom. When he returned, he had several notifications.

DEREK: Do u remember that thing?

DEREK: It's in my dreams man.

DEREK: I'm terrified.

Wyatt's jaw hung agape in shock. It couldn't be. They both had experienced something impossible, had *seen* something impossible, and were reeling from what they had been through. That's what it was. That's what it had to be.

WYATT: Me 2

DEREK: What?

WYATT: It's in my head 2

DEREK: What is it?

WYATT: It's that thing sitting on top of your neck

DEREK: Not my head. I'm being serious

WYATT: So am I

There was a five-minute pause before the next message came in. If the wait was any longer, he would have panicked.

DEREK: I'm going to text the rest of the team and see what they say.

WYATT: They're going to call you a wuss.

WYATT: Most likely ask if you pissed the bed.

WYATT: I know I would.

DEREK: I don't care.

WYATT: You do you, bro.

Time passed as he grew impatient, waiting on a response. He started to walk out of his room ever so quietly, trying not to wake his parents.

His parents.

He had to see if they were alright after hearing them scream so realistically in his nightmare. Suddenly, his phone started to buzz rapidly. One after another. At first, he assumed Derek was calling, but the vibration didn't have a pattern like it should. Those were texts.

DEREK: Wy

The next was one of his teammates. A linebacker.

CONNOR: Dude

Then another from a different player.

DANTE: Bro

His phone was blown up with notifications from his teammates. They all consisted of "Hey" or "Wake up". But one stood out to him. A final message from Derek that sent shivers down his spine.

DEREK: THEY ALL HAD THE SAME DREAM. THEY ALL SAW IT. WHATS GOING ON???

A sudden wave of nausea struck when he thought about walking to his parent's bedroom again. He froze in the dark hallway, then decided to slowly back into his room. He locked the door, leaving the light on before he wrapped himself in his covers.

****

Ruttledge Waters focused on the screen in front of him, his eyes searching for any sign of weakness from his opponents.

The strategy game he was playing was his favorite. The premise of the game was based around several countries that the player had control of. Several opponents also possess nations, and the goal of the game was to take over the world. It was something he was good at, and he played it at least an hour every day. Most times he would win because he was good at predicting the enemy's movements, but every so often, his strategies would fail him. Usually, this was because there was always one wildcard. It was a player who couldn't be predicted. Their strategies were chaotic, and the movements were without reason. This happened more often than he liked, and every time he would lose to these people, he wanted to pull the hair out of his head.

Not this time, however. He had just jumped into the game, and Ruttledge could already tell it wasn't going to be an easy victory. His blue markers advanced onto the northern countries, snuffing out the little competition that challenged him.

One down, two to go.

TAKEN BY THE NIGHT

There was a nation covered in black to the south, and another in red that was sandwiched between them. They had all their forces trying to drive away the dark force below them.

Ruttledge advanced while the red nation was distracted. He took over the border between them, pushing further into the mainland.

Suddenly, the red began to pull its forces away from the black zone and focused on defending against him. He became overwhelmed as he was being driven backwards.

What are you doing? I can win this! Let me have your land and I win! He mentally began screaming at his opponent to surrender.

It wasn't long before the dark zone below them surged forward, swallowing the red zone whole and creating a massive power that Ruttledge wasn't prepared for.

He did everything he possibly could, but the black color spread through the land like a disease, snuffing out the red and blue all together.

'YOU LOSE'

The bold letters blinked on screen, mocking him as they danced along in front of his eyes. Ruttledge grasped at his hair in frustration just as a knock came from his basement window.

He looked up over his laptop screen and peered at the glass. He could see his friend, Jesse Davis, opening it to try and slide in. It was something he did often when he was visiting, mainly because Ruttledge's parents had cameras on the front door, and they didn't want the two boys hanging out together.

Jesse slid a leg in, then Ruttledge could hear him wail in pain outside.

He stood up from his chair and walked over to the window, catching the behemoth of a boy as he finally fell through with a groan.

"Jeez, what happened to you?" Ruttledge stared at his friend's injuries as Jesse limped over to the lounge chair that sat in the corner of the room.

He sat down with a moan as he grasped his leg. "I ran into a tree."

Ruttledge stared at the bloody nose Jesse had, then focused on his injured leg. "You…ran into a tree."

Jesse looked at his friend as he wiped the crusted over blood from his upper lip. "Yeah, and I don't want to talk anymore about it, man."

Ruttledge nodded as he walked up stairs to grab a first aid kit. He tossed the pack into Jesse's lap.

"No, forget that." His friend coughed out. "Where are my cigarettes?"

Ruttledge reached under his desk, then pulled a strip of tape away, letting the white packet fall to the ground. He kept it there to keep his mother from finding it.

He picked up the pack, then tossed it to Jess.

"Don't smoke in here. Go outside. I don't need my parents smelling that filth every time they come down here."

Jesse stuck a cigarette in between his lips as he held his arms out in protest. He leaned back in the chair, the leg rest lifting his hurt knee up in the air.

"Does it look like I'm in any condition to go outside?" He mumbled as he held the lighter up to his mouth and began clicking at it with his thumb.

Ruttledge balled his hands up into fists as he walked forward and yanked the lighter out of his friend's hand. He threw the lighter up against the wall next to the window and then stared into Jesse's eyes. There was a glimpse of anger, but Ruttledge wasn't scared. Even though Jesse was taller and broader, he knew the guy wouldn't try anything. They had started out as the bully and his victim. Ruttledge had been homeschooled most of his life, and Jesse's family used to be close to his own. Once Jesse's mother had left his family, his father cut off all communication with their old acquaintances. Jesse had become a 'bad influence' during middle school. The event of his mother leaving humbled the bully, and he found solace in a friendship with Ruttledge.

Jesse smirked as the anger washed away, then he stood and limped over to the window. He struggled to bend over and pick up the lighter, so Ruttledge did it for him.

"How thoughtful."

Jesse lit his cigarette, then blew a pillar of smoke out the window. It seemed as if it calmed him.

"Do you want to tell me what happened now?"

Jesse sighed another exhale of smoke, the stack of gray billowing out the window.

"I, uh…I was at the football game tonight. I ran into this dude trying to make a move on my girl, so I chased him off. He was a scrawny little sucker who goes to the high school. I recognized him, so I corner him, right?"

Ruttledge nodded in response.

"Then suddenly, he lunges at me and overpowers me! Dude stepped on the back of my bad knee repeatedly. I think he re-injured it." Jesse palmed his jeans as he spoke.

The two boys sat in silence for a second. Ruttledge didn't know how to respond. Jesse was tall and large and threw his weight around whenever he felt like it. Ruttledge was done trying to convince him to be kinder to others, especially when it came to boys trying to talk to his girlfriend. He wasn't the best-looking guy in town. His face was square, and his haircut resembled a sort of bowl cut. His mother was gone, and his dad was deranged. Betty was all he had.

He knew why Jesse was in his basement. He was afraid to go home. He didn't want his dad to know he hurt his knee again. Ruttledge had seen the bruises on his friend some days when Jesse would do something stupid the night before.

"Jesse," Ruttledge sat at his table, his eyes focusing on his computer screen again. "You have to do something about him."

"Who?"

"You know who, your dad."

Jesse paused, which Ruttledge assumed was a smoke intermission.

47

"He's my dad, man. There's nothing I can really do. He's all I have left, you know?"

Ruttledge shook his head and was going to say something. He was going to start another argument with his friend involving his dad's antics. He wanted to initially, until he heard the basement window slamming shut and Jesse's hoarse screams.

Startled, Ruttledge quickly looked up from his computer screen and his eyes met that of a hideous creature that stared at him through the glass. They were bright red, and the face was nothing but a disgusting darkness. It smiled a grin that shook him to his core with repulsive, gnarly teeth.

Jesse let out a string of expletives as he fell backwards, stumbling across the floor in a mad dash to get away from the thing.

Ruttledge stood up from his seat as the creature's eyes widened and it let out a sickening cackle, a laugh that sounded like a hyena had inhaled a helium balloon. It waved what could only be assumed as a hand before it backed away from the glass and into the night.

"What was that thing?!?" Jesse could only yell curses as he continued to stare at the window. Ruttledge headed towards the

48

basement door, hoping to go find his phone so he could call the police.

He stumbled up the stairs before his hand met the metal knob.

Locked.

Ruttledge swallowed hard as he shook the knob once again.

They were trapped.

He looked at the watch on his wrist. 12:01 AM.

He turned back down the stairs, his hands shaking in fear as he turned to Jesse.

"Wha-what was that thing, Ruttledge?!?"

Ruttledge looked at the window where the creature had been, then back at his computer screen. The words 'YOU LOSE!' were still blinking across the screen.

"I don't know."

****

Robbie was visited by the shadow once again, wrapping him in a fear like he had never experienced before.

A silhouette with sharp teeth and red eyes stood in the corner of his bedroom, watching him as he stared back from his bed.

Its mouth opened, laughing along with an earth-shattering screech. Robbie covered his ears and started to sob, a panic

49

grasping at his chest. His breath wouldn't return to his lungs no matter how much he inhaled. His face flushed a cherry red in his cheeks as a sharp tingle danced across his skin. He scrounged up enough courage to fall over the other side of his bed and grab the revolver he stole from his dad. He had taken it from his dad's gun safe after an argument the two had one night. Robbie thought he was old enough to keep a gun, while his father advised against it. At that moment, Robbie considered himself intelligent for going against his father's wishes. The revolver was the only thing between Robbie and the creature that stood in the corner of his room.

He aimed at the thing as the screech grew so loud his ears began to trickle with blood. He fired the gun in the direction of the shadow, an echoing *thoom* bouncing off his bedroom walls.

The screeching stopped. Robbie searched the room, his eyes darting back and forth in paranoia. It was gone, once again leaving Robbie bewildered and curious.

He stood and walked over to the wall he had fired the gun at. He felt the bullet hole with his finger, pulling away loose chips of paint. This assured Robbie that he wasn't dreaming.

TAKEN BY THE NIGHT

Dad isn't going to like this. He thought to himself as he shook his head.

Not one bit.

Chapter Four

The morning light glimmered through Wyatt's bedroom window, waking him from his sleep. It had been a restless night as he continued to think about the...he didn't even know what it was!

He sat up in his bed, clearly in need of more than the two hours of sleep he had received. He knew that wasn't an option, though. He wondered if the night before had really happened as he checked his phone for the messages.

All of them remained. Every single one.

Wyatt still felt the grip of anxiety, so he stood up and moved over to his stereo. He needed his tunes to calm the inner stirrings of his mind. He flipped through his phone's music and pressed shuffle. His morning routine took over as the opening verse of

Cheap Trick's "Surrender" echoed unnecessarily loud through the speakers. As his feet hit his bathroom's cold tile floor, Wyatt was overwhelmed with a sudden sense of nausea, and he threw up from the stress of it all. He knew the day wasn't going to be a good one.

"Mom!"

There was no answer. He spit into the toilet in a futile attempt to remove the taste from his mouth.

"Mom! I'm puking!"

Still, no one responded.

"I could be dying!"

After a few minutes of nothing but the music booming from his bedroom, the morning fog finally left his mind and the realization of the night before took hold. He had no idea if his parents were okay. He flushed the toilet, then walked out of his room, his feet sinking into the carpet as he moved to the master bedroom. His steps were cautious as he recalled the night before and how he had hesitated to do the very thing he was attempting now.

The door creaked as he shoved it open.

The room was wrecked. The sheets were thrown wildly off the bed. The dresser was knocked over, its drawers splintered all over the floor from some type of violent impact. Clothes were everywhere. The ceiling fan now rested on the floor where it was smashed against the foot of the bed. Clearly, something was seriously wrong. Wyatt yelled.

"Mom!"

His phone suddenly began buzzing frantically in the pocket of his gym shorts. He looked at the caller ID. It was Derek.

"Wyatt, you need to meet us at the bookstore!" He spoke with a panicked tone.

Wyatt rubbed his eyes with his fingers, picking at the inside corners for crust.

"What? Wait, what's happening?"

Derek started to sound concerned." Dude, the town has gone nuts! No one can find their parents! It's just chaos down here! Get here fast! Run if you have to!"

Wyatt rolled his eyes as he hung up and slid the phone back into his pocket. *Derek was going to have to wait for whatever it was he was doing!* Wyatt's brain had to get adjusted to being awake before he even decided to do anything! He made a pot of his dad's coffee, then took a shower. As he was drying himself off, the thought occurred to him that his parents' disappearance could have something to do with what his friend needed him for. He grabbed his wrinkled white t-shirt, spiked up his hair with as much gel as needed, then slipped on his red sneakers. He poured the steaming hot liquid into a thermos, grabbed his skateboard, then made his way out the door.

****

Desmond woke from his slumber, the morning sun casting its warmth on his face through the blinds in his room. He had a nightmare, but he was too old to care, really. You only freaked out about that stuff if you were little. He was more mature than that, until he remembered what he had seen the night before, and how that was real. He leaped out of bed with an urgency.

"Dad?!? Dad, are you okay?"

He rushed into the living room. The house only had two bedrooms, and when they moved to Lyonside for his father's job, he had decided to give them to his kids.

God, he gave up so much for us after Mom passed, he thought to himself.

The couch was turned awkwardly, its bright red cushions sloppily thrown on the floor, and the coffee table was overturned in the corner of the room, one leg smashed into the drywall. Desmond felt an unnerving sensation in his gut that something was terribly wrong. His dad was a neat freak. He would always fold up the blanket and drape it over the back of his chair. This mess was very unlike him. Another thing that kept coming to Desmond's mind, was how heavy the coffee table was. He remembered having to pick it up with Molly after his dad threw his back out trying to lift it when they moved into the house. It would take an amazing amount of force to move it a mere few feet, let alone toss it across the room hard enough to break through the wall. He rushed into his sister's room, which was filled with books of all sorts piled on her desk, the reading light still on and shining down on one of her textbooks. Her purple sheets were still made neatly on her bed. His sister had sleep apnea; a disorder that makes it hard to breathe when sleeping. Her insomnia often drove her to all-night reading sessions.

"Marcella!" He yelled her birth name throughout the house.

He moved into the kitchen, his bare feet smacking against the cold tile as his eyes still attempted to adjust to the sun as it penetrated the back-door window. He could hear the birds chirping outside, almost as if the world was bliss. The animals paid no attention to his predicament.

TAKEN BY THE NIGHT

"Molly! Dad!" The world had gone silent, then faintly he could hear a distant, muffled shouting coming from the back yard.

He stepped through the screen door as the muffled voice became understandable. He could feel the sun slicing through the cold November morning air, as it shined bright into his eyes, causing him to squint as he scanned the area. He could smell the morning pine from the couple of trees towering above their yard.

"Dez! Dez! Get me out of here!" It sounded like his sister, her voice unusually panicked and croaking hoarsely. The yells originated from their dad's tool shed that sat cozily in the right corner of the yard, its foundation dug deep into the soft grass. The padlock jostled as the plastic doors jumped on their hinges from his sister beating on the other side.

"How the heck did you get in there? The door is locked shut!"

"I'll tell you, just get me out first!"

"Alright, alright! Where's the key?" Dez responded, pressing his eye up to look through the gap between the doors. He could see her, still in her silk pajamas and hair tied back.

"How should I know? You were the one that helped Dad with this stuff, not me!"

Dez backed up from the door as he scratched his head. He couldn't remember where his dad stashed the key. He ran back inside and checked everywhere he could think of, but finally concluded that it must be on his father's key ring. He must have taken it with him, wherever he had gone. He grabbed a heavy brass candlestick, then rushed back to Molly. He bashed it against the lock until it fell off, clinking on the ground. Molly came staggering out, before hugging her brother.

"Dez, you're okay?" She asked, pulling back and looking him in the eyes, her own squinted as she studied his expression.

"Yeah," he responded. "Where's Dad? It's a Saturday, so he shouldn't be working, and I found the living room a wreck."

Molly's expression went cold. "Dad's gone?" Dez knew that look on her face. She knew something that he didn't.

"Marcella....why were you in the shed?"

She backed up, her golden eyes wide and her head moving slowly from side to side. "Last night something bad happened, Desmond. I was in my room studying until around midnight, when I went to get something to drink. I heard a noise outside and it didn't sound like an animal or anything, I thought someone was trying to break in. Here." She handed him their Dad's handgun.

58

"Jeez, Molly!" Dez let out, flustered. He yanked the pistol from her hands and popped the empty magazine out, checking for bullets. There were none. "What were you planning on doing with an empty gun?"

"Check it."

He pulled the slide back as something shiny jumped from the opening. She caught the unused bullet in mid-air, then played with it in between her purple nails, a smirk on her face as one eyebrow went up.

"One bullet? What would you have done if it *was* an intruder?"

"That's all I'd need. Did you forget that I'm a better shot than both you and Dad?" She crossed her arms and leaned on her left leg. "I'm only a year younger than you. I'm a big girl, Dez. I can take care of myself." She tossed him the bullet.

"Yeah, baby sis? And what if it was the neighbor's cat?" He responded, checking the gun to make sure it was empty this time.

"I guess they'd have a missing cat." She joked, before going back to the original conversation. He had never seen her convert emotions so fast. She went from happy and joking to scared out of her wits again. "Dez, I heard a sound inside of the shed, and the door was swung wide open. Then....all I remember was a sharp pain in my head. It was like an insane migraine set in or something. It was enough to knock me out cold. When I woke up, I was in there and the doors wouldn't budge."

Dez eyed her suspiciously, then turned and looked at the shed. His expression went from confused to laughing. "Alright, you both are hilarious. Knock it off, where's Dad? Is he hiding somewhere?" Dez snapped his head from side to side, looking through the bushes that aligned the backyard fence.

"What?" Molly asked, her expression replaced with confusion of her own. "No, no! Desmond, this isn't a prank!"

"Yeah, whatever Molly. This is just like the time you two put that spider on my pillow!"

"First: That was hilarious. Second: I wish this was one of those times. I really do."

He looked her in the eyes, then squinted. She squinted, too. Neither would back down if not for him being interrupted by his phone ringing. He pulled it out of his back pocket and up to his ear without forfeiting the staring contest.

"Hello?" He said.

"Dez, my man." It was Derek Hoff, one of Desmond's classmates and starting quarterback for the Lyonside Lions. "We have some problems in town, and I need your help. How fast can you get down to the town center by the bookstore?"

"I still need to change and find my dad. I'm sure whatever it is can wait."

"Good luck with that, so is the rest of the town. Everyone's parents are gone and its chaos around here. That's why I need you, ASAP. Bring your sis, maybe she can help, too."

Desmond hung up the phone, then looked at his sister.

"What? What's happening, Dez?"

He swallowed hard, remembering the monster from the night before.

"I don't know, but it isn't good."

****

Robbie hadn't slept the rest of the night. He sat against his headrest, cradling his father's revolver. He spun the chamber with his fingers then clicked it back into place. Ever since the creature had shrieked at him, he couldn't shake the ringing in his ears. He wasn't sure if it was real or some sort of hallucination. All he knew was that the blood that dried inside of his ears was real. He knew the hole in the wall where he had fired the gun was real.

No one would believe his story about a creature breaking into his room in the middle of the night. He wasn't sure if his dad would think he was defending himself. He didn't know if anyone would think he was defending himself from Jesse the night before, either.

Nobody is going to see it my way.

He would be harassed by Jesse's wrestling teammates, even though he was defending himself. He would be considered a psychopath by other people in town, all because he was defending himself.

No, no. It'll be okay. Dad will have my back. I know he will. He always does.

Robbie didn't like the way the air around him felt in his lungs. His chest rose as he took in oxygen, but something stuck in his airways. It was almost as if he couldn't breathe.

Robbie shook the feeling away as his footsteps creaked down the wooden stairway. He walked through the kitchen, his socks sliding across the smooth wood flooring.

He opened the door, letting the morning air hit him as the cornstalks in the field in front of him swayed back and forth. The blue sky hung overhead, without a cloud to blemish its color.

TAKEN BY THE NIGHT

Robbie could feel that something was off. The hair on the back of his neck stood up on end, and goosebumps began to form across the skin of his arms. He slipped his tennis shoes on and stepped out the door.

He turned his gaze away from the stalks as he walked, an unnatural shiver tingling his spine. The air was cool around him, and he regretted not grabbing his jacket before heading out. He was already outside and on his way to the barn, however. He knew his dad would be inside and he wanted to see what chores he needed to do for the day. He wanted something to take his mind off the events of the night before. He would even clean out the pig pen if it meant he could focus on something else.

He opened the big, gray, rotting barn door, and it creaked on its hinges as he stepped inside.

"Dad?"

He scanned the inside of the barn, and his eyes focused on a bale of hay that sat against the wall.

There was some motion on the other side, a dark figure moving just beyond where Robbie could see.

His jaw clenched as he stepped forward, his hands quaking as he moved.

63

"Dad? Is that you?" He asked again.

Robbie received no answer. His thoughts raced to find an explanation for the movement. He couldn't help but remember the silhouette. Its hideous teeth chilled him to the bone, and the red orbs that resembled eyes burrowed into his memory.

Robbie peered around the hay bale, expecting to see the hideous creature once again.

"Shhh." His father held a finger up to his lips to quiet the boy. He was cradling a baby pig that Robbie didn't recognize. It was suckling on a bottle of milk.

The tension left Robbie's shoulders as he exhaled. It appeared that Janice, the pregnant pig who lived in that terrible pen he had to clean out occasionally, had finally given birth during the night.

"You okay, son?" His dad asked in a whisper.

Robbie shook his head as he thought of a response. Before he spoke, Robbie could have sworn he saw a glint of red in the green of his dad's eyes.

"I'm uh…I'm okay, Dad. I'm okay."

****

Ruttledge awoke slowly, his eyes adjusting to the light that shined from outside the basement window. He leaned up from his chair,

64

the muscles tightening up in his neck as he winced in pain. He had never slept sitting up before, and he didn't want to do it again.

He turned his head and looked at Jesse, who was reclined back in the leather chair. His mouth hung open, a loud growl of a snore emerging from his nostrils.

Ruttledge rubbed his eyes before turning them towards the window. The frame hung open, as if the events of the night before had not taken place.

"Woah…" He groaned to himself. "Jesse."

Jesse snored again.

"Jesse, wake up!" Ruttledge picked up a balled-up sock, then flung it at his friend. It popped him in the forehead, causing him to suddenly sit up. His eyes were wide as he searched the room.

The window Jesse had entered the basement through was now wide open, letting in a nice, cool breeze that offered some relief in the humid, warm room.

"Wow," He muttered as he stood up from the recliner with a huff. "Well…uh…thanks for letting me stay over."

Ruttledge looked at his friend suspiciously, wondering why he wasn't mentioning the creature they had seen.

Had I even seen it? He asked himself. *Had it just been a nightmare?*

Ruttledge wasn't about to admit to having a nightmare, knowing that Jesse would tease and hurl cruel jokes at him. "Yeah." Ruttledge coughed as he stood and stretched. The muscles in his back had stiffened from the position he slept in and his neck had a cramp. "No problem."

Jesse stared at the window. He hesitated, a look of terror flashing across his face before he shook it off and began climbing up and outside.

The expression Ruttledge saw from his friend convinced him that what they had seen the night before wasn't from a dream. They had both witnessed the figure. They had both looked into its merciless, blood red eyes. It was real.

Ruttledge closed the window, alone within the silence of the basement. He closed his eyes, breathing slowly.

A familiar beep rang from behind him. His computer needed charging.

He plugged the cord into the wall and as the screen came on, he once again saw the letters 'YOU LOSE' spread across the game map he had been looking at the night before.

TAKEN BY THE NIGHT

He shook off the chill he felt come over him and began walking up the basement stairs to the door, that was now unlocked for reasons unbeknownst to him.

****

Derek was right. Kids were running through the streets. Some playing, others desperate to find their parents. Some laughed and enjoyed their newfound freedom, while others cried and blubbered for their parents. This was serious. Wyatt kicked it into high gear as he turned, hooking a lamp post with his hand and skating down into the town center. He saw Derek standing inside the bookstore, the glass pieces from the door still on the sidewalk. He stood with the girl they talked to the night before, and another guy, who looked to be Wyatt's age, but taller and much bulkier. Dez Martin, who played basketball for the Lyonside Lions was there, along with another girl whose face seemed vaguely familiar, but he couldn't place her name. Her black, wavy hair had a slight frizz to it, and was pulled back into a ponytail with some strands hanging near her temples. Her nose was perky and her lips small. Her skin seemed to be a bronze shade that was a little darker than her golden eyes.

Wyatt swerved out of the way of a group of children playing and hopped off his board, walking over the glass shards.

Derek looked slightly ticked. "What took you so long?!?"

He set his skateboard on the counter. "I took a shower."

Derek looked at him in slight surprise. "Y--you took a shower?"

"D—did I stutter?" Wyatt mocked his tone and facial expression. Wyatt new his lack of effort was wrong, but he wasn't going to admit it.

Derek displayed a fumed expression. "Dude, I told you to hurry!"

Wyatt sat on the counter and pulled out a pocket screwdriver. He started tightening the front axle of his board as he doubled down on his reasoning. "After last night, be glad I took one! I smelled like our locker room after summer workouts."

Derek grabbed the bridge of his own nose in frustration. Dez spoke as he walked forward. "Wyatt, quit being you for a minute, okay?"

Wyatt sat up and looked at him. "You weren't complaining about me being me when I was distracting our chemistry teacher long enough for class to end."

"You put pudding in his chair! He spent the rest of the period trying to get it out of his shorts!"

Wyatt laughed, then shrugged as his eyes shifted back to his skateboard. "Ah, that's not how I remember it."

Alex finally spoke up." Will you idiots please just shut up!?!"

Wyatt scoffed as he set his board down. "The men are talking, sweetheart."

Alex's face grew red as she marched towards Wyatt, ready to blow his hair back for the sexist remark, but Derek stepped in between them. Wyatt turned and looked at the other girl again, who was peering at him with an eyebrow raised and a frown as she studied his demeanor.

"Who are you, again?" He asked, pointing a thumb in her direction.

She didn't answer, as she continued to look him up and down. It was apparent she did not approve of what was in front of her. Dez spoke up.

"This is my little sister, Molly." He nodded towards her. That explained why their eyes matched. Other than that, there didn't seem to be any other physical feature they shared. Wyatt thought about the name, trying to place it in his recent memory.

"Molly...Molly Martin? The girl who sucker-punched Jesse Davis and threw milk in his face during lunch?!?" He threw his head back laughing. "That was you?!? Oh, man! That was priceless! His face was as red as a tomato for the rest of the day!" He held up a fist to bump, but she didn't change her expression and remained still.

"Okay, then." he turned to Dez. "She's a charmer."

"Has anyone attempted to...I don't know...call their parents?" Alex presented the idea with crossed arms.

"They're dead numbers. All of them, but if we call each other...." Desmond responded.

"They go through perfectly fine." Derek finished for him. "Same with text messages. Even the emergency lines are out!"

"Has anyone tried reaching out over the internet? What about radio and TV signals?" Molly asked seemingly to anyone within the group who had an answer.

"Yeah, try getting any sort of data or connection. Let me know how that goes!" Wyatt said, grimacing at his phone screen as he shoved it back in his pocket.

Derek rubbed his head. "TV seems fine. Nothing on the news about any catastrophic events."

TAKEN BY THE NIGHT

Down the road, tires squealed from a vehicle turing a corner at a high rate speed. The group ran outside to see what caused the sound. An armored security van was barreling towards them, swerving back and forth as children ran inside the buildings to avoid the speeding mass of metal. A kid, who only seemed to be in his preteens, had his hand out of the window. He was motioning for the people in the streets to move, and they could barely hear what he was screaming over the roar of the engine.

"I can't stop! Move! Move!"

Alex snapped out of her trace like state and raced into action pulling a child out of the street by his shirt collar. A little boy tripped and fell into Molly's arms as he was trying to escape the oncoming behemoth. She pulled him onto the sidewalk along with a mass of little children desperate to get out of the way. Wyatt grabbed Derek's keys off the desk and ran for his truck that was parallel parked across the road. He was missed by seemingly inches when the van soared by at lightning speed.

"Hooooly crap!" He yelled as he felt the turbulence that signaled how close he was to getting squashed.

Dez chased after him.

"Wy!" Derek yelled from the bookstore, hobbling over on his crutches.

He had already started the truck and was moving out of the parking space as Desmond opened the passenger side door and hopped in.

"You're a psycho, man!"

"I'm trying to save lives! Can we put a pin in the insults until later?!?" Wyatt yelled frantically. He slammed his foot down against the accelerator as the truck approached highway speed in order to catch up to the runaway van. Both vehicles began heading downhill out of the town center.

****

Chloe grabbed a water bottle out of one of the football player's tattered bag. She pushed her blonde hair out of her eyes, cringing as it tickled across the wound breaching vertically through her left eyebrow. She had hit the window of the bus when it crashed, putting a small gash down her forehead. She was lucky the shattered glass didn't take out her eye. The morning after, when the survivors of the crash awoke, she found that the bus driver was gone. There was a blood trail that began a mere few feet beyond the street the teenagers rested on and continued into the forest that stretched for miles around them.

"Why hasn't anyone called 9-1-1?" Amy asked.

Jobe, the senior quarterback who had ironically suffered a broken arm in the crash, spoke up.

"We need to head back into town."

A few of the survivors turned to him, confused. This included Chloe. He sat on the spare tire that had fallen off during the crash.

"We need help," he explained.

" Again...just call 9-1-1." Amy spoke up again.

Chloe rested her forehead in her hand. "We can't. There's no signal."

The redhead checked her phone. "That's so weird! I had four bars last night."

Jobe lost his temper as he stood, cradling his injured arm. "Yeah...and we also had Frank last night, but now he's dead in that pile of yellow crap with wheels!"

He walked off in a huff as Amy moved over to sit next to Chloe.

"He didn't have to be a jerk about it," she said, a sort of pout in her tone.

Chloe sighed. "Give him some time. He just lost his friends. We all have."

"Yeah, I guess." Amy said turning to her. "You know, there's something about your accent that seems to give you these magical powers of influence."

Chloe laughed. "One of the perks you get being from London." Chloe Fuller had moved to America from the United Kingdom when she was only sixteen. Now a year later, she missed Britain and her family more than ever. It was hard to understand some people here. The American lifestyle was like what she was used to, but still different in some ways. It was hard to adjust, and now she was stuck on the side of the road with no help in sight. She played with a strand of her messy blonde hair, a color that wasn't even authentic. She really had jet black hair, but she admired the glow of golden locks like her godmother.

Chloe had been orphaned as a baby, before her Godmother Stephanie took care of her. She had the most beautiful shade of hair, and the most gorgeous personality. When they had moved to America, she decided to get hers dyed to match.

Chloe's thoughts were interrupted by the sound of roaring engines in the distance. Two speeding vehicles were rocketing

74

towards them from the direction the bus had been traveling before the crash.

****

Wyatt had taken the truck up to nearly fifty miles an hour. That's what it took to pull up next to the out-of-control van.

"Woah, look at that sucker fly!" He looked at Dez, who seemed more stressed than he was.

"Grab this!" He handed Dez the wheel to stabilize the truck. He rolled down the driver's side window and began to climb out.

"What the heck is this?!? Are you serious?!? Wyatt!" Desmond let out as he positioned himself in the driver's seat.

Wyatt turned his head and quickly gazed at the terrified kid in the speeding beast's front seat.

"Let off the pedal!" He yelled as the truck swerved an inch closer. He snapped his head around. "Easy! Easy, Dez!"

"I can't!" The boy's voice broke as he tried to yell over the chorus of engine revs.

"It's stuck!"

"Oh, lovely!" Wyatt grabbed a bar that was welded horizontally to the roof of the van and leaped. His body slammed violently against the metal side of the dark gray security van. The breath was knocked out of him as he gasped, but he hung on for dear life. The wind stung his face as he reached into the passenger side window of the van.

"Holy crap! This is just like *Raiders of the Lost Ark*!" He yelled above the wind that screamed by, slinging his hair all around. He looked at the kid.

"What?!?" The kid stared back at him for a second, bewildered by the statement.

"Never mind!" Wyatt screamed again.

He leaned onto the rear-view mirror, one hand still grasping the metal bar. His feet rested on a step located underneath the door.

The kid continued yelling, this time at people in front of them. Wyatt looked through the wind, struggling to keep his eyes open. A yellow school bus was turned over in the road, as boys in letter jackets and cheerleaders dove out of the way of the impending danger. The vehicle was slowing, its tires screeching as it burned across the asphalt. However, it would not stop in time to avoid hitting the bus.

Wyatt thought quickly and yanked the door open, diving inside. He unbuckled the seat belt and pushed the driver side door open. He rolled out of the opening, pulling the child from the driver's seat by his arm. They plummeted to the ground below, rolling a few feet before coming to a stop. The van had swerved onto the grass surrounding the asphalt, where luckily, both boys hit a bush to break their fall and soften the impact.

The sickening sound of metal scraping across metal rang through the air as the van collided with the bottom side of the bus. The impact sent both skidding further down the road with a screech that echoed through the forest around them. The kids that were in the way screamed as they made the effort to escape the danger. Dez pulled Derek's truck over next to Wyatt and the boy, who were laying in the brush a yard away from the road. Wyatt's body ached as he sat up, pain revealing itself in the shoulder he landed on.

"My leg!" The boy yelled as he cradled his right shin. "It hurts! It hurts so bad, oh jeez!"

Dez knelt. "Alright, buddy. Calm down. You'll be okay. My sister is smart, she can help!" He rolled the boys right pant leg up and looked at his ankle. It was clear he needed medical attention, as around the rim of his shoe was purple, swollen flesh. He pulled the dark-haired boy's shoe off, revealing more of the injury and making him shriek in pain. He picked up the kid and set him in the backseat of the truck.

"Wyatt, I'm going to take him into town to get help!"

Wyatt was too busy puking in the grass to hear him. He watched Dez hop into the truck and drive off as he started becoming less disoriented.

"No problem!" He yelled to the truck as it pulled away. He laid back down where he had originally fallen, out of breath. "I'll just chill here."

He closed his eyes. However, it wasn't long before a pair of hands grabbed the front of his shirt, yanking him awake.

"Hey! What's your deal?! You trying to kill us?!" Wyatt opened his eyes to see a teenager twice his size, whose face was as red as his hair, staring back at him menacingly. Wyatt looked down at the guy's arm sleeve, which had sewn to it the number ninety.

"I know you!" Wyatt said with a childish enthusiasm. "You hit me in last night's game! I thought you'd hit harder than that!"

The giant of a teen threw Wyatt back to the ground, then planted his foot in his side. He spoke again. "What's going on?!? Why did you try to hit us?!?"

TAKEN BY THE NIGHT

Someone stepped in front of Wyatt, who was on his hands and knees. He spat out blood from his lips. It sounded like a girl was speaking in a British accent. It wasn't extremely thick, but present. He could only see her shoes, which were white athletics. The kind that cheerleaders always wear.

"Tony, stop for a second!" She stepped in front of the raging football player.

The boy tried to push passed her. "Chloe, he almost killed us!" He took a step back as his rage started to subside. "Besides, he probably knows what's going on!"

Wyatt looked up, propping himself up on one knee.

"Now hold on. Let's just figure this ou--"

"No, he's right, blondie." Wyatt spoke to the cheerleader, but he kept his eyes locked on the jock." I somehow managed to kidnap all the adults in town, steal this van, then decide to hit you with it! What a stellar observation, Sherlock!"

The girl turned to him, revealing her face. "Wait...what did you just say?" He felt a tickle in his stomach as he smiled that cocky grin at her.

"I'm sick of your smart mouth!" The player became enraged again.

Wyatt's lips moved before his brain could finish processing, a very dangerous habit. "I'm sick of your face! Guess we both have to suffer."

Not even the cheerleader could stop the left boot that connected with Wyatt's jaw, sending him spiraling into the ground.

****

Robbie huffed as he swung the scythe in front of him, clearing out a portion of overgrown weeds that spanned the perimeter of his father's farm. Despite the cool breeze that continuously caressed his face, sweat had begun to drip down his face and arms. He could feel the warm drops fall from the hair on the back of his head onto his shoulders, soaking into his shirt.

Robbie brought the scythe back over his shoulder again, then swung the blade horizontally. The weeds severed with a *woosh*, plopping onto the dirt below his feet.

His anxiety was eating him alive. He could feel it within the pit of his stomach. Something was seriously wrong. He couldn't reason with himself as to what it was.

I should never have taken it that far during the fight with Jesse.
He began to reason with himself, thinking maybe that this was the

source of his stress. *Something just came over me. That...that*
never should have happened. I'm not like that. That isn't me!

It never should have happened. It wouldn't have happened had
that kid come and helped him. He could have stopped me from
stomping on Jesse's bad leg. It wouldn't have happened had Jesse
not chased me into that alley. He had it coming.

He wound-up the scythe once again, bringing it down on
another patch of weeds that dotted the landscape. Robbie began to
feel a tickle in the back of his head, a quick and sharp sensation
that caused him to hesitate before beginning his next swing. He
stopped and began to breathe as the feeling faded.

The birds that had been chirping around him stopped abruptly.
Robbie hadn't noticed until the silence had begun to assault him,
sending an unnatural chill down his back. The breeze had stopped
as well.

Robbie began to look around, his green eyes scanning the
cornfield behind him.

Robbie.

Something said his name. His skin turned pale as his motions
became frantic, desperately searching for the source of the
whisper.

Robbie!

His eyes focused on the cornfield ahead of him. The wind began to pick up once again, swaying the dead, yellow stalks back and forth, contrasting against the blue sky above him.

Robbie began to walk forward, his footsteps carefully trotting across the dirt as he squeezed the handle of his scythe.

"Hello?" His voice trembled as the words left his mouth.

Something inside of him was telling his body to keep going, even though his mind was shouting at him.

He reached a clearing he didn't recognize, a circular area of dirt among the stalks with a cross-shaped wooden stand in the middle. It looked like it was meant for a scarecrow.

Where did this come from? We don't even use a scarecrow!

Suddenly, a crow began to call from somewhere within the stalks. The tickle in the back of Robbie's head exploded into a violent headache, causing him to fall to his knees in agony.

He grasped at his ruby hair and gritted his teeth, a hoarse yell seething from between his bared lips.

He squeezed his eyes shut, begging for the pain to go away. A warmth overcame his skin as the air around him suddenly became thick. Hot, humid air was entering his lungs. The smell of smoke flooded his nostrils. He peered up for a second, attempting to ignore the surging pain in his skull.

Red painted his face, as the glow of a flickering, surging flame overcame his senses. The corn stalks were on fire; his dad's farm was ablaze.

No, no, no, no!

A bird fluttered over his head, landing on the scarecrow stand. The crow from the alley.

Tears began to fall from his eyes. He rubbed them away, then turned around to find his way out of the burning field.

A figure stood behind him, causing Robbie to catch his breath. It was his father, but something was off. His skin was pale, and his eyes did not reflect the dirty green color that Robbie had inherited. They were a burning cardinal color that reminded him of the fire that surrounded them.

A gruff, monstrously hoarse voice arose from his father, a voice that he did not recognize.

Robbie...

Robbie shook his head as he attempted to find the words.

A.P. JENNINGS

Is he angry about the hole in the wall where I had shot? Is he upset about me assaulting Jesse the night before? Where did the fire come from? Does he think that I had something to do with it? The tears fell from Robbie's face in streams as he began to babble. He could feel the rage radiating from the figure in front of him. He tried to speak, but all that arose from his dried, smoke-filled throat was a desperate croak.

His father charged at him with a vicious growl. Robbie was caught off guard by this and began to stumble backwards as his dad wrapped his callused hands around his throat. His dad had always been loving and understanding. He had always been a warmth in Robbie's life. Even through the hard times, he had always been a source of comfort. He was everything that Robbie wanted to be.

Now, his fingertips felt as cold as ice on Robbie's throat. Robbie pulled his scythe forward to keep himself from landing on it.

His body hit the ground, sending a cloud of dust into the air. He heard a sickening *schink* as he felt the blade penetrate something. The hands that were wrapped around his throat had vanished, and all that remained was the gentle feeling of a palm on his cheek.

84

TAKEN BY THE NIGHT

The dust settled as Robbie looked upon what he had done in horror.

His father had fallen on the blade, its end piercing into his chest. His eyes had glazed over, reflecting back Robbie's terrified expression. He could feel the warmth of blood soaking his shirt as he turned over. He rested his father's head on his arm as he begun wailing.

"Oh my God! D-dad! I'm-I…"

The smoke that surrounded them dissipated as the flames mysteriously vanished, leaving Robbie with his father's body in his arms. He collapsed forward, crying into the crook of his dad's neck.

The sharp pain in the back of his head assaulted his brain once more, causing him to squeeze his eyes tight as tears of anguish rolled down his flushed cheeks.

The grasp he had on his father began to loosen as the sensation of touch faded.

He opened his eyes again.

His father's corpse was gone.

Robbie's breathing intensified and his eyes widened in realization.

Was this real?

The chirping of birds began to ring in his ears once more. The cool November breeze once again caressed his face. As he peered up, he noticed the crow was gone.

His eyes fell directly in front of him. Another figure was staring at him. This time, it was the shadow monster from the night before. Its scarlet eyes focused on him as Robbie's bottom lip began to tremble.

It held up a hand, then began to move its fingers as if it was playing the piano, a rhythm that looked as if it was waving.

Robbie screamed at the top of his lungs as his voice returned. He scrambled to his feet, then took off through the stalks toward the road away from his house.

****

Dez pulled Derek's truck up next to the bookstore, trying to avoid the broken glass. He could see him, Alex, and a few other teenagers trying to calm the town center full of children. He knew this would happen. Well... he didn't know, but he knew. He could feel it. In his mind. He knew something was dreadfully wrong. Things would never be normal.

TAKEN BY THE NIGHT

Dez helped the kid out of the backseat. He led him into the bookstore and set him on the desk, the wood still sticky from Alex's soda.

Derek grabbed his shoulder. "What happened?"

Dez turned to him, ignoring the sobbing kid in front of him. "Boy decided to take a joy ride and the accelerator got stuck."

Derek turned to him, hobbling on his crutches. "You could have died!"

The black-haired boy just nodded and wiped a tear. "I want my mom." He said with a sniffle. He seemed much too old to be pouting like a toddler, but in a time of such panic, nothing more could be expected of anyone.

Derek sighed and put a hand on his forehead.

"What's going on?" He whispered to himself.

"Where's Molly?" Dez asked as he examined the boy's ankle. He knew of her extensive medical knowledge, remembering that she had wanted to be a doctor since she was five and had started the studies early, spending a lot of her allowance on medical textbooks when she was old enough to understand it.

"I'm right here. What happened?" She spoke, making her way from behind one of the aisles of books in the back of the room.

Dez pulled her aside to explain, while Derek approached Alex, who had a glare in her eyes that signified she was deep within her own thoughts.

"Every adult in town has disappeared. Teachers, doctors, parents...everyone." Alex spoke up, twisting her long brunette hair into a ponytail, much to Derek's liking. Now he could see her face.

"Ahem--Yeah, but I saw that plenty of the eighteen-year-old guys from the team are still around. I even saw Keith earlier, and he's nineteen." Derek said, breaking the trance he put himself in by looking at Alex's deep brown eyes.

"This doesn't make any sense."

A Hispanic teen walked into the bookstore, avoiding the glass. Two more followed him. All three boys had letter jackets on. Alex didn't recognize them, but Derek sure did.

"Carlos, brother..." He said to the teenager they referred to as Eight-Ball. His hair was buzzed evenly along the sides with the top longer and pushed upward with gel.

"Sup, one-leg!"

They fist bumped, then Derek explained some of the things he knew were happening.

"Wow." Carlos spoke, swallowing the lump in his throat. Alex could see the goosebumps growing on the skin of his arms.

"Yeah," Derek turned his head and remembered the kid. "Hey, guys I need you to go look all over town for any sign of an adult. Go into basements, attics, anything. Don't be shy about it either. Break down doors if you must. If you see anyone please send them down here to take control of all this." Derek pointed a finger out the window at the children playing in the streets.

The football players left as Derek hobbled over to the desk, keeping his gaze fixed on the kids outside. Something was missing.

"Hey, Dez," He asked in a curious manner. "Where's Wyatt?"

Dez let out a frustrated sigh and looked down. "Crap."

"Is he alright?"

"Yeah." Dez placed a hand over his eyes and massaged his temples. "At least I think so. Last I saw him, he was sitting by the side of the road with that same stupid punk grin he always has...then he puked..."

Alex laughed as Derek's mind drifted off to other, more important things. *How were they going to take care of a whole town full of kids? Forget that, the question to ask is what the heck was going on? Why are all the moms and dads gone?*

"Hey, Alex?" He let out as he turned his head to her.

"Yeah?"

"How good are you with children?"

"I have a knack for taking care of them. Apparently, I'm good enough to be paid as a babysitter around town occasionally. Why?"

"I may need you to watch the kids tonight, at least until we can set up a system."

She peered up at him, a look of contempt on her face. "Okay. Anything to help."

Derek raised an eyebrow. "Something the matter?"

Alex shrugged. "I don't know. You and the others seem to have a hold on things, but you're setting me up on babysitting duty? Come on, dude. Wyatt's out there playing superman stopping a runaway car and that's the best you've got for me?"

Derek shoved his hands in his pockets. "Wyatt's going to play superman no matter what I tell him. I just need someone to watch the kiddos and make sure they don't get into any trouble until we can establish some kind of system, okay?"

Alex shrugged again, then sighed. "Okay."

Derek began to back out of the door. "We have to do whatever is necessary to survive, right? You okay with that?"

TAKEN BY THE NIGHT

Alex smirked at him. "Yeah, I got it."

Chapter Five

Wyatt opened his eyes, only to wince at the sunlight. He sat up, then felt a shooting pain in his jaw. As he propped himself up on his hands, he noticed someone sitting on a discarded tire next to him, which had apparently come off one of the vehicles during the collision.

"Here," the person said as she handed him a plastic bag full of ice. It was the cheerleader from earlier.

He looked at the bag, then switched to her eyes. They were a beautiful bright hazel. The left side of her face had a gash running from her forehead to across her brow. Her hair was short like most boys, but still long enough to have a sort of fluff. She was a blonde, with some brunette highlights evident. Her nose was short and perky, with her cheeks narrow. Her jawline was sharp, and her eyebrow straight with a small arch. Her smile showed straight, white teeth between her red lips.

"Thanks." He took the item from her and pressed it to his jaw.

The group of teens were packing up their things, and a few knelt beside the totaled, yellow bus using different colored sharpies to write something.

Wyatt turned to her. "So, what's your name?"

"Chloe."

Wyatt stood. "Ah, Chloe. A Greek name. It means beautiful flower."

She laughed and looked at him. "Really?"

"No," he responded, stretching. "I just made that up."

She let out a slight laugh and brushed a strand of hair out of her eyes. "What's yours?"

"Wyatt."

She stood and brushed some dirt from her red cheer skirt. "What does that mean? Sarcastic ninny?"

Wyatt snickered. "Close, but I'm pretty sure it means sexy beast."

He handed her the ice pack. "Here. Put that on your boo-boo." He pointed at the gash in her forehead.

"Thanks."

Wyatt nodded. She was probably the prettiest girl he had ever seen. She also knew how to keep him in check with his comments, quick to respond withnasty comebacks herself. This seemed even more attractive to him. She could handle him. This was different than the others, who would blow him off at the first sign of flirting. However, she may have been too different. Wyatt didn't know if he could mentally compete.

"So, uh...Wyatt?" She said, removing the ice pack from her head and standing up from her chair. "Earlier, before you ate Tony's boot, you said something about...all the parents disappearing?"

He nodded. "Yeah. Woke up this morning, and they were just...gone. Their cars were still in the driveway and their room looked like a wild animal attacked. Same with every other kid."

Chloe thought about this for a second, remembering what she saw right after the crash. How that…thing…dragged the bus driver away into the woods.

"You guys should come into town. We're still trying to...do something about all this. Corral the tikes, contact the police, things like that. If all else fails, there are plenty of houses for everyone to stay in until help arrives."

"That sounds good," She responded, biting her thumb nail. "I'll tell the others."

"I can do it." Wyatt walked forward with confidence, but Chloe grabbed his shoulder.

"Not the brightest move to make. I'm pretty sure I'm the only one here that doesn't completely hate you."

"Oh c'mon. I didn't hit anyone with the van, did I? They're still pissed about that?"

"Wyatt," She tilted her head as a concerning tone took over. "The car crash you caused mutilated the bodies of our friends, of course they are still upset at you!"

Wyatt wanted to interrupt and explain his case, how he was trying to save a kid's life, but he could tell from the look in her eyes that she wasn't up to hearing it. He nodded slowly then stuck his hands into his jean pockets. Chloe walked off to the group of West Side High School students gathered around the wreckage. He watched the football players trying to move the van to no avail. He noticed something, then walked over to them, despite Chloe's warning.

"What do *you* want?" The one who kicked him, Tony, said while flashing him a dirty look.

He ignored the vile eyes, threw open the passenger side door, reached in and pulled the gearshift from drive to neutral. Stepping out to see their confused faces, he pressed his hands on the front end of the vehicle and started to push. It nudged backwards, then the players joined in. Slowly it progressed in reverse, until one of the boys had to jump in and apply the brakes.

Wyatt ignored the teenagers around him, then started walking alone down the road and back into the town of Lyonside. He caught a glimpse of the side of the bus, which had memorials of the dead written in different color markers.

****

A crow cawed somewhere above him in the sky as Robbie shuffled his way down the street, bumping into kids that ran rampant. They laughed, as if their parents disappearing was the greatest thing to ever happen to them. They didn't see what he saw, though. The thing. That shadow creature was everywhere. In the corner of his eye, he could see it smiling at him. Just smiling.

TAKEN BY THE NIGHT

He pulled his hood over his head, letting the material brush his earlobes. The night before, it felt as if he was stabbed repeatedly directly through his eardrums. He remembered feeling the blood trickle down his fingers as he tried to protect his ears from the shadow's scream.

Oh, God....the scream.

A shiver was sent down his spine at the thought. He could hear it. He could feel it. Like tentacles pulling at his fear. *No.... no..... it pulled at his hate*. Everything he loathed. Everyone he despised. Jesse, the kid who chased him into the alleyway. Betty Mulburrow, Jesse's stuck up girlfriend who thinks she's too good for anyone. His father for attacking him....

No, no, no, no, no! That wasn't my dad! That was some sort of creature created by my imagination!

Even so, he could still feel a burning rage in his chest as he reminisced on the feeling of icy cold fingers on his throat.

Why did he attack me? He shouldn't have attacked me. He shouldn't have. He wouldn't have attacked me if I had just been good, if I hadn't had attacked Jesse. But I had to defend myself! I shouldn't have even had to defend myself! He shouldn't have chased me, and the boy who saw me shouldn't have ran away!

He began to feel a burn in his stomach, a flaming hatred for the guy who witnessed the events the night before. The kid did nothing. He didn't even speak up! Who just stands there and watches a guy get assaulted, then runs away like he has something better to do?!?
Now that his head was somewhat clear, he remembered the face of that boy. *His name was...was...Riley? Walker? Wally? Wyatt?*

Yes! Wyatt! They were in algebra class together. He played football.

Freakin' typical jock. Always thinking they're better than everyone else.

Robbie could feel the rage underneath his skin. His blood was boiling as his face became bright red. He stopped and grabbed his head as a breathtaking headache set in.

That's when the whispers began.

He looked up, and suddenly he wasn't in the center of town anymore. Robbie stood on the side of the road that lead out of Lyonside, and after a long journey, would eventually take you to the interstate.

"Wha--?" His voice cracked as he turned himself around in a panic. He could see trees behind him.

In front of him stood a cornfield.

His father's cornfield.

The whispers continued as Robbie grabbed his hair violently, a look of desperation on his face.

Robbie.

A voice rang out in small, yet echoing whispers. It sounded as if it was coming from within the...

Roooooooobbieeeeeeeee....

The voice grew into a childish tone, as if this were nothing but an afternoon game of hide and seek. Robbie stared in between the stalks, attempting to locate the source. His eyes moved quickly from one row to the next, but all he saw was darkness.

Darkness.

Robbie turned back towards the town and sprinted full speed, his tennis shoes slapping the asphalt as the whispers grew silent.

He dared not turn around.

****

Derek finally had the chance to sit down to try to figure things out. What would they all eat? He assumed they should loot the grocery store down the street. Ugh, he didn't like that word. *Loot.* It sounded wrong. *It was what they were doing, though. Did that make it right?* They were doing what they had to in order to survive. Jeez, it hadn't even been a day yet and he was already trying to rationalize things to himself. He told himself it was just what they had to do. He pulled out his phone to send a text he knew would never be received. He opened his mom's number, then began typing.

Where r u?

He stuffed it in his pocket, then hobbled over to the road outside of the bookstore. He turned to the grocery store parking lot where a lot of kids were running out with arms and mouths full of junk food.

Someone needed to take charge. Alex was busy locating toddlers and babies in a neighborhood a little further up a dirt road that intersected with the main street. There weren't that many babies in town as far as Derek knew, but Alex would still have her hands full with the toddlers. They would then take them to the town church further up that same road. She had taken many other teens with her, some football players who knew nothing about childcare. He laughed at the thought of Eight-Ball trying to comfort a little one.

Dez whistled from outside, grabbing his attention. "We got company!"

He pointed down the road, where Wyatt and Dez had tried to stop the runaway security van earlier that morning. A large group of kids were walking towards them, none he recognized, except for Wyatt in the front.

As they got closer, Wyatt opened his arms in a gesture, letting out an impossibly loud sigh.

"Miss me, losers?!?"

Derek smirked. "Not really. Who're your friends?"

Wyatt turned to the group of battered teens behind him. "I believe you know the West Side Knights."

Derek was confused as to why they were there. The West Side game was always one of rivalry. Expletives were always thrown from both sides, and harder hits were always promised. Derek thought about this and put those emotions aside. He walked up and tried to shake each of their hands.

"I'm Derek."

"Yeah." The first boy responded solemnly, refusing to offer his hand back.

"Oh, get over yourselves." Derek refused to take the attitude. "Just shake hands so we can start talking about the actual important things."

"You talk a lot, Lyonside dweeb." The tall redhead responded back.

A blonde cheerleader made her way up front from somewhere inside the pack of athletes.

"Tony, you said you'd be alright with this." She remarked.

He scoffed, refusing to remove his eyes from Derek's in a match-up of dominance. "Yeah, well I've changed my mind."

His eyes snapped away from Derek focusing on Wyatt, who was glaring at him curiously.

"What're you looking at?"

Wyatt cocked his head like a bird. "I don't know. I haven't figured it out yet."

Tony gritted his teeth and started towards Wyatt with balled up fists as the organized pile of teenagers began to cave in and try to keep the towering boy from knocking Wyatt out again. Desmond, who was around the same size as Tony, shoved him backwards and held his arms out.

"All of you just stop acting like children! We need to just chill out for a minute and figure out what's going on, together!" Dez yelled over the skirmishing group.

The road went silent for a moment before Derek spoke up. "He's right."

"Hey, now I know what I'm looking at! It's bigfoot!"

Dez turned to Wyatt and pointed at the ground in irritation. "I'm about to choke you out myself if you don't shut it, Richards!"

Wyatt shrugged, then crossed his arms like a scolded child.

"Everyone in town is all on main street. It's as organized as possible, given they're all...kids."

"Right." Derek hobbled back to the bookstore with the West Side gang behind him and stood in front of the crowd of Lyonside kids. He let go of his crutches, allowing them to smack the ground.

Silence.

"Hey, everyone. I know...I know this is weird. Our parents are...well, they're gone. In the middle of the night, I guess. No trace of where they've gone."

"Are they dead?!?" A voice from the crowd yelled out.

He swallowed the lump in his throat. "God, I hope not! But....we must...we have to be prepared for the worst. No one can get a hold of the police! So...we will have to take care of this ourselves!"

"How?!?" Someone yelled.

"Yeah, How?!?"

"Why should we listen to you?!?"

Dez thought about the missing parents. Everything that happened the night before. Seeing the monster, the nightmare....

The nightmare.

He walked up next to Derek. "Raise your hand if you had a nightmare last night!"

No one moved a muscle for a few seconds until Wyatt, who was leaning against the wall of the bookstore, raised his hand. One-by-one, the crowd of kids and teenagers began raising their arms. The younger children raised both in a playful fashion. None of the West Side teenagers raised theirs. Derek looked at Tony curiously.

"We...we didn't, our bus was attacked last night. Something happened and we crashed...we crashed and the next thing we know, half of our friends are dead...and...and the bus driver was missing."

"Something took him." Chloe spoke from behind him. "I didn't want to say anything before because I thought I was crazy...but now...I know it was something." She peered at Derek.

Derek's eyes widened. She had the same look on her face that Wyatt had the night before. It was the same expression that Alex had. Fear.

"Exactly! Something bad is happening now! Right freaking now! Our parents didn't just disappear. They were taken…by something that lives in there!" Dez threw an arm violently in the direction of the trees that acted as the gateway into the forest. This was new information to Derek, as he looked at his friend with crossed arms. Dez continued yelling towards the crowd of kids.

"Now, sure. Don't listen to us! Go out and do whatever you want, but the thing that took them is not done! It has only just begun! How long until you disappear?!? The only way we survive is if we all stick together!"

The crowd grew silent as the color was drained from some of their faces. Others didn't dare look him in the eyes.

Dez turned and looked at Derek, who had a look of desperation on his face.

"Don't worry, man. You don't have to do this by yourself."

Derek smiled and looked down at the concrete below. With the kids a little more willing to cooperate, they separated the crowd into groups, each led by an older teenager. As they were organizing who would do what to benefit the town, Derek bumped into Wyatt.

"Hey, man," He said, adjusting the crutches under his arms.

He watched as Wyatt's eyes trailed through the crowd, then they stopped on the group where a few of the West Side kids were gathering.

"I might join in on scavenging the grocery store with them," He said, shifting his head sideways.

Confused, Derek paused and then looked at Wyatt before asking, "This coming from the same person who just called their guy an ape?"

"That is false. I called him bigfoot."

"And at practice, said you'd take one of their heads off at the game...then proceed to shove it down their throat?"

Wyatt turned to him and smiled in his sarcastic way. "Call it a change of heart."

Derek looked back at the group, then as his eyes caught a glimpse of a blonde cheerleader, he figured it out.

"Holy balls! Wyatt Richards has a crush!" He said louder than he intended.

Wyatt's expression remained unchanged. "I don't know what you're talking about." He suddenly kicked Derek's right crutch out from under his arm, sending the crippled boytumbling to the concrete below. Wyatt walked off to join the group, leaving his friend chuckling on the ground.

Once Derek returned to his feet with some help from another teammate, he looked around. His eyes focused on Desmond and his sister walking down the road. Derek called out to them.

"Hey, Dez! Wait up!" He began hobbling forward on his crutch. Desmond turned to Molly and told her to go on, then sprinted over to meet Derek.

"What's up, man?"

Derek had to approach this topic carefully. He couldn't come across as condemning or suspicious. He was just genuinely curious as to what his friend was talking about during his speech.

"Nice little rallying monologue you had back there." He commented.

Desmond leaned back with a smile. "That was nothing but the truth, dude."

Derek chuckled a bit to prevent tension from setting in. He rubbed his chin. "Yeah, um...speaking of that. I...uh...I didn't know that the thing was from the forest."

Desmond seemed confused by the statement, as his grin turned downward. "I don't think, I...I didn't say that, did I?"

"Yeah..." Derek's throat tightened slightly. "Yeah you did."

Silence hung in the air between them.

After what seemed like an eternity, Desmond muttered, "I guess it was just an assumption. Scary...uh...scary things usually come from forests, right?"

Derek could smell the bull behind that statement. "Oh...okay. My bad, bro! You can go on. I was just curious!"

Dez smirked as they bumped fists. "Yeah, man. Let me know if you need anything else."

Derek nodded. Desmond held up a peace sign, then turned around and began jogging away. Derek was contemplating on what his friend really knew when his phone began buzzing in his pocket. He looked at the notification from Alex. He really needed some stress relief, and she was the perfect person for it.

****

Ruttledge was walking along the sidewalk with Jesse, both boys heading towards the school in order to find supplies.

"I really don't like them," Jesse grunted out as he pulled his bum knee along.

"Who?" Ruttledge looked up at the pinkish sky as the sun began to set on the mysterious town. The beauty of the sun's rays casting through the gray clouds above captivated him.

"That whole group. Derek, Desmond…especially Wyatt."

"I've never met them." Ruttledge ran a hand over his thick black hair.

"Be grateful," Jesse said as he spit something out of his mouth on the ground in front of them. "They're a bunch of pretentious jerks, thinking they're better than anyone else. They just took control, if you even want to call it that."

"Control is important. Without it, there's anarchy."

Jesse held his arms out wide and smirked. "Look around, old pal. It's nothing but anarchy!"

Ruttledge looked at all the kids that surrounded them. They were all beginning to spread out, moving to either their separate stations or just playing with their friends in the street. It wasn't normal. It felt chaotic. It was an organized chaos, but it was chaos, nonetheless.

"I see what you're referring to."

Jesse nodded. "See, I'm not as dumb as you think."

Ruttledge watched one of the kids walk up to the group entering the grocery store. He believed this person was Wyatt.

"I never said you were dumb, Jess." He turned back towards his friend.

"Yeah, well, let me lay a little more knowledge on you about the situation. Someone is going to end up dead if we don't get a handle on things. I haven't felt right since we saw that thing the other night."

Both boys turned their heads and stared at the sky as the darkness of the night fell upon them.

"Neither have I," Ruttledge exhaled a shaky breath, unable to release the tension in his shoulders. "Neither have I."

****

Derek: You all ok?

Alex was cradling a baby, letting it suckle on a bottle as she walked back and forth across the chapel's main room looking at her phone.

Alex: We're good.

Derek: Ok. Heading home. My phone is about to die, so in case I don't get the chance to say it later: Goodnight.

Alex: Night.

She sang softly to the little one as she cradled her. Her voice was quiet, but if one was listening close enough, they too would be able to hear her through the walls. She ran out of song ideas after a while and started improvising using the poem she had read the night before. Edgar Allan Poe's writings had a way of sticking into one's memory. She simply added a tune to his words, letting out a gorgeous melody.

"That was beautiful," a voice behind her said. Alex turned and saw Carlos cleaning out a bottle of milk that had gone bad.

"Oh, it isn't mine. It's Edgar Allan Poe." She explained.

"Last time I checked, Poe didn't sing his poems, especially not like that," he said as he dried his hands with a discarded dish rag.

The lights flickered. The sun was setting, which made the half second of darkness send a chill down Alex's spine. Her breath went cold, as the hair on the back of her neck stood on end. Carlos seemed to feel the same sensation.

"Alex?" He said with a hint of worry and shakiness in his voice.

The lights shut off completely, sending the little ones they had rounded up around town into hysterics. The bulbs flickered to life, much to her relief, until her eyes met Carlos.

The creature she had seen the night before had its hand wrapped around his throat, lifting him off the ground. The children screamed at the sight of the horror and fled in her direction.

Carlos desperately pulled at its fingers, but the grip was supernaturally strong. His eyes bulged and showed a look of horror as he struggled to let out a scream, though one would not come. The smaller kids howled in terror and cowered under the church pews.

It turned to her, and smiled, bearing its horrific teeth.

The lights flickered once again, but once they returned to normal, the thing was gone, along with Carlos.

Alex tried her best to hold in a scream, as that would only send the children into more chaos. The sun was setting, and she was paralyzed by the fear that ran like ice water through her veins.

Where was Carlos?

TAKEN BY THE NIGHT

Chapter Six

Desmond was screaming, and the sound gave Molly goosebumps.

It was two o'clock in the morning, and as usual, she hadn't been able to sleep, so she had decided to bury her head in a book. The house had fallen silent like every night, until the sounds of her brother's cries abruptly broke the tranquility. Desmond had a very stoic demeanor, only revealing emotion when needed. She had never heard such fear in his voice. It shook Molly to her core.

"Desmond!" She called out as she raced out into the dark hallway. She turned the corner, sprinting to her brother's door. She jostled the handle, but it was locked.

Was he being attacked by that thing?

"Dez! Desmond, open the door!"

114

He responded by screaming once again, his voice cracking as his deep tone erupted into a high screech.

"Desmond!" She banged on the door with her fists.

He screamed again. She threw herself against the door to try and knock it down.

She was contemplating grabbing something to ram into the handle to try and bust the lock off, when she heard the unmistakable sound of metal clicking.

The door unlocked.

It creaked on its hinges as it slowly opened, giving her a full view into her brother's room. The lights were off, painting the wall with a thick blackness. She could see the figure of her brother standing in front of her, his head down and his hands rubbing at his eyes.

She reached into the room and felt along the wall for a switch. When her finger finally flipped on the light, her eyes were suddenly bombarded with flashes. Images seared into her brain. A glance at something inside of her big brother.

Her eyes gazed upon a figure that was larger than life, standing tall above her. It looked like the beast the others had described. It had no definition, like a shadow, however this monster was glowing red, like a thriving flame. The smile was the same, way too big for its face and filled with gnarly teeth. The eyes, however, had thrown her off. The other kids had said it had bright red, wild orbs. This thing had black, soulless holes within its head.

She screamed as the lights flickered revealing her brother once again. His eyes were swollen, as if he had been crying for hours. She was now shaken to her core. She had never seen a tear fall from his face. Never. He was the strongest person she had ever known.

"Desmond?" She let out, her voice quaking.

Her older brother sniffled, then locked eyes with his sister. "Yeah, sorry."

He was trying to regain his composure as he turned away from her, wiping his face on his shirt.

Molly spoke louder than she had intended. "Dez, what on earth was that?!?"

"Nothing." He explained. "Just another one of those night terrors everyone else has been getting. Go back to bed, sis." He walked over to the door and tried to shut it on her. She slapped the wood with an open palm and pushed back.

"No, that was something else entirely! I…I've never heard you scream like that in my life! I've never seen you…" Molly began to choke on her words as hot tears welled up in her eyes, "I've never seen you cry! Something is seriously wrong!"

Desmond couldn't stand to see his sister cry, so he pulled her into a tight hug, letting her sob into his pajamas. After a minute she pulled away.

"Tell me, Desmond! What's happening?!?" She begged him.

He looked into her golden eyes, reflecting the same color from his own. He nodded towards his chair by the desk for her to sit down, and she walked over and curled up on the seat as he plopped onto his bed right across from her.

"I….." Desmond paused, unsure where to begin. *Should I explain why I was screaming? Should I start from the other night when we last saw Dad?*

"I knew this was going to happen. I knew it the night before the parents disappeared." He opened his mouth, allowing the floodgates to open and the truth to spill out. "Something inside me…it told me it would happen."

The red creature Molly had seen inside her brother popped into her head as he continued. "I didn't really know, you know, not in detail. It's like...I get these...feelings."

Molly wrapped her arms around her legs. Desmond stared at the ground with glazed eyes and continued.

"When I last saw Dad, I knew it would be the last time, but that's all I was aware of. These little moments of dread and anxiety in my chest that tell me these things, but it just got worse...so much worse when...."

"When you went to sleep." Molly finished his sentence. "That's why you were screaming."

He looked up at her. "I didn't scream, did I?"

She nodded, obviously still scarred from the experience.

"Wow. Okay," He ran a hand through his hair. "In my dreams, I can see these...moments. Things that haven't happened, yet. I can feel the cold, sharp metal of something through my body, and see it...sticking from my chest. I can feel myself sinking to the bottom of a body of water. Sometimes I see myself in a straight jacket, the kind they put on crazy people. I can never move my arms. Then sometimes, I see myself out in that forest. That's how I know where the beasts are coming from."

Molly nodded slowly; the shock still fresh to her senses. After what felt like forever, she finally spoke. "Something tells me the adults won't be back for a while, huh?"

Dez nodded.

"Why didn't you tell anyone before?" She asked.

Desmond stood up from the bed. "Would you believe me if I weren't your brother?"

Molly contemplated on this for a second, sucking on her teeth. *If I were anyone else, I would think you were a nut-job! Plus, you're telling me that you are feeling things and seeing experiences that haven't happened yet, and I see this...monster inside you?!?*

Neither spoke a word. Both Martin siblings just stared at the ground, their minds racing for an explanation.

****

It had been a long, gruesome, and paranoid-filled night. Nobody wanted to sleep. Younger kids were crying in symphony for their parents, and even the teenagers who strive for independence, were caught up in the desire for safe arms to protect them from the dark. Even Wyatt, who had been sure he could live on his own, felt this need desperately. He slept in his own bed inside of his own house, but he felt no safer than if he was laying in the dimly lit street outside. Every sound he heard, whether it resembled the house settling or the wind whistling outside his window, made him bury his head deeper into his pillow and wrap himself tighter in his blankets.

Come morning, he had gotten at the most three hours of sleep, possibly less. He walked groggily outside in nothing but a worn-out pair of red shorts and a Lyonside football t-shirt. He looked around at the sunlight shining on the grass he had neglected to mow. The dew shimmered as he yawned, stretched, then scratched the inside of his ear with his pinky.

There was movement at the house across the street. With many new kids from the bus crash in town, some needed places to stay for the night. They had taken residence in houses that belonged to the adults without children. Wyatt happened to notice that Chloe, a girl he admittedly had a thing for, was walking out the front door.

He quickly pulled his finger from his ear, suddenly caring about how he looked. He wasn't exactly appearing classy, with his light brown hair stuck out in all directions, and the crust in the corners of his eyes.

He waved.

She smiled and waved back.

TAKEN BY THE NIGHT

After Chloe went inside, he heard a truck engine down the street, and after a few minutes, the source of the sound pulled into his driveway. The engine shut off, and out hopped Derek, who greatly contrasted Wyatt in appearance. His black hair was perfectly aligned, and his clothes were casual and pressed.

"Hi," he said in a melancholy tone as he hobbled on his crutch over to his friend.

"How'd you sleep?" Wyatt asked with an attitude implying he knew the answer.

"Like a freakin' baby." Derek answered with heavy sarcasm.

"Man, I think these boxers I picked up from the store are too small. They are crawling up my legs." He picked at his wedgie, glancing over to the house across the street to make sure Chloe had not returned.

Derek smirked. "That's what you get for randomly grabbing crap off the shelves without checking the size."

"You weren't there so you don't know!" Wyatt awkwardly trotted towards his front door.

"No, but I know you."

"God, it's making me walk like a *Looney Tunes* villain!"

"Who? Yosamite Sam?"

"No, no. Remember that one movie where they mixed the animation with real actors?"

"Oh, *Space Jam!*" Derek guessed.

"Just forget it."

"*Who Framed Roger Rabbit*?"

"That's not even *Looney Tunes*!"

Wyatt went back inside and got dressed, then met Derek back at his truck and proceeded to the town center. Everything was quiet now that the restless, motherless, and fatherless night had passed. Very few kids were running around, and most of them had bags underneath their eyes from lack of sleep. Wyatt considered everything that could have happened to cause this. *Did all the grown-ups just run off into the forest without telling anyone?*

"Aliens," he muttered.

Derek turned to him just to send a confused glance. "Say what now?"

"That's probably it. Aliens."

"Right," Derek spoke sarcastically. "I doubt that thing that was chasing us the other night was an alien."

"How do you know? Have you ever seen one?"

"Well, no."

"Why don't we wait until we find more substantial evidence before we start leaping to conclusions, huh moron?"

Wyatt turned and looked at him, clicking his tongue. "You know, words hurt sometimes."

"Would you rather I use my fists?"

Derek parked alongside the curb in front of the bookstore, where a crowd of kids had already gathered to list complaints. Most were things they couldn't control, like how to get the grown-ups back. Derek hobbled over on his crutch to the group as they erupted into questions.

"Have you found my mom yet?!?"

"Did you hear anything last night?!?"

"I'm scared!"

"I want breakfast!"

Derek waved his hands in the air. "Wait, wait! One at a time!"

He became consumed by the crowd of kids as Wyatt stood back and watch the natural leader take the wheel. He was a second-string quarterback, second only to the great Derek Hoff. Everyone liked Derek. He had a winning personality and a victorious smile that could tame a rabid dog. Wyatt didn't exactly have that ability. He could turn a tame dog rabid.

123

"He's rather good at that," a recognizable voice said as it approached from behind. It was Chloe, in a pair of denim jeans and a gray t-shirt. They were clothes she had grabbed from the store when they stockpiled the night before. Wyatt had on a green *Ghostbusters* t-shirt, along with a pair of cargo shorts.

"Yeah, he is. You should have seen him on the football field!"

She looked at him. "How's your head?"

He put on his infamous sarcastic smile. "Oh, lovely. I'm still just as insane as I've always been."

"Well, good. Wouldn't want you in your right mind, now would we?"

Wyatt felt a tap on his shoulder. He turned and looked down slightly, his eyes meeting those of the kid he saved from the runaway van.

"Hi," the boy spoke, his voice slightly sheepish.

"What's up, Frodo?"

"Uh, my name's Isaac."

Chloe held in a laugh and looked towards the sky as Wyatt closed his eyes and shook his head. "Okay then, Isaac."

"Uh, can you help me?"

"If you need the mayor," Wyatt pointed at Derek, "that's your guy."

Isaac shook his head. "No, I want you."

Wyatt looked at Chloe, who just shrugged. He turned back at Isaac.

"Okay kid, on a scale from one to a hundred, how important is this? Because I swear if you send me on a mission to find your missing Gameboy, I will...I'll probably keep it."

"What's a Gameboy?"

Wyatt ran his hands down his face in frustration, "This generation is screwed."

Chloe helped them get back onto topic. "What do you need?"

Isaac looked down at his feet. "I can't find my sister. She's somewhere all alone. I'm scared for her and her baby."

Chloe raised an eyebrow. "Her baby?"

The kid nodded. "Yeah, she's pregnant."

Wyatt remembered hearing rumors about one of the town teenage girls becoming pregnant. Her name was Lucy Letrail, and she had pulled out of school a few months before.

Wyatt crossed his arms. "Why do you want me for this? I'm the kind of guy who looks for his sunglasses when they've been on my head the whole time."

"Because I trust you. I don't know that many older people in town, so I…I thought you might be able to help."

Wyatt turned and looked at Derek, who had been completely swallowed by the crowd, but was now being assisted by Dez.

"Alright, Frodo." Wyatt said as he crouched next to the boy. "Tell me where she was the last time you saw her."

Chapter Seven

Alex woke up from her restless sleep, a napkin stuck to her cheek. The children surrounded her, scattered around almost as if they fell asleep right where they stood the night before. One boy was even covered in the building blocks from the toy bin.

She looked around for any sign of what happened the night before. There was nothing left of Carlos except what she remembered. She knew it happened; it was too horrifying to forget. The poor children also witnessed and were probably scarred for life.

She had to get back to town and tell the others, but she couldn't leave the kiddos wandering around the church. Especially not with that...thing...still out there.

She gathered them to the center of the room. Some were quick to awaken, while others yawned and rubbed their eyes. She half expected terrified grimaces on their faces and questions about the night before, however, they didn't seem bothered by it. Maybe the moment of Carlos' disappearance was too much for their tiny brains, and as a protection mechanism they blocked it out. There was one boy in the back, sniffling. He kept his head down and didn't say anything. She told them they were playing follow the leader, and that they would get a prize if they stayed with her, the leader, until they reached the town. *What would she give them?*

"Miss Alexandria?" a little girl spoke up.

"Just call me Alex, sweetie," she responded as she led them down the dirt road into town.

"Alex is a boy name, though. You're a girl!"

Alex laughed." It's a unisex name."

Half of the kids jumped like she had just spoken the worst word known to mankind.

"You said a bad word!" The little girl exclaimed.

Alex giggled at the premise of them getting "sex" and "unisex" confused.

"No, no. Unisex. It means that it's for both boys and girls!"

The group groaned in understanding as they continued walking. They had gotten a good distance away from the church, and after a few minutes, they rounded the corner into the town square. Derek emerged from a group of kids who were rationing food. Alex assumed it came from the town grocery store.

"Where have you been?" Derek asked with a smile. "And where's Eight-Ball?"

Eight-Ball. Carlos.

Alex broke down crying in his arms. He caught her, letting her sniffle and sob into his shirt. He could feel her tremble with every gasp of breath, so he didn't rush her, but decided to let her finish.

"Alex," he pulled her back and looked into her brown eyes with his blue ones. "What happened?"

The little boy who had been keeping to himself in the back made his way towards Derek and Alex. He couldn't have been any older than nine, which was way too young to be experiencing these atrocities. He spoke up. "The monster got him!"

Derek looked at the child, then back at Alex, who had long strands of brown hair dangling in front of her still-wet face. She nodded in agreement.

"That thing?" he raised his eyebrows.

She nodded again. One of the little kids must have run off to tell their older sibling and spread word while Alex had been crying, because before Derek even realized it, a crowd had begun to form around them.

"I thought only the parents were taken!" A preteen voice spoke from the gathering.

"We don't know the parents were taken!" Derek responded.

"Yeah, right!" A taller, scrawny boy with pale skin spoke up. "We all saw it in our dreams!"

Derek surveyed the crowd." Listen to me! We're still trying to figure this out! Please, just go back to your responsibilities!"

The crowd dispersed reluctantly. He turned to Alex, who had removed the hair from her face.

"Take them to the ice cream shop and I'll have someone else take care of them for a little bit," he said, a hint of dryness in his voice. "It's in the center of town, so there's less of a chance of anything dangerous happening there."

She nodded and began to round up the children, before turning back to him.

"You okay?" He asked for what seemed to be the millionth time. She nodded.

"Yeah." She crossed her arms as she swooped her hair out of her face. "I'm fine."

****

The pain in Robbie's skull wouldn't stop. He felt the urge to throw up. Something was terribly wrong with his head, but going to his house wasn't an option. He didn't want to run into the thing again, or some sort of perverted version of his father. The flickering memory of him stabbing, murdering his father continued to play over and over in his mind. He wandered the streets, until his eyes locked on a familiar face.

It was him. Wyatt. *The kid who left me, abandoned me while I was being beaten in an alleyway by Jesse.*

Coward!

Just the thought of the guy made Robbie want to puke.

He watched him talking to a blonde girl, a student from West Side high school. He remembered seeing her in that group, the ones that came back to Lyonside. They must have gotten stranded when the adults disappeared.

Kill him.

A voice rang out, but it wasn't his ears that heard it, it was in his head, and it was loud, very loud. His headache worsened.

Wyatt began speaking to a child.

Do it now!

Robbie pushed his way out of the crowd around him in the opposite direction, grasping at his head and likely drawing stares. Robbie Burnett had had enough. He took off, full sprint down the road.

Away from anyone he could hurt.

****

Dez walked into the bookstore, reading glasses in hand. He moved through the isles surrounded by the few shelves, searching for something.

"Hey, Alex!" He said, refusing to remove his eyes from scanning the books.

She walked over to him, holding a pen in between her fingers. "Hey." She said with a little more confidence than she had earlier during her return from the church.

"Where are the horror books?"

A confused look grew across her face. "Um, I don't think we have anything like that, except maybe a few books on urban legends."

"That would work."

"Huh, good luck," she responded, walking out of the isle and to the desk. "They aren't on the shelves."

"Then, where are they?" Dez responded as he followed her.

"Well, they were organized neatly into a column, but that was before Wyatt came in here like a bat out of Hell the other night and knocked all the piles over."

"Great," Dez sighed. "The guy isn't even here, and he still finds a way to make me want to punch him in the throat."

Alex sat on the desk. "What do you need those books for? Last I checked, we're living in a horror novel."

Dez plopped down on the floor and started rifling through the hundreds of books scattered around. "That's exactly why I need them."

Alex thought about this for a second. "So, you think you'll find an answer to all this in a few campfire stories?"

He put his reading glasses on without moving his head. "Got any better ideas?"

He began searching, but it wasn't long before he started to feel something. A sort of force urging him to reach further within one section of the piles. It was like a temptation of some sort. It felt almost wrong to reach for what he felt a pull towards.

His hands inserted into the endless abyss of novels. His fingers lightly grasped a leather-bound novel, pulling it from the pile and out into the open. The outside cover was an inky black, with no words on the front or back. It was way too big to be a journal and seemed too ancient to even be in a small town used bookstore.

"What's this?" Desmond held it up for Alex to see.

She raised an eyebrow as she studied the front cover. "No clue. I just watched the shop for the elderly woman who ran this place. Does it have a price sticker on the back, or maybe a bar code?"

Dez inspected it.

"No, none of those."

She crossed her arms and huffed in bewilderment. "Then it most likely isn't from this store."

Dez flipped through the pages, his eyes skimming over dozens of words as the paper slipped through his fingers. He slammed the book shut once more before turning to Alex.

"How much?"

Alex looked at him as if he were crazy. "Are you serious? Just take it, goody-two-shoes!"

Desmond hesitated for a second, before breaking out into a chuckle. "My bad."

TAKEN BY THE NIGHT

He made his way out the door and onto Main Street, his new book tucked tidily beneath his arm.

****

Wyatt had gone over the story a thousand times in his head. The girl, 15-year old Lucy Letrail, had disappeared a full day after the parents. According to her brother, she had left in the dead of night to smuggle some food from the rations for her brother. The food was stocked in the school gym, up a dirt road a short distance from where her and her brother had decided to take residence. An unlit dirt road, which meant it was near pitch black during the night, apart from the moonlight to navigate. Wyatt remembered running sprints down this long road during the summer, right before football. He remembered the blistering July heat. It seemed like torture at the time, training for yet another uneventful season with the Lyonside Lions. Now he would give anything to have that back.

He had asked Isaac for a picture so he could identify her if found. She was your average teenager. A face in the background at a small-town public school. She had brown hair, a bit overweight, and had pale skin. From her clothes to her facial features, there was nothing extraordinary about her that would cause anyone to stop and take note.

He had to admit it to himself: the only reason he was helping Isaac was because his missing sister was only fifteen and expecting a child. This hit home for Wyatt, because he knew that his own mother became pregnant with him at a young age. Isaac had gone on to explain that the baby's father had moved away, and this caused Wyatt to choke up slightly. He was once an accidental baby, and he didn't know where he'd be without his dad.

He pinned the picture to his bedroom wall and hung a printed photo of a Google Maps satellite view of their small town right next to it. He drew a blue circle around her, then he placed a blue splotch on the map to suggest where she had last been. One at the house, then a dotted line down the dirt road. He then placed a photo of Carlos; a cut out of a team picture they had taken earlier that year. He pinned it next to Lucy, used a red marker to circle him, then placed a splotch on where he was last seen: the church. *How would he find them both? Would more kids disappear?*

Focus, Wyatt, he told himself. *One step at a time. Starting with Lucy.*

Next, go walk down the road where she disappeared.

He grabbed a water bottle he had stashed underneath his bed, then he waltzed out the front door and towards the road.

Wyatt took a swig of his water and walked past Derek at the school parking lot, surrounded by kids volunteering to stock food. He had a checklist in his hands.

"Wy! Wait up!"

Derek waddled over to him, crutch under his right arm, checklist in his left hand.

"Yo," Wyatt responded.

"Where did you get that water bottle?"

"Your mom."

Derek's expression grew agitated. 'Your mom' wasn't a valid response, especially when no one's mom has yet to turn up after disappearing days before.

"Wyatt!"

"What?" The two paused, perhaps recognizing what they heard in one another's frustrated voices. Maybe it was fear or maybe they were resigned to the inevitable. Wyatt kept walking forward, eyes dead ahead down the dirt road.

"Where did you get that?"

"I found it."

Derek sighed. "You can't be stashing stuff! We have to have order around here!"

"Whatever you say," Wyatt said as he stopped dead in his tracks. His eyes were fixed on two pink objects on the side of the road where the gravel and the grass met.

"Here," he tossed the empty bottle at Derek, who had to drop the clipboard to catch it. "I'm finished with it, anyways."

He walked towards the objects, and as he got closer, it became clear what they were.

A beat up, dirty pair of hot pink tennis shoes.

Chapter Eight

After he removed the itchy cast from his leg, that night, Derek had decided it best for everyone to stay together. Nobody truly wanted to sleep separately, especially with the news of Lucy disappearing under mysterious circumstances. Wyatt explained what happened but refused to go into detail about exactly what he knew and how he knew it. He said it was personal business he had to take care of alone.

He, Dez, Wy, P.B n' J., and a group of other teens helped set up the tables they gathered from the high school cafeteria. They were set up close to each other, with a small aisle between them to walk around, in the middle of the street right outside of the bookstore. Just in case there wasn't enough light, a packet of glow sticks was placed on the plastic white top of every table. They would have dinner together. They would have fun and joke around. They would have one night with no worries, then they would all huddle together in the school gym. However, Wyatt advised against this, mainly because the only path to and from the school was the dirt road, the same place where Lucy Letrail had been taken.

After around 8:00 p.m., Alex helped gather the kids to the town center. Soon, the whole town was present and seated all around. It was then that Derek got his first look at how many people there really were. At least a hundred, maybe one-fifty. It was a lot to take in. This many needed to be taken care of, these many lives were at stake.

He grabbed his nightly rations, sat down next to Alex and began a deep conversation. Molly sat across from her, listening intently to the discussion before nudging her brother to get his head out of the book he had found. Desmond adjusted his glasses, then peered up towards his friends.

Derek had his head turned towards Alex when a sudden slap on his shoulders broke him out of his trance. It was Wyatt.

"Alright," The wild-eyed boy interrupted as he opened his palm above the table. Three cherry red dice blocks knocked against the table abruptly, resting on the wood with the numbers one, three, and five facing upwards.

"When I was nine, I threw up on a girl's back in the playground."

The group all stared at Wyatt in silence, all with looks of confusion or disgust.

"I'm…I'm sorry," Desmond said. "What?"

"If you don't mind, I'd rather not repeat it." Wyatt sat down to the left of Derek, his metal chair scraping against the concrete.

Derek's eyes focused on the dice blocks as Wyatt collected them again, then began rattling them in his hands.

"Roll the dice," he threw the blocks down again, this time the numbers adding up to thirteen. "Do a little bit of mathematical mathematics, then you have to tell an embarrassing story from whatever age number you roll. For example, when I was thirteen, I ran my dad's dirt bike into our backyard fence."

The table went quiet as Wyatt reached for the dice once more. However, Molly's hands beat him to it.

"Hey, now!" He exclaimed. "Look at little miss sunshine warming up to my ideas!"

Molly rolled her eyes and grinned, then dropped the dice on the tabletop. She peered at them. She had rolled four ones.

"I don't remember anything from when I was four. What do we do then, Einstein?" She turned to Wyatt with her arms crossed.

"I do." Desmond added. "You once pretended you wet your bed."

The group collectively looked at Molly with confused expressions.

"What?" She turned to her brother, equally as confused.

"Yeah," Desmond laughed. "You had been bugging Dad for these Wonder Woman bed sheets that you just had to have, right? Do you remember those?"

"Yeah, they're still in my bottom drawer."

"Well, you decided you were going to dump a huge bottle of apple juice on your old sheets and say you wet yourself, but he could still smell the apple."

Desmond took a swig of his cola can. "He bought you those new sheets the next day."

The table went quiet for a second, then Alex started giggling, which caused a chain reaction of laughter.

"Oh, come on, guys! I was four!" Molly pleaded with her hands out.

"Maybe, but you were also a little evil mastermind," Wyatt added.

She giggled, a slight smile growing on her face. Wyatt wondered if she was laughing at his comment or just the situation in general.

Desmond grabbed the dice and tossed them.

"Eleven." He said. He contemplated to himself for a second, then spoke. "I backed my dad's car out of the driveway and ran over our garbage can."

The group laughed again. Wyatt propped his feet up on the table as the next person took the dice. Alex rolled a fifteen.

"I got to the top of the rope climb during gym class and was too scared to come down."

"You're scared of heights?" Derek asked.

"Deathly!"

Derek laughed as he grabbed the dice. He rolled three sixes.

"I'm, uh…I'm not eighteen yet."

The group collectively looked at Wyatt for an explanation of what to do next.

"Now you have to say something you'd want to do by the time you're that age."

Derek sat in silence for a second as he contemplated his answer. He drummed his fingers on the table, then spoke.

"I want to go camping one day. By myself. Alone in the wilderness."

Wyatt threw his head back with a huff. "God, why are you so boring?"

Desmond chuckled and added. "Yeah, come on. Something fun!"

Derek scoffed. "What? Camping can be fun!"

Wyatt shook his head as he grabbed the dice for a third roll.

Eleven.

Wyatt's smirk began to fade. His expression turned serious as he retreated into his own thoughts. He sat up and cleared his throat.

"When I was eleven, I uh…I killed a lion."

The group was collectively shocked. Alex put her hand to her mouth.

"You what? No way." Desmond leaned forward on his elbows as he crossed his arms. "Quit playing, Wy."

Wyatt scoffed nervously and adjusted in his seat. "I wish I was playing, dude."

He looked into the eyes of his friends before he spoke again.

"It was my eleventh birthday. My dad took me to the zoo to celebrate because I was obsessed with lions at that age, right? I was bouncing this rubber red ball back and forth off the walls, up and down as we walked."

Molly raised an eyebrow as Derek leaned back and crossed his arms.

"We...uh...we got to the lion exhibit and I was excited, like *really* excited. I bounced the ball so hard that it flew over the gate and into the den. It bounced into a bush and I couldn't see it. I thought I would get in trouble if my dad knew, so I didn't tell him, and we went along our way."

Wyatt sucked on his teeth for a second as he leaned forward, tapping his fingers on the table.

"When we got home that night, we saw on the news that one of the lions at the town zoo had died. The report said he had choked on a toy. I...I never told my dad what happened."

The table went quiet as Wyatt leaned back in his chair again. Derek could see the look in his friend's eyes. He was clearly uncomfortable reminiscing on the memory.

"That was a nice story, Richards." A slurred voice arose from behind Wyatt. The group turned and saw Jesse Davis with a flask in his hand, waving it about as he spoke.

"I especially liked the part where you killed that lion like you did our playoff chances." He chuckled. "You killed the Lions' chances at a championship, and you murdered an actual lion!"

Molly noticed something in Wyatt's eyes as he stared at the table in front of him, fondling the dice in his palm. He was trying not to respond; he was holding back.

"You're clearly too wasted to be talking trash," Derek responded. "Where'd you get the alcohol, Jess?"

Jesse leaned on Wyatt's chair to steady himself. "None of your business. Besides, Wyatt Earp over here can defend himself. We all know his mouth is faster than his legs."

Wyatt clenched his right hand into a fist with the crimson cubes inside. His hands were shaking. Molly could hear his breathing intensifying. He suddenly calmed, his tensed shoulders relaxing as he casually turned around.

"I'm glad you liked the story, Jesse. I really am. I mean, at least I had a chance on the football field, right?"

Molly's gaze switched to Jesse, who had his head cocke, curiously looking at Wyatt. She then looked at Derek, who had a look of pure exhaustion on his face because he knew what was coming next.

"What's that supposed to mean, choker?" Jesse responded.

"Well," Wyatt's motor mouth began to rev its engine, then it took off like a rocket. "I'm a decent student. I at least have enough brain capacity to use on the field. I mean, we blamed the bum knee for why you couldn't play, but we all know it's kind of difficult for someone who was held back twice in middle school to use their head."

Alex had been taking a swig of soda when she heard the comment. She choked for a second, then covered her mouth as she coughed. Desmond turned to his sister and gave a smile that told her he was entertained.

"Oh, yeah? You want to go, Richards?" Jesse leaned back with his arms out wide, an invitation for a brawl.

Wyatt chuckled. "Sure, I'd love to knock your teeth out, assuming you had any left in your head, you uneducated hillbilly."

Jesse turned red in the face as he began moving towards Wyatt with harmful intent in his eyes.

Wyatt shot up from his seat to defend himself, but Jesse never made it over to the table. Derek had suddenly launched out of his chair and swung a fist in his direction, contacting his jaw and sending Jesse staggering backwards. He fell to the sidewalk, the sound of his palms smacking concrete echoing over the tabletops and demanding the attention of the crowd of children.

As he struggled to stand, Wyatt walked over and picked up the flask he dropped, then tossed it across the table to Desmond.

Jesse waved a hand in their direction, and Wyatt took this as a prideful form of surrender. Derek crossed his arms as he stood next to him.

"Batman and Robin!" Wyatt held out a fist. Derek rolled his eyes, then bumped knuckles with his friend.

****

The time was 10:00 p.m. Derek was leading the pack of kids down the dirt road, Lucy's road, as Wyatt preferred to call it. After a couple of minutes in complete darkness, apart from the flashlight in his hand, he started hearing things. The whistle of the nighttime wind serenaded his ears, as the snap of a twig somewhere in the forests surrounding them echoed just below the murmurs of the crowd. He may have let Wyatt's paranoia get in his head, but he had a feeling the situation was about to get very bad, very fast.

Wyatt walked along the back of the pack, separating himself from the group from West Side. He wanted to be alone again and think about finding Lucy. It had consumed his mind, and in a way, he felt it was his responsibility. This was his way of rationalizing the situation. He had no clue where the parents had gone, but he did know where Lucy was, however. She was somewhere in the forest around them....

"Wyatt!" Dez's voice rang out for him as he felt a hand grasp his shoulder. He had a book open in his other hand.

"Sorry I can't take your call. Leave a message at the beep."

Dez ignored the sarcasm with a face that displayed a grim look.

"Wy, when you were looking for the missing girl, what did you find on this road?"

"A pair of pink shoes. Why?"

Dez put a hand over his mouth slowly, as if he was contemplating the words just said and what to do next. He held the book up to where Wyatt could see, and he lowered his voice so that none of the other kids would overhear.

149

"Check it." He said.

The page was pure white, with a single paragraph of black ink at the top, and a single word in bold letters.

NIGHTCRAWLER

This urban myth sprung from tales told by farmers to keep their children from wandering the dirt trails in the nights of the early 1900's. The legend speaks of a creature, at least 10 feet tall with broad shoulders and long arms that stretch to the ground, that would take children back to its cave and devour them. It left nothing but the shoes exactly where they were snatched. The eyes range from bright red to a yellow that's hardly noticeable in the darkness. No further description available.

Wyatt's eyes widened. *Could there be more monsters besides the one they had seen the other night?*

"I thought that.... only thing out there was the...wait...what?"

He looked around in the darkness in quick movements. His head jerked from one side of the road to the other, until his eyes locked on something. A faint color in the inky blackness surrounding them.

Two yellow orbs stared back at him, shifting slightly as twigs snapped in the forest in front of him. Something big was shifting as it moved towards them.

"Oh, no."

Chapter Nine

Wyatt sprinted through the group of confused kids, with a determination motivated by the pure terror that coursed through his veins. Dez followed not far behind, book under his left arm. He stopped right behind Chloe and the West Side gang.

"Chloe!" He spoke with urgency. She turned to him; one eyebrow raised.

"What's going on?" she asked, an urgency in her eyes. It was almost as if she knew and was attempting to hold back a panicked reaction.

"This will sound nuts, babe, but take off your shoes," he said, as if it wasn't the craziest thing he had spoken all day, which it was not.

"First: don't call me babe," She scolded. "Second: What? Why?" She tilted her head to the side, one earring dangling, gently swinging back and forth.

"I don't have time to explain! Just trust me!"

Dez reached for his shoulder. "What are you planning?"

She removed her white tennis shoes, revealing yellow socks underneath. Wyatt grabbed them, pulled back, and launched them down the road in the opposite direction. He turned around and spoke to the crowd.

"Everyone! Take off your shoes!"

Some kids had a little more faith than others, as they removed theirs and mimicked his pitch in the same direction he had thrown Chloe's sneakers. A few others were more reluctant.

"Screw that!" Jesse yelled back at him. He was slightly more sober than before, since Dez had confiscated his drink. However, he approached through the crowd, making his way along the outside ever so closer to the center. "I am not walking on this gravel barefoot!"

Some of the others joined in the protest.

"Fine, Jess. You know what?" Wyatt responded angrily. "Go boil your head! On second thought, that thing that took Lucy might do it for you!"

Jesse yelled an expletive back at him as Derek, who only had socks on his feet, had heard the commotion and was trying to settle everyone down.

"Wy," he said. "What's going on? Something took Lucy?"

"I'm about to lose it on this dude, Derek!" Wyatt exclaimed. "I'm about to beat him down like it's a Tarantino movie!"

Jesse held up an unpleasant gesture as Wyatt tore from Derek's grip and marched towards him.

A loud screech suddenly broke the tension, sending many kids into hysterics after already being in a panicked state. The sound seemed so sharp that it was other-worldly. There was no way it came from any of them. It was too animal-like to be human, but it was unlike any other animal heard before.

Wyatt could see Jesse in the group, on the edge of the darkness by the road, and then it was as if he was yanked away by the collar of his shirt, his body flailing like a rag doll in a panic. The night swallowed him whole, as his teenage, voice-cracking scream echoed through the silence.

TAKEN BY THE NIGHT

"Jesse!" Wyatt yelled as the nightmare commenced. The group of kids and teens alike bolted down the road for the school gym. None of them seemed phased by running on a gravel road in nothing but socks and bare feet.

As his friends were amid the chaos, Wyatt let the adrenaline take over instead of the fear, and he ran against the crowd, like a horse pushing against its herd. He broke out of the other side in full sprint towards the darkness where Jesse was taken. Skidding to a halt, he stared down at the ground. An unstoppable flood of terror suddenly gripped him as his eyes caught a glimpse of Jesse's blue tennis shoes, then moved down to the red sneakers on his own two feet.

Oh, crap.

Wyatt saw something grasp his leg. It was a dark, wet limb covered in matted black fur and fingers supernaturally long. It pulled his legs out from under him, causing him to hit the gravel hard, then yanked him into the forest brush before he had time to scream.

****

Derek, Dez, Alex, and Chloe had taken off along with the crowd, which finally began settling down when everyone had entered the school gym. Derek looped a chain through the bars, not to keep them in, but to keep whatever was out there from entering.

"Is everyone here?!?" Desmond spoke loudly, letting his voice bounce off the walls and ceiling.

"What just happened?" Derek said as he was bent over onto his good knee, breathing heavily.

"I don't know," Chloe spoke, hand to head. "Wy said something about taking off my shoes, then he told everyone else to."

"Why?" Alex spoke up, leaning over the water fountain, the liquid running down her chin.

"We should know by now that there's no explaining what he does," Derek said.

Chloe started looking around.

Dez walked forward. "It started when I showed him a page in my book about what might have happened to Lucy."

Chloe turned her head, scanning the group of children and teenagers. "Where's Wyatt?"

"I thought he was running with us," Dez said.

A cold bead of sweat ran down Derek's forehead as he unhooked the chains and threw open the doors, instantly letting the darkness and the cold of the night inside.

TAKEN BY THE NIGHT

"Wyatt!"

****

Robbie limped into town, his sleepless eyes dreary and his head bent over. The pain had not ceased. It was turning him into a mindless zombie. It was making him crazy.

He peered through his eyelids down the main street of Lyonside at the tables and chairs set up. They looked abandoned. Tugging on the sleeve of his black hoodie, he walked down the dark road out of the reach of the streetlight. He could see nothing but the pitch black in front of him, but he didn't care. His sense of fear had long since diminished along with his sense of sanity.

His foot touched something.

Shoes.

Tons of them. Red. Blue. White. Yellow. It looked like a Foot Locker had been looted and all the inventory was scattered across this gravel road.

He turned towards the forest, just as the sound of rustling got his attention.

"Go away!" Robbie yelled. He thought it was that thing coming back for him. The pain in his head was so intense he couldn't even hear himself.

A boy leapt out of the forest brush, panicking as he stumbled towards him. His face was battered and bruised, but Robbie recognized him.

Jesse.

"Please, Robbie!" Jesse said, his voice cracking. "Help me! Something is after me!"

An intense rage began to build inside of Robbie.

"Oh, I'll help you." He kept his head down.

"Thank you, man! I owe you!"

Robbie pounced with supernatural strength and speed. Jesse's face displayed panic as he attempted to fight off the much smaller, much thinner teen, but something wasn't right. It was like he was possessed, breathing heavily and screaming as he took Jesse to the ground. Robbie wrapped his hands around his throat and squeezed. There was resistance, but the shock was too much. He slammed Jesse's head against the gravel, over and over until he heard nothing but gasps and the crack of crushed bone.

The pain stopped. Everything stopped. Robbie stood.

"Don't worry," He spoke through a dry throat. "We're even."

Chapter Ten

Wyatt was being drug through the leaves and forest brush, his mouth and clothes filling up with dirt and twigs. Even while being dragged by his legs, he could feel the thing tugging away at his shoes, trying to remove them and leave behind what Wyatt assumed was its trademark. The beasts large, meaty fingers struggled against the double knot Wyatt always tied, but it was beginning to make progress in sliding them off. His left cherry red sneaker was almost completely untied when his flailing hands managed to grab a tree trunk. This caused the creature to stop dead in its tracks, then screech again in frustration. Wyatt kicked his legs out of the abomination's grip as he screamed for his life. His hand grasped something thick and covered in bark. It was a large branch that had fallen from one of the trees.

Wyatt swung it around with all his might, *thwacking* the wood against the darkness in front of him. The beast screeched again, recoiling in pain and let go of Wyatt's leg.

He scurried to his feet, his knees shaking in terror as he began to stumble into a run in the other direction. He took off like a rocket, leaping over more fallen logs and crunching over endless piles of leaves. The only light guiding him was that of the moon and the phone he had fished out of his pocket. The dim beam shook around as he sprinted, only lighting up certain parts of the path.

He stopped where he thought he was safe and leaned up against a tree to catch his breath. There was a stitch in his side from the intense amount of inhalation. He couldn't hear the lumbering steps of the monster behind him anymore.

"Jesse?!? Derek?!? Anyone?!? Hello?!?" He whisper-shouted. His calves were burning like hot coals under his skin.

The woods were silent. He could hear himself inhale and exhale at an extreme pace. The lack of noise sent chills all over his body. When his family moved to Lyonside, they had passed the thousands of trees that aligned the roads in and out of town. He had wondered what was out there. He now had his answer.

Terror. It was pure terror.

Suddenly, his beam caught something standing in his path. His heart skipped a beat as he stopped in his tracks.

"Holy jeez!" He wheezed to himself in shock.

"Help...me!" A young girl, covered in dirt and hair in her face with a slightly protruding belly, begged in a raspy tone. She had no shoes on.

"Please!"

Lucy Letrail.

"Lucy?!?" Wyatt said, as if he had known her his entire life.

"Yes! Yes, please!" She wrapped her arms around him. Her skin was pale, and her fingernails were dirty, as if they had not been cleaned in a while. Her socks looked rough and worn. He didn't want to touch her. He almost didn't believe it was her.

" Help me! It's coming!"

Wyatt heard a deep growl, causing him to spin around searching for the source. Once again, his eyes locked on a pair of yellow orbs in the dark, swaying bushes to his right. He could feel the cold, unforgiving thoughts that ran through this creature's head. After a moment of silence, Wyatt grabbed Lucy by her shoulder, refusing to break eye contact with the beast.

"When I say," He let out, his voice shaking with fear, "you run in the direction I came from." He knelt and started to unlace his cherry red sneakers.

"Three."

The bushes rustled. Lucy let out a whimper.

"Two."

Wyatt pulled both of his shoes off.

"One!"

He gripped the white shoestrings in one hand, then hurled them into the darkness of the midnight forests like an Olympic hammer throw. He didn't see where they landed, because as soon as they left his hands, he made a break down the path he had just ran, right behind Lucy.

****

Robbie was shaking violently as he lay curled up in the corner of the barn. He had passed out not long after his encounter with Jesse and had awakened here. His skin was red hot from the fever that had set in, and his eyes were bloodshot. He felt like a zombie. He felt dead inside. His throat was sore, and his mouth had started cracking from the dryness. He couldn't walk into town to get a drink. He was afraid he would hurt someone. It had taken time to settle in Robbie's head what he had done to Jesse.

He threw up once more on a haystack to his right. A pig, who had been sleeping in the left corner opposite of him, snorted and kicked, then settled back into its slumber.

He could still hear the whispers coming from the cornfield, only a few feet away from the swinging doors. It seemed the closer he got to it, the less his head would hurt. He watched the stalks sway with the whistling wind in between the cracks in the wood of the walls.

Someone was moving among it, flashing like a shadow in front of the openings. *Something.* If he blinked, he would have missed it.

Against his better judgment and his own body, Robbie stood on wobbly legs, his knees so weak they could give out any second. He took a step at a time, spending what seemed like an eternity spanning the length of the barn to the doors.

He placed an eye to the crack in between the barn doors, then immediately regretted it.

Another eye was staring back, sending a rush of adrenaline through Robbie's system and making his headache return. The eye was blood red, like the creature in his bedroom the night the parents disappeared.

He fell backwards in shock and terror, letting out a hoarse yelp as he hit the ground. The doors swung open, sending dirt flying into his face.

Robbie.

Something snapped inside of him. He didn't want to fight it any longer. Robbie stood, then turned to the creature.

Follow.

A crow screeched from nearby as the midnight air cooled his skin. The monster faded into the corn stalks, and Robbie's head finally stopped hurting as he followed.

****

It was midnight. Most of the kids had fallen asleep on the sleeping bags that were found in the grocery store and had been set up beforehand. Some were snoring, and some slept silently. A stocky Hispanic boy, who seemed to be around twelve years old, was becoming quite loud in his snoozing. A kid nearby hurled a pillow at the boy's face, then scolded him to quiet down. Alex had fallen asleep over with the smaller kids, who had grown attached to her. It was as if she was a temporary mother hen, making sure they were safe from any harmful creature of the night. It was just like their naive minds to think such things. She herself knew very well if they were attacked again, she could do nothing but scream along with the children. The kids were only alive because the monsters had not yet chosen to approach.

Chloe had settled over with the other West Side cheerleaders. Even during such a catastrophe like they were experiencing, the order of popularity and social groups still applied. The football players stayed near each other, unless they had a little sibling to comfort.

Derek and Dez sat next to each other, leaning against a wall just behind the bleachers, a few yards from the chained doors.

"Did your sister make it in?" He asked.

Desmond nodded. "Yeah, she went to help Alex with some of the kids."

Another moment of silence hung in the air between them.

"He's an idiot," Dez bellowed out in the silence.

Derek turned his head to look at his friend, who took a swig from a half empty bottle of water.

"Who's an idiot?"

"Your boy, Wyatt."

Derek scoffed. "Tell me something I don't know."

"He's narcissistic," Dez held his fingers out as he counted. "He's immature, he's insensitive, he's irrational, and overall a jerk."

Derek didn't particularly like hearing about his best friend's flaws, especially since the teenage boy was missing and could be lying somewhere hurt at that very moment, or even worse. However, what he was saying was true, so he let Dez continue.

"You know, the weirdest part of it all is that I'm genuinely worried about him." Dez said.

"Someone have a crush?"

Dez shot him a look. "Nah, man," he laughed as he let the comment roll off his back. "I don't roll that way!"

Derek laughed and pushed his hair out of his eyes.

"So, who *do* you like, then?"

Dez adjusted himself in an awkward motion, crossing his legs and folding his hands.

"I don't know." He took a sip from his water bottle.

Derek smirked. "You know, if we don't figure this thing out, we may have to live like this. Settle down with someone and establish a community."

Dez choked on his water, suddenly being thrown into a fit of laughter.

"What?" Derek responded. "I'm serious."

"Listen to Lord of the Flies over here!" He exclaimed. "Man, we're just kids! That's all we are, kids. You can't build a society out of children. This isn't a movie, bro," He said, with a smile on his face. "Though, it has been feeling like a horror flick lately. Plus, we still don't know what is even going on. I could be dreaming for all I know."

Derek laughed, then ran his fingers through the hair on the back of his head. "Like seriously. A shadow demon thing and an urban legend. What's next? Zombies?"

Dez laughed. "No way am I dealing with that! Couldn't we just have like, I don't know, corny 1930's Dracula vampires?"

"Or *Twilight* vampires."

"All we would have to do is hide all the glitter, lipstick, and hair gel. They would just die from that."

It was Derek's turn to choke on his water in laughter.

Chapter Eleven

Wyatt walked along the dirt road, wincing as he stepped on the gravel beneath his feet. Lucy was right next to him, still rattled by what they had seen. Not just the monster in the forest, but something else was bothering her. He knew because the same thing was happening to him. He couldn't scrub the image from his brain.

Once they had broken free of the forest, he had assumed the nightmare was over. How ignorant of him to think that way. It was still too dark to really see where they were going, and the battery in his flashlight was dead. He didn't originally spot it, Lucy did.

She screamed.

The night was so silent and still, that such an abruptly loud noise rattled him. He couldn't see her at first, until he looked down.

She had tripped over something, because in the pitch black she was as blind as he was. He looked down at the ground, where she was laying on top of something.

A body.

"Oh, God," He let out in an exhausted manner.

The streetlight flickered on for a moment, long enough for him to recognize the pale, lifeless face.

It was Jesse. His head had been cracked open and was surrounded by a dark red pool of blood. His eyes were glazed over, a look of shock plastered permanently across his face.

Lucy hadn't spoken since then. As they made their way up the gravel path, the high school gymnasium came into sight. It was when they entered the parking lot that she finally spoke in a hoarse voice.

"He was cold."

Wyatt beat fiercely on the heavy metal door, making sure to get the attention of anyone inside. He hoped everyone had made it during the hysteria the night before. He beat on it again, listening to it rattle on its hinges.

The door swung open, and on the other side was a half-asleep Derek, dazed and confused with his hair sticking up in all different directions. Once his eyes adjusted, his expression shifted to relief. He gave Wyatt a bear hug. "Dude."

Wyatt held his arms out in an unwelcoming fashion. "Yeah, this got weird fast."

Derek pulled away from him.

"You look like crap," Wyatt said.

Derek smirked. "Oh, like you look any better!"

Wyatt scanned himself. He was right. Dirt and leaves covered him from his socks all the way up to his neck.

Derek sniffed. "You smell like something died, too!"

"Nah," Wyatt flicked his wrist in a dismissive manner. "I always smell like that."

The commotion had awoken everyone. Derek's eyes were looking passed his right shoulder, and a surprised expression grew on his face.

"You found her?!?" He let out.

"Lucy!" A voice yelled from the crowd behind the doors.

Isaac came running through the crowd, then he blew passed the teens and embraced his sister.

TAKEN BY THE NIGHT

The reunion brought a smile to Wyatt's muck covered face. It remained until Derek asked, "Where's Jesse? Did you find him, yet?"

Wyatt shoved his hands in his pockets and looked down at his socks.

"Yeah," he answered with a sniffle. "I found him."

****

The light of a dawning sun cast its beam onto the moving group. After spending the rest of the night in the gym, the group of Lyonside kids walked down the infamous dirt path back into town, this time a lot slower and more cautious than before. No one in the group of kids spoke a single word.

Wyatt lead Dez and Derek ahead of them to keep the little ones from seeing the body of Jesse Davis, head soaked in his own blood.

"Bet he wishes he took his shoes off now, huh?"

Derek shot him a dirty look. "Don't be a tool, Wy." He knelt beside the body to study it.

"Speaking of which," Dez put a hand on Wyatt's shoulder. "Why *did* you tell everyone to remove their shoes?"

Wyatt let out a sigh and scratched his messy head of hair. "That book," He said with a scratchy tone until he cleared his throat with a brief cough. "It said the Nightcrawler's calling card was to leave the victim's shoes. I figured if you didn't have any shoes, he wouldn't snatch you."

Dez scoffed and shook his head. "That's idiotic and genius at the same time."

"Aw, I'm blushing," Wyatt replied in a sarcastic tone.

"How did you know it would work?"

"I didn't."

Derek stood and interrupted. "Dez, did that book say anything about how it kills its victims?"

"Not in detail," he replied. "Just that it eats the poor soul. Why?"

Derek kept looking at the body, an unsure glare in his eyes.

"Then why isn't Jesse eaten? Why is he here?"

"Maybe Wyatt and Lucy spooked it before it could finish the job." Dez said, starting to reflect an uneasiness.

"No," Wyatt was thrown off by Desmond's assumption that he chased after the monster. He felt the urge to correct him and say that he was grabbed as well, but his pride made him keep his mouth shut. After all, the other way made him sound a lot better.

"No. If he was dead, I would have seen him before I went in. Plus, Lucy was still alive, and she had been taken days ago. The monster lets its prey sit before it eats it, so I don't think it would have done this to Jesse."

Derek leaned down and tilted Jesse's head to the side, revealing red marks along his neck. His hair was soaked in blood that seemed to be dripping from the back of his skull and onto the ground in a massive pool.

"Something isn't right about this. He was choked, but there's a lot of blood. Something must have slammed his head on the ground."

He took off his letter jacket and placed it over the body to keep the little ones from witnessing the gruesome scene as they passed. It covered the face down to the hips, but the legs stuck out from the bottom.

"We'll come get him later," Derek said.

The only one who heard him was Wyatt. Dez had run into the tree line to puke.

****

Wyatt made it home and jumped into a hot shower, his mind focused on a long overdue nap. His legs were cramped and sore, more so than anything he had ever experienced on the football field. Bruises and cuts were all along his arms and face. The morning sun had finally risen and was shining through the east windows of his house. He left all the lights off as he wandered over to the pantry, feeling the scrapes along the bottom of his feet caused by running through the forest with no shoes on.

His shoes.

Last night, he had thrown his sneakers away in an effort to avoid being taken by the monster. Although they were his favorite shoes, he sure didn't want to go back and search through the leaves and trees for them.

He fell on the couch with a loud grunt. His body was recovering from the adrenaline overdose from when he was running through the forest. His muscles felt like they wanted to fall off his bones, and his eyelids felt heavy.

Knock, knock, knock,

Someone was at his door. The sound rang through the silence of his house. For a split second, he considered calling for his mom to answer it.

"Wyatt?" A heavily accented voice muffled from the other side. Chloe.

He sighed. If it was anyone else, he'd have ignored it.

As he stood, dizziness set in. He moved fast, his body resisting the effort. As he shuffled over to the door, the disorientation refused to go away.

A flash blinded him just before he reached the door. He groaned, squeezing his eyes shut before opening them again. The room had suddenly gone dark, as if the sun outside his window burned out like a mere light bulb. An eerie fog had drifted into his home from somewhere unknown, covering everything within sight. Wyatt blinked a few times in shock.

He shook his head violently, trying to clear his thoughts. *Was this a dream? Had he fallen asleep on the couch that quickly?*

As he opened his eyes again and regained his focus, he felt his blood run cold. There was the face of a boy before him, one he could somewhat recognize, but it was grotesquely twisted and morphed with that of a scarecrow. Wyatt stumbled backwards, trying to put as much distance between himself and the horrific image in front of him as he could. Someone was screaming, a blood curdling scream. It only took a moment before he realized the screams were coming from him.

"Coward! You would leave a boy to be beaten?!?"

A voice rang out somewhere within his mind. No, not one voice, but two, blended together. That of a teen boy, and that of something darker, like a gargling, hungry beast. They spoke in a horrific rhythm that sent him sprawling onto the carpet. He screamed again.

"Coward!"

Another voice. This time it was Chloe, back in reality and on the other side of his front door.

"Wyatt?!? Open the door! Are you okay?!?"

His ears were ringing along with a sharp pain in his head. He wasn't sure if what he was seeing was real. The flashes in front of his eyes of a creature that wanted to harm him and anyone else he cared for.

"Chloe, stay away!" He didn't want whatever this thing was to get a hold of her.

"Don't run away from me! You coward!" the creature roared.

There was a thunderous crash, as shards of glass soared through the air and pelted his face.

Wyatt blinked again. The image was gone, along with the fog, and the sun had returned. He was sucking in air at a rapid pace, his chest rising and falling as his heart thumped against his rib cage. He noticed that one of his mom's metal lawn chairs that sat out on the front porch had been thrown through the window.

"Wyatt!" Chloe climbed through the opening. She hurried over and knelt next to him, placing one hand on his back and the other on his arm.

"What happened?" He asked, still struggling to catch his breath.

"I don't know!' Chloe let out. "You tell me! I was just coming over to check on you, when I heard you screaming! I didn't know if something was wrong, so I busted the window to get in!"

Wyatt nodded manically, attempting to rationalize what had happened. He ran his hands through his hair, pondering what he had seen.

Who... he had seen.

Chapter Twelve

Jesse hadn't stopped by that morning to visit, which was out of his routine since the parents mysteriously vanished.

Ruttledge texted his phone and received no response. He looked around town everywhere, but still couldn't find his friend.

His anxiety began to build, until he finally asked one of the teenagers about what happened the night before. Ruttledge had locked himself away in his parent's basement researching the creatures and strange occurrences hoping to find some answers as to what was happening in Lyonside. In doing so, he had missed out on everything that had happened.

"Yeah, one of the football players got dragged into the forest and everyone panicked." The teen responded.

Ruttledge's face went pale as he swallowed the lump in his throat.

TAKEN BY THE NIGHT

It's okay. Everything is okay. He is probably just still at the school where everyone was staying.

Ruttledge began walking down the road towards the school in between the endless rows of trees. He came across a figure in the road, its face covered by one of the football player's jackets. As he removed it, he gasped sharply.

Jesse Davis' lifeless body lay in front of him with his head surrounded by a pool of crimson.

Ruttledge wept, then punched the ground in rage.

No, no, no, no! This is their fault!

He remembered what Jesse had told him not long before. Someone was going to die because of the chaos.

This town needs order so this will never happen again!

Ruttledge wiped away the tears on his sleeve as he stood, a vengeful glare in his eyes as he began slowly walking towards the school.

****

Chloe put a hand to Wyatt's cheek. It was burning hot and his face was flushed. His eyes were tired as he caught his breath and put a hand to his chest.

"Wyatt, what happened?!?"

He turned to her and felt himself relax, comforted by her presence.

"I…I-don't know." He answered. Even though he was sweating, a cold chill came over him.

She curled his arm around her neck and lifted him up to the couch, resting his head on a burlap throw pillow.

"Do I need to go get someone? Molly, maybe?"

Wyatt shook his head and placed a hand to his forehead. "No, I'm...I'm okay. Thanks."

She grabbed his half empty water bottle off the floor and placed it in his lap.

"Here. Drink."

He shook his head again. She crossed her arms and stated, "I wasn't asking. Quit being stubborn and let me help."

He reluctantly twisted the cap and sipped, letting the satisfying liquid drizzle down his dry throat. "It's just a lack of sleep. That's all."

She sat next to him, grabbing another pillow off the floor. She brushed the glass off and hugged it tightly to her chest, then she pulled her legs up onto the couch as she curled up. Her blonde, dirty hair shimmered in the sunlight that shined through the opening where the window had been.

"This is crazy," She let out.

"I've seen crazier."

She looked at him and smirked. "Oh, really?"

He nodded as the plastic of the water bottle crinkled in between his legs. They both sat quietly for a moment lost in thought about the occurrences of the last few days.

"What's your full name?" He asked.

She turned to him, breaking the trance she had entered.

"Chloe Marie Fuller."

"Hm," Wyatt huffed.

"What's yours?"

He shifted in his seat, taking another swig of water.

"Wyatt Sexiness Richards." He spoke with a completely straight face, until Chloe elbowed him in the ribs.

"Anthony," He said with a laugh. "Wyatt Anthony Richards."

She let out a chuckle as she turned to pick a string out of the pillow threading.

"So," He spoke again. "What happened with your parents?"

"What do you mean?"

"Well, the rest of us...our parents were taken from our homes. But you weren't home when it happened, so...where do you think your parents are?"

Chloe sat and thought about this.

"I don't know, she said. Wyatt could sense the sadness in her voice. They didn't go to the game that night because my sister was sick." As she brushed a strand of hair out of her eyes, Wyatt noticed that her eyebrows were beautifully shaped and had a darker tint than her hair. She also had a few faded freckles scattered across her nose and right underneath her hazel eyes.

"I'm assuming they were taken, too," she continued. As major as this is, Lyonside can't be the only town affected!"

He nodded in understanding. He missed his mom and dad. He remembered how his mom had taught him to cook when he was younger, and how he had burned the grilled cheese his first time. He missed the smell of her perfume when he got home. His dad had taught him how to change the oil in his pickup truck and how to mow the lawn correctly, with great precision and a perfectionist's attitude. Every single blade was cut evenly. His dad had also taught him how to use and clean his gun.

His gun.

TAKEN BY THE NIGHT

Wyatt shot up off the brown leather couch like a rocket and raced up the stairs before Chloe had a chance to yell out.

"Where are you off to?"

"I just remembered something!" He yelled back as he reached the top step and stumbled into his parent's room, still wrecked from that night they were taken.

He searched through the drawers of his father's dresser. Nothing. Lifting the mattress to their queen-sized bed, he revealed a set of narrow, thin boxes underneath. He tossed the mattress from its frame and up against the window, blocking out most of the light in the room. Kneeling, he started opening the boxes underneath, trifling through them like a starving animal looking for food. There were stamps, letters, old clothes from the 1980's, and some VHS tapes.

"C'mon, old man," He mumbled to himself. "Where'd you put it, Dad?"

The light from the ceiling fan switched on suddenly.

"This might help," Chloe leaned against the doorway, one finger still on the switch.

He smiled in a way that a small child would, jokingly, and then continued opening boxes.

Nothing.

He stood and scurried into the closet, flipping on that light and tossing out his Mom's clothes. Some of his dad's jackets hung in there as well, but it was his mother's dresses that took up the space.

"She's pretty."

Wyatt turned to Chloe again, who was studying the wedding picture that was resting on the dresser.

"Yeah," He answered as he continued his mission.

There it was.

Wyatt reached up onto a hidden shelf and grabbed his Dad's shotgun. It was double barrel, which meant it could fire two shells at once. The barrel was shorter, because his dad had illegally cut it off with a saw. The stock was different. It wasn't a long stock to place against your shoulder, but it had a pistol grip, to allow you to shoot it like a pistol. He turned it over to look at the name engraved in the wood. James Richards.

"Thanks, old man."

****

Dez stood in front of the cornfield reminiscing about when he was younger visiting a cornfield for the first time. His mother had taken him not long before his sister was born.

"This is where they grow corn, sweetie," she had spoken in such a soft, touching voice.

"And cows and chickens and pigs?" He remembered asking.

"Yes, and cows and chickens and pigs," she responded with a laugh.

Dez started to tear up from the memory. *What was happening to this town? What had turned Lyonside into a freakshow?*

The sound of footsteps broke him from his trance. He turned his head and saw his sister, Molly, walking towards him, with her curly hair hanging in her face and hands shoved in the pockets of her plaid jacket, the gray hood covering her head.

"Hi." She said, waving.

"Hi." Dez nodded.

She flipped her hair out of her eyes, as Dez hurried to wipe the tears from his eyes before they fell. "You good?"

"Yeah," She responded. "You're thinking about mom again, huh? I can tell from that look you get in your eyes."

Their mother had passed not long after Marcella was born from a car accident. She had been suffering from postpartum depression, and car rides would take her mind off things.

He had heard of a lot of cases where one sibling hated the other when put in a similar situation, but he had never held that over his sister's head. He knew it wasn't her fault. Even at such a young age, he had always subconsciously understood that such a tiny being as his sister was when she was born, couldn't have killed his mother.

"She was tough," He said, sniffling before he wiped his eyes again on his shirt sleeve and smirking. The cold wind stung against his face as it whistled by. "And you're just like her. You don't take crap from anyone."

"I know," She responded, her eyes looking at the ground below her feet.

"Hey," Derek had approached them from behind. "Am I interrupting?"

Dez was about to say yes and to give them a minute. He wanted to continue remembering with his sister, but she intervened before he could respond.

"Uh, no. I was just leaving actually." Molly said as she placed her earbuds back in her ears, then turned to leave. Dez watched her walk away.

"You good, brother?" Derek asked.

"Uh," Dez responded, regaining his composure. "Yeah. I'm going to guess you called me 'brother' as in 'friend' and not 'brother' as in 'a black dude'." He was attempting to turn the tables on his friend. Derek rubbed his neck, obviously feeling awkward by the conversation.

"I'm kidding, man." Dez laughed.

The sound of the trees rustling in the wind was interrupted by a phone buzzing. Derek pulled it out of the back pocket of his jeans as Dez scoffed.

"I can't believe those still work."

Derek shrugged as he opened his messages. "I'm not complaining."

Wyatt: Hey

Derek: Sup

He waited for a reply.

Wyatt: Where do u find guns in this god forsaken place

"Dear Lord," Derek let out.

"What?" Dez asked, keeping his gaze on the cornfield in front of them.

"Wyatt wants to know where all the guns are."

Dez broke into laughter.

Derek: I don't think u should have 1, Wy.

Wyatt: Jokes on u

Wyatt: I already have 1

Wyatt: But where r the others

Derek ran a hand down his face in an exhausted expression. "Oh, he has one."

Dez kept laughing, a slight wheeze coming out. "He's going to shoot himself in the foot!"

Derek: Just chill for a few minutes while I round everyone up. Meet me at the grocery store

Derek: Bring witnesses

Wyatt: K. Gotta find my shoes first.

Chapter Thirteen

Wyatt had finally gotten the nerve up to retrieve his signature cherry red sneakers from where he had thrown them in the forest. They had been covered in leaves and muck. It was a lot less terrifying during the daytime.

They had all made their way to the back of the almost empty sporting goods store. Three aisles down there was a steel case holding several types of firearms, everything ranging from pellet guns to rifles with mounted scopes.

"We saw it here when we were scavenging," Derek spoke. "We couldn't get it open, so we just left it."

Wyatt looked at the lock for a second and decided without hesitation what he would do.

"Ladies and gentlemen!" He spoke as if he was talking to a crowd at a concert, but really the only people present were Derek,

Dez, Alex, and Chloe. He felt a wave of freedom as he waved his gun in the air above him. "Would you kindly take a few steps that way, por favor?" He pointed further down the aisle.

They each looked at each other with curiosity as they stepped away, someone's sneakers squeaking along the linoleum floor.

"Oh," he rested the barrel of the gun in front of the lock. "Cover your ears!"

Wyatt squinted his eyes as he pulled the trigger, anticipating a loud bang. It didn't come immediately, not until he applied more pressure than he thought necessary. The shot rang out at an ear-piercing level. He felt the concussion from the shot as the pistol bucked in his hand from the recoil. The metal from the lock went flying in all different directions.

"That felt lovely!" He yelled, clearly still deaf from the experience. He dug at one ear with his pinky.

Chloe laughed as Dez and Derek forced the dented metal gates back. The smell of gun cleaner and finish overwhelmed them.

"Note to self: wear ear protection!" Wyatt let out, again louder than necessary. Derek rolled his eyes, tossed Wyatt a pair of orange foam ear plugs he found on a shelf, then proceeded to check the chamber of a lever-action rifle.

Chloe reached in a cabinet and pulled out a gray revolver with an abnormally long barrel. She propped it up on her shoulder, and asked jokingly, "Does it match my outfit?"

"Yeah," Wyatt responded sarcastically. "Looking like a real femme fatale.*"*

Chloe laughed, then broke out her best Ellen Ripley impression.

They both laughed, as Dez turned around from the gun cabinet with a confused expression.

"Oh, don't tell me you didn't get that!" Wyatt said with a smile.

"No, I got it," He said. "I'm just surprised she did, too!"

Wyatt laughed, looking at her. She pointed the revolver further down the aisle and mouthed a bang, along with a mimicked recoil.

"Wy," Derek finally spoke up. "Why are you so interested in these guns?"

"Thought they would be good to have."

"For what reason, exactly?"

Wyatt leaned against the shelves behind them that had once held tennis rackets. "Look, we still don't know what's going on, what we're up against. I just think that we would feel a lot safer with them on our hips rather than locked in the cage." He tapped the steel with the barrel of his gun.

"Well, we can't just hand these out like candy to a bunch of kids." Derek said.

"I'm not saying that. Just give them to the older people, maybe, if we can trust them."

"That would be the safest option," Dez spoke up, this being one of the rare times he had ever taken Wyatt's side. "We can have groups each night. Everyone with an older kid and a gun in different houses. People would be a lot less scared. They would get more sleep, plus it would give poor Alex a break from babysitting."

Derek thought about this for a second. It wasn't a bad idea. There would probably be less disappearances, too. Although, chances were the creatures didn't understand firearms nor what they were capable of, so they would probably have no fear of them. *Do they even feel fear? Were they like wild animals, or more intelligent?*

"Alright," He finally spoke after heavy consideration. "Let's do it."

****

Alex started handing the afternoon's rations out, attempting to be as conservative as possible. She was stubborn about handing them out. Supplies were starting to run low and would not be replenished until they could loot the homes and stores further. Most of what was left was beef jerky and cans of Dr. Pepper. She spotted Derek approaching from the crowd, weaving in and out of kids.

"I have good news," he said, arms out and a smile spread across his face.

She smiled. "And what would that be?"

He rested his arms on the rations table. "You don't have to babysit the little ones anymore. We've come up with a system that would keep everyone safer and hopefully let us get more sleep."

He grabbed her arm and pulled her aside, opening his red-letter jacket revealing the handle of a semi-automatic pistol sticking out of the waistband of his jeans. Alex's eyes grew wide and she grabbed his jacket, hiding the weapon before any of the other children saw.

"Are you insane? Where did you get that?" She whispered in between clenched teeth as she reached over, attempting to conceal it.

"The store had them. Surprisingly enough, this was Wyatt's idea."

She let go of his jacket and put her hands on her hips. "And you're considering this, coming from him? You aren't going to go handing those out, right?"

"No," He said, resting a hand on the bulge from the handle. "Only older kids that are trustworthy. We're splitting everyone up into houses, and each will have an older kid with one of these." He patted his hip. "Good plan?"

She crossed her arms. "And the little ones?"

"It will all be established tonight. Dez is back at the bookstore figuring out the logistics. Do you want one?" He asked as if it was a common question.

"What, a kid?"

"No, a gun."

Alex shook her head and held out a hand. "No thanks. Not much of a gun person."

"Then you'll have to be housemates with someone who has one."

She raised an eyebrow. "Seriously? I can take care of myself."

"I know," he responded, "But still. No exceptions."

"Fine," she peered into the gathering of kids on the main street. Her eyes caught Chloe in a group of girls, the cheerleaders from West Side. "I'll stay with them."

"Alright, that's good. Chloe's a carrier. I'll set everything up."

She laughed and punched him in the arm. "Who died and made you the king?"

He smiled. "Someone had to take the reins."

She smiled back at him, admiring his complexion. "Yeah, well I'm glad it was you."

Chapter Fourteen

The dark sky came upon the town faster than the night before. It was as if the clock moved quicker than usual. The sun had set, but no one was sleeping. The streetlights lit up the roads, and many were wandering around in groups. No one went out alone anymore.

Wyatt had taken a desperately needed shower and started getting antsy in the lonely silence of his own home. He knew Derek and Dez were busy with whatever they were doing, and he was too afraid of appearing needy to walk over to Chloe's place. He put on a clean pair of jeans along with a plain white T-shirt and opened the windows to his house, letting in the cool night air, as well as turning on every light in his house just in case any of those nightmarish suckers decided to show. He set up his dad's old MP3 player they listened to occasionally.

God, he missed him.

He ran down the stairs, mimicking an air synthesizer solo as the first verse of Cutting Crew's "I Just Died in Your Arms" rang throughout his home. He ran into the kitchen and grabbed himself a can of cola he had gotten from rations that morning. It was warm, but he was content as the carbonation burned his throat as he guzzled it down. He let out a sigh.

"Wyatt!" Someone yelled into his house through the shattered living room window. He walked into the living room, letting out a small burp as he stepped passed the shattered glass. He could clearly see who it was through the opening. Derek, along with his beloved checklist. Wyatt opened the front door, stepping out on the porch.

"Need something?" He leaned on the doorway and crossed his arms, soda can still in hand. He hadn't noticed right off the group of little kids gathered in his driveway. He turned his head to them, then back to Derek, this time with a look of anger as the realization dawned on him.

"No, no, no!" He let out, waving his finger in Derek's face before he walked back inside, slamming the house door for dramatic affect. The closed door really wasn't necessary considering the gaping hole where the front window once was. Anyone could enter or exit as they please.

Derek yelled back through the opening. "Wyatt, c'mon now! We discussed it this morning! Everyone in a group. Every group with a teen carrier."

"No!" Wyatt turned back around to face him. "Not only no, but heck no! I'm not babysitting just because you want your girlfriend to have a break! Nope. Sorry. That isn't my job."

Derek climbed through the broken window, stepping over the section of wall. "You need to pitch in and start helping, man!"

"Oh, don't pull that card! I went scavenging! I went out and found Lucy! I mean, for Pete's sake, I saved everyone from a freaking monster attack!" He guzzled the rest of his soda, crushed the can, then tossed it at Derek dismissively. Derek wanted to remind him that not everyone was saved, but he thought mentioning Jesse was too crude.

"Alright, Wy," He spoke with a tired expression, like he didn't have the energy to argue. "Look, you can't be alone. Everyone is pitching in." He put his hands on his hips and sighed. "But I will let you choose who stays with you if you don't fight me on this."

Wyatt thought about this for a few seconds, keeping his gaze on the shattered glass in his carpet.

"Alright." He said finally." Give me Isaac and his sister."

"The Letrails?"

"Yeah."

Derek held his arms out. "You have to take in more than two people."

"Too bad. I only have two beds, not including the couch."

Derek ran a hand through his hair. "Not a problem. We can put some mattresses in here!"

"Isaac and his sister," Wyatt said again to emphasize his point. "Or no one. Take it or leave it."

Derek squeezed the bridge of his nose. "Fine. Be that way."

He disappeared out of view for a minute, allowing Wyatt enough time to grab a vacuum cleaner and clean up most of the glass on the floor. He had been procrastinating but decided to get it done in order to keep his new guest from cutting up their feet.

Derek eventually returned with Isaac and Lucy, both with pillows and blankets in their arms.

Wyatt welcomed them somewhat apprehensively, trying not to be too obvious with his feelings about the whole idea.

"Great," He muttered under his breath. "I'm living in a sick and twisted version of *Adventures in Babysitting*."

****

Chloe helped Alex move a mattress in, plopping the queen size down on the white carpet of the master bedroom. It was quite large, big enough to fit three of the girls on comfortably. The previous owner had taken very good care of the home itself. A bright, sunshine yellow painted the walls, which gave a quaint, cutesy feel to it. Molly had decided to room by herself in the guest bedroom, while Alex and Chloe agreed to room with Amy, the redhead, even though none of them had even known each other a few days before. That went for everyone else in this town. Chloe liked West Side, but she was too fiery for the girls at her school, except her cheering teammates. That was different though. They had to get along. She scared off boys, as well. That didn't stop them from trying to flirt occasionally. She liked Alex, who sat quietly in the corner, reading a book on poetry. Their personalities, at first glance, seemed like opposites. Chloe was outgoing and passionate, Alex simply wanted to be left alone.

She could hear the music blaring from Wyatt's house across the street and wondered what he was doing now. He seemed interesting to her. He had many flaws, sure. His comments were sometimes uncalled for and got him into more trouble than it was worth, and he seemed defiant simply for the thrill of being a rebel. He was cool, though. He found Lucy, and he helped them remove the van from the wreckage of the school bus. Plus, they got along a lot better than she did with the other boys. They were both outsiders. Maybe they really did have a lot more in common than she realized. *Yeah. He's pretty cool,* she thought with a smile as she moved a handful of pillows into the room.

Chapter Fifteen

"I was born here," Alex explained to her new housemates. "In this town. I grew up in a house down the street with my mom and dad and older brother. He isn't here, though. He's serving in the military, somewhere overseas. "Anyways...yeah." She took a swig of cola and flipped through her book with her thumb in a nonchalant fashion.

"You don't have to talk about it if you aren't comfortable," Molly said as she crossed her arms.

"He sounds cute," Amy said with a smile. Molly nudged her with her foot, attempting to quiet her.

"What? Just curious."

"I remember how sad I was when he left," Alex kept explaining. "I was afraid I would never see him again." She took another short sip from her can. "I knew Andy, though. He was tough as nails, and that's what kept me going. That simple amount of faith I had in him. I guess now I really don't know if I *will* ever see him again. I don't know if I'll see any of my family anymore." She stared off, in her own thoughts.

The room grew silent, letting the melancholy tone of her story hang in the air, bringing a cloud of gloom over the girls.

"So," Amy spoke up, awkwardly breaking the silence. "Do you like any of the boys in town?"

Molly kicked her in the leg.

"Ow!" Amy screeched as she reached down and rubbed her leg.

"Can't you think of anything other than that?" Molly let out.

"I was just trying to take her mind off it!"

Alex laughed as she glanced over to Chloe, who hadn't been paying attention to the conversation. She was entranced as she sat by the window, staring at the night sky and marveling at the stars. She looked over at Alex, smiled, then went back to her daydreaming, leaning her pretty head on the wall beside her. Alex smiled back, then turned back to Molly and Amy.

Chloe continued to fix her gaze on the stars above them. She wondered if they were real. She wondered if any of this was real.

Is it all a dream?

Maybe she was still asleep in her bed back at home. Maybe any moment she would wake up in her West Side home. Maybe any moment her mom would walk into her room and give her a big hug, along with a kiss on the forehead. Maybe she had died in the bus crash and this was Heaven. It sure didn't feel like it. Maybe it was Hell. She wasn't particularly into religion, even though she was raised Christian. She was never a bad child. She went to Sunday school. She got good grades. She prayed. Not as often as she should, admittedly, *but it had to count for something, right?* No, this couldn't be Hell, but it couldn't be Heaven either. That only left the dream theory.

Laughter erupted from the girls across the room causing Chloe to turn around to see what the commotion was about. As she turned back towards the window, a face appeared just inches from hers, snow white and expressionless. Its eyes were dark, with a yellow ring where the iris should have been.

Chloe let out a scream as she stumbled backwards, trying to flee. Her blood ran cold. Her heartbeat thumped against her chest at a rapid pace. She knew that this was no dream.

****

TAKEN BY THE NIGHT

Wyatt awoke from his sleep to the sound of screaming. He shot up off the couch, disoriented and groggy. The TV was still on, halfway through *Indiana Jones and the Temple of Doom.* The DVD player remote flew off his lap, across the living room and smacked against the carpet. His first instinct was to bolt into the master bedroom, where Isaac and Lucy were snoozing. He remembered he had tucked them in after a movie marathon.

Another scream. This time he was awake enough to hear it originate from across the street at Chloe's house. Without hesitation, he leaped through the living room window opening, his bare feet smacking against the concrete porch. He barrel-rolled through the bushes that lay in his way, getting poked and prodded through his pajamas. He didn't care. Dashing across the dark, lonely road in between the homes, the only light was the dim streetlamp that stood like a sentinel on the opposite sidewalk. He leaped the curb as his field of vision lessened. His eyes hadn't adjusted to the darkness yet, but the lights were on in the home, so he ran towards the lights. Wyatt didn't break his stride, running full speed straight at the living room window. The house had a mirrored layout to his own. He hurdled the bushes, his feet clearing them, but it slowed his momentum down as he launched off the concrete. Bracing his shoulder, he bounced off the window like a rubber ball. It cracked in its frame from the impact but didn't break as he collapsed to the ground.

"Okay, then."

He shook it off, then grasped a rock from the soil beneath the leafage of the bushes. He turned and hurled it in one quick motion, followed by a loud crash as the glass shattered and fell inwards. He stepped inside, cautious of where he placed his feet.

"Chloe!" He yelled. His voice echoed off the empty halls. He heard commotion from one of the rooms.

He braced his shoulder once again and banged against the wood door, knocking it free. He looked around the room.

The four girls had bunched up against the wall to his right, except Alex. She was slowly approaching the window. Their faces were all drained of color, shaking as if they had seen a ghost.

"Alex!" Chloe yelled loudly at her friend. The other girls were crying, mumbling the same words. "Oh my god, oh my god, oh my god!"

Wyatt ran over and knelt beside them, grasping Chloe's shoulders.

"Are you okay?" She turned her face to him. Her hands were cold as they grasped his arms.

"Wy, stop her, please!" She pleaded between quick breaths.

He turned to Alex. She had gotten a tiny bit closer to the window. He approached her, placing a hand on her shoulder. His eyes caught a glimpse of what they had been so scared of.

Carlos.

Wyatt yanked Alex away from the window and out of the trance she was in. She sat down on the carpet, tears in her eyes.

"Go get your brother!" He grabbed Molly's shoulders. He could see that her skin was lacking color and was as cold as ice. Oddly, this magnified the color of her eyes as he stared into them trying to get her attention. She stared wide-eyed, looking at him for the first time without any sort of contempt in her expression.

"Molly, please! I need Dez! He's one of the fastest people in school!" He begged her again as he let go of her and took off out the door. Chloe chased after him, looking to offer a hand in whatever he was planning.

Wyatt burst into a full sprint through the back door. Carlos was his friend. His teammate. His brother. Not by blood, obviously, but he had put on the football pads and stepped on the gridiron with him. It was a brotherhood only those who had experienced the comradery of a football team would understand. Wyatt remembered during one game when he scrambled out of the pocket and into the open field where he lacked protection. He remembered a humongous linebacker had him locked in his sights and was coming in like a missile. The hit was going to hurt, he knew it. He recalled an almighty bang ringing through his ears, and a groan from the crowd. The impact hadn't affected him, though. Carlos, a fullback, had caught up to Wyatt, then ran ahead. He had abandoned his passing route he was supposed to run when he saw Wyatt scrambling and laid the linebacker out about a yard in front of the back-up quarterback. Carlos had cracked his helmet against the backer's chest as if it was a weapon and not just for his own protection. If that wasn't brotherhood, he didn't know what was.

As soon as Wyatt had exited the house, Carlos took off, leaping the back fence into the neighbor's yard. Something was off. In the darkness, Wyatt watched his friend's movements. He was familiar with Carlos' running form, as he had watched him take the field many times before. Now, his arms and legs seemed lanky. It was like he was just now learning how to run properly. He didn't pump his arms like they were taught during training. They hung at his sides, bouncing limply as he ran. It almost resembled that of a puppet.

Wyatt turned around and ran back through the house, bumping into Chloe.

"Wyatt!" She said hysterically. "Where is he? What's wrong with him?"

He wiped the sweat from his top lip with the back of his hand. He didn't want to stop moving, for fear he might lose his friend. Carlos was a lot faster than him, there was no doubt about that, but he wouldn't give up. He refused.

"He's hopping fences!" He explained as he rushed to the front door, "But I know where to cut him off!" He let the adrenaline fuel him. His heartbeat was pounding against his chest like a caged animal. He got his second wind as he took off down the dark street, not caring about anything but bringing his brother home.

****

Molly had almost beat down her brother's door. He opened before the ruckus woke up any of the little ones he was taking care of. She was in hysterics and couldn't catch her breath. He reached over and hugged her, trying to calm her nerves.

"Easy Mol'. What's wrong?" He could feel the sweat running down her back and neck.

Carlos showed up!" She sputtered in between coughs.

"What?" He stepped outside and shut the door, then crossed his arm as she explained what had happened. She didn't even have to mention Wyatt chasing him, because Dez's eyes had wandered from her to the main road behind her.

Wyatt was running down the road in his pajamas, his bare feet on the asphalt.

"Come on!" He yelled.

Dez stepped off the porch, then turned to Molly. "Watch the kids!"

Alex and Chloe were not far behind as Dez turned onto the dark road and followed. Dez could hear Wyatt's controlled breathing. In through the nose and out of the mouth. In. In. Out. Out. This was a technique well known to most athletes, football players and basketball players. He never really thought about it before, whether it helped while running, but at this moment, he was frantically bringing in air trying to catch up with Wyatt.

They had blown through main street, shooting straight past the buildings. The silence was abnormal and nerve-racking. Wyatt brought himself to a halt at the turn-in for the grocery store parking lot. He could see the opening behind the main street stores as his eyes scanned the area. With his hands on his hips sucking in oxygen, he noticed that his clothes were drenched in sweat and his hair had fallen out of shape and stuck to his face. This pause gave Dez and the two girls enough time to catch up.

Dez had his hands on his knees and was choking on air.

"Dude," he coughed out.

Alex was breathing just as heavily. She didn't do sports, or much exercise at all. She never really needed to; she had been scrawny all her life. Now, her lungs were burning up inside of her and it was a struggle to keep up with the boys and Chloe.

"Where is he?" She had wide eyes and her movements were frantic, quickly jolting from one direction to the other. This greatly contrasted Wyatt's slow scanning process with halfway squinted eyes.

"I don't know! I don't know! I had him; I swear!" Wyatt broke into his own panic, grasping his wild hair in efforts to focus his mind on the task at hand and not get emotional.

"Frickin' jeez, Wy. We need to slow down and figure this out first!" Dez said, brushing off the dirt on his jeans

There was movement from behind one of the stores. It wasn't clear who it was in the midnight moonlight, but Wyatt was pretty sure he had an idea. The silhouette hit the parking lot, then sprinted in a limp fashion diagonally, heading straight for the turn-out on the other side.

"You can slow down if you want to," he said to the other three who were still breathing heavily. "I'm saving my friend!"

Wyatt took off like a rocket, and the others, determined to keep up, broke into a sprint. They had no idea where he was going, but suddenly, it was almost as if a vision had popped into Dez's head. A flash in front of his eyes. It didn't last long enough for him to catch colors or details, but his brain immediately recognized the location. He stopped running, hands on his knees and shaking his head rapidly. A headache began to set in.

Alex stopped, turning back to him. "Dez!" She hurried back to where he was.

"Farmer Burnett's cornfield," He whispered.

"What?" she asked frantically, placing one hand on his back. She felt his lungs expanding.

TAKEN BY THE NIGHT

"The cornfield!" He yelled ahead of them to Wyatt and Chloe as he sucked in the cold night air. "He's heading for the cornfield!" he yelled again, breaking into a sprint.

Chapter Sixteen

Chloe had followed Wyatt and the figure into the corn stalks, their steps crunching on the dead plants as they moved through them. He was a considerable distance ahead of her. The last she saw of him was the back of his head as he ducked through more foliage, then he was gone.

"Wy!" She let out.

Her foot caught on something, sending Chloe tumbling down to the ground. The soil flew into her eyes and mouth. She spit it out and stood, her clothes covered in dirt. She couldn't see anything due to the lack of light.

She called his name again.

What am I doing? she thought.

She didn't even know Carlos. Maybe she was doing this because it meant so much to Wyatt. She had seen the look on his face when he realized it was Carlos, his teammate, in the window. She knew the bond that football players formed from watching her own high school team. They were unbreakable. She didn't know Wyatt as well as she wanted to, but she knew from the glimmer in his eyes that this meant something to him.

She looked around. *Which direction did they go?* She had gotten her directions mixed up when she fell. She ran directly ahead, continuing to call his name. Something didn't feel right. She felt a cold shiver down her spine. It felt as if someone was watching her...

Stop it, Chloe. You're getting paranoid, she thought. She looked around. The only thing she could see other than corn was a scarecrow, hanging from its perch. It was dressed in a ragged brown shirt, some old torn up jeans clung to its legs, and a straw hat obscuring its face. A single crow hopped along the arm.

She broke through another line of stalks, this time coming out at the other side of the field. Directly in front of her stood a barn, dark gray in color. It seemed rickety and rotting. Its swinging doors barely hung on their hinges and grass was growing between the cracks. She felt it. Cold. She felt cold. There was an overwhelming stench coming from the barn that smelled putrid,

215

like something had died. She retched, covering her nose and mouth with her hand. She walked slowly forward, taking caution with each step, fighting off the urge to run, and ignoring her intuition that screamed at her to not open the door.

But she did.

The door creaked slowly open as if screeching at her to stop, but she refused. The smell's intensity rose as she walked through the opening. The floor was splattered with a thick coat of red paint. No, not paint, blood. She studied it for a second, wondering what had happened. *What could have bled so much?*

Something gently struck the top of her head, and she felt her hair, then looked at her fingers.

A sticky, crimson liquid reflected from her fingertips. The hair on the back of her neck stood on end, and a cold sweat set in. Her eyes grew wide as she tilted her head upwards.

A pig, at least what seemed like a pig, it was hard to tell because of how bad it was mangled, was pinned to the roof with nails stuck in its eye sockets. It had been skinned and the legs were chopped off. Blood was seeping from its mouth.

Chloe let out a scream, stumbling backwards out of the barn losing her balance and falling backwards to the ground. A cold breeze struck her as she started hyperventilating. She continued to push herself backwards scooting along the ground, away from the barn, tears welling up in her eyes. A hand grabbed her shoulder, causing her to scream again, until another covered her mouth.

"Hey, hey, easy, girl." Wyatt was on his knees next to her, his eyes filled with tears as well. She hugged his neck.

"I couldn't find him, Chloe." He spoke with a shaky voice as he buried his head in the crook of her neck. She felt his warm tears soaking her shirt, and she soaked his with her own. They cried for a few minutes until both their eyes were red.

After a minute, he pulled away. "C'mon," he said with a sniffle. He grabbed her hand and helped her stand.

"We need to go. The others will be waiting for us," He wiped his face clean with his already tear and sweat soaked shirt.

"Yeah, okay."

They wandered back through the field, trying to find their way out. Chloe had his hand as they moved. She abruptly stopped, pulling him back.

"Wyatt." She said with a shaky voice. Her eyes were locked on something in the field beyond them. Something was wrong, he could tell from her tone.

217

"What is it?"

He followed her gaze outwards, locking on a large wooden stake that stood in the distance. A crow cawed from somewhere in the distance.

"There was a scarecrow there earlier," She whispered, almost inaudible. Her eyes were wide in horror.

Wyatt was hoping he hadn't heard her correctly. He wished, with every fiber of his being, that they hadn't stopped moving. He remembered the mental flashes of the scarecrow he had had earlier that day. Oh God how he hoped she was just seeing things! He hoped she was going crazy. Better yet, he hoped he was going crazy!

"We need to keep moving, Chloe," He swallowed hard then began pulling on her arm.

She teetered back and forth, until her body had given up. Her knees buckled as she fell to the ground suddenly, Wyatt scrambled down next to her quickly.

"Chloe!"

She had blacked out, her face a bright shade of red. He wrapped her arms around his neck and picked her up, curling his elbow just under her legs and the other holding her back.

"C'mon, babe, wake up!"

Her gold earrings jingled as he ran with her, the wind striking his face with a ferocious sting. His arms were going numb as well as his legs. He thought something was rustling behind him with each step, but he kept moving. He kept going. He had failed Carlos; he would not fail her.

****

Dez and Alex had entered the maze of corn stalks as well. They tried to stay together in the dark.

"Keep your eyes peeled," He said to her as she turned from him, wandering forward. He wished he had grabbed his gun from the house before running off, and Alex was wishing she had agreed to take one from Derek.

They heard Chloe's voice yell from somewhere deep within the stalks.

"Chlo-"

Something covered Alex's mouth from behind her. It felt as cold as ice. She assumed it was Dez, until she heard his voice in front of her, his face appearing from the corn.

"I don't see anyo-"

He gasped, stopping his movement forward. He coughed out words she couldn't make out, as if he was choking on something. He grabbed ferociously at his shirt, as blood started to drip from the corners of his mouth.

She let out a muffled scream and started flailing her arms. She kicked and shook, but she couldn't break free. Dez started rising into the air as a crimson stain formed through his shirt, radiating in a circle dead center of his chest.

Something stepped into view from behind him. It looked like a strange mixture of a boy and a scarecrow. It was as if someone had sown the face of a kid into the sack head of one of the straw dummies. The eyes were human, green even. Red hair and freckles were visible underneath the long brim of his straw hat. The rest seemed to be made from a burlap sack tied at the neck, with the twisted, toothy smile of a carnivorous beast. He lifted Dez's body and hurled him deep into the cornfield, blood falling from the blade of his scythe. The thing turned to her, staring into her frightened eyes.

"What's wrong, sweetie?" A hideous hybrid of an adolescent's voice and that of a horrific monster spoke. "You look like you've seen something scary. Don't worry, Robbie's here now."

TAKEN BY THE NIGHT

****

She was let go. She didn't know why. He simply said she wasn't worth his time, and the hand moved from her mouth. She ran for dear life in the direction they had come from, tears hot in her eyes. She turned around for a brief glimpse and caught a flash of a pale figure in a red and white letter jacket standing next to Robbie.

It was Carlos.

Once Alex's feet met the road, she doubled over crying and puking from her experience.

Desmond! She hoped he was okay.

Quit being stupid, Alex. He's dead. No way he survived that! she thought to herself. She sniffled again. Suddenly, there was the sound of an engine revving in the distance.

She turned her head and recognized the headlights of Derek's truck.

Alex stood on wobbly legs and attempted to move forward. She guessed she probably looked like a zombie.

She started walking towards the truck. Derek would help. Derek would fix it. He would find Dez in the cornfield, and he would be okay, just a little shaken.

Alex started running.

A.P. JENNINGS

****

Desmond stared at the sky above, amazed at the beauty of the night. He was choking on a warm fluid that began oozing its way up from his lungs.

Desmond.

It sounded like his dad, but something was off. The voice seemed different. It seemed perverted, almost monstrous.

Let go Desmond.

N—no." Desmond groaned as blood trickled from the corners of his lips.

Molly needs me! I can't go!

Dez closed his eyes as he began to feel himself fading.

****

Wyatt broke into the first house he found when he exited the cornfield, kicking the back-door inwards. Farmer Burnett's home. It wasn't the best option, but it would have to do. He could hardly move, let alone carry Chloe any further. He gently set her down on the couch, letting her rest comfortably. He sat in the old rocker and faced her. His lungs had given up, and his eyes felt heavy. Despite the lack of comfort, he fell asleep with ease.

TAKEN BY THE NIGHT

He awoke to the sound of thunder outside, the back-door slamming from a gust of wind. He was wide-eyed in the darkness, looking around frantically. Someone was there, next to Chloe. No, *something*.

"Hello, Wyatt." A gravelly, dark voice spoke out. It stroked Chloe's cheek with a finger that had a nasty, overgrown nail protruding out.

He wanted to bolt forward, shouting obscenities at it. This was the thing he had seen when he had his panic attack earlier that day. It terrified him, so he coped the only way he knew how.

"Sound a little congested there. I have some allergy medicine that does wonders for my-"

It stood and faced him, revealing a set of green eyes and a hideous smile. It had too many teeth to fit in its mouth, and it held a long scythe. In what seemed like a second, the scarecrow pounced on him wrapping its claws around his neck and slamming him against the wall.

"You've got a big mouth. Clearly, you don't have the brain to back it up," it snarled, the stench of its breath assaulting Wyatt's nostrils.

"Even without a brain, I've been known to talk a lot." Wyatt choked on the words. His eyes drifted over to the sleeping body of Chloe Fuller.

The scarecrow grew angrier, as it followed his gaze to Chloe. It smiled. Wyatt felt nothing but immense hatred for that horrid face. He had never hated anything this much in his life.

"Oh, don't worry, I won't hurt her. Not yet, anyways. Soon though," It nodded its head in her direction.

"You'll pay." The scarecrow continued; its voice trailing off into a whisper as the blade of his scythe nicked the skin of Wyatt's throat.

"You'll pay for everything!"

The scarecrow pulled the blade back, then brought it down suddenly. Wyatt quickly closed his eyes as he gasped.

****

Wyatt was suddenly shaken awake, his head bouncing a couple of times off the wooden rocker he slept in.

"Wy!" Chloe was standing over him, leaning in his direction. She was different. She seemed to have lost that glow that separated her from everyone else. She seemed gloomy, as if a dark cloud hung over her.

TAKEN BY THE NIGHT

He opened his eyes slowly as his brain attempted to process what had happened the night before.

The scarecrow.

He jolted out of his seat, almost pushing her over. He moved across the wooden floor in a mad rush. Searching, looking for that thing. Chloe yelled for him, but he ignored her. He was in a frenzy, his face red with anger and his hands balled up into fists. His knuckles went white as he slung the door he had kicked in the night before open, staring out at the cornfield revealed by the sunrise. The morning air smelled fresh, almost as if everything that had happened that night before was a sick fantasy.

Did it? Or was it a dream? He placed a hand on his throat. Something was stuck to it. He picked at it and pulled off a flake.

Dried blood. *The scarecrow was real. That thing was...real.* Why should he be surprised, though? He threw his sneakers at a creature straight out of a horror flick a few days before.

He heard the screen door open. It swung violently and smack against the wall. Molly, Dez's sister, marched towards the living room where he stood. Once they locked on him, he could see a burning fire in the gold of her irises. She bared her teeth before reeling back and planting a roundhouse kick behind his knee, sending him tumbling backwards and hitting the floor. She may have been almost a foot shorter than him and much smaller, but she could fight. She had him pinned to the ground quickly, before wrapping her hands around his throat.

"Molly! Wai-" He choked out. She was squeezing hard, and he was already weak from the night before. She pulled back and swung a fist, connecting with his lip. The punch stung, but it gave him enough time to gain leverage, and roll her over pinning her down. Drawing the shotgun from the scabbard on his back, he held it on her to try and restrain her.

"What is wrong with you?!?" he yelled.

"You killed him! You freaking killed him, Wyatt!" She blubbered out, tears erupting from her eyes. They were puffy and red from crying and not sleeping after what had happened with Desmond.

Chloe knelt over her. "Killed who, Molly?" She then looked at Wyatt, eyeing his gun. He got the message and stood up, sliding the shotgun back into its scabbard. Chloe helped a calmer Molly stand, after which she pushed Chloe away, then ran back towards Wyatt, swinging wildly at his face. This time he saw the attack coming as he grabbed her wrists.

"Molly, please!" He asked, desperate not to hurt her.

"Desmond, you idiot! He's dead!" She struggled against his grip.

Wyatt's face went cold, as he let go of her wrists. Instead of attacking, she fell on him, sobbing in the crook of his shoulder and his neck. Not even the warmth of her tears on his skin could prevent the cold feeling that overcame him. He wrapped his arms around her, his expression still in a state of shock. Tears burned through, but he refused to blink them away. He looked at Chloe, who herself was fighting back tears as she stared at the ground in disbelief. She walked towards them, then pulled Molly away.

She walked Desmond's little sister outside.

Wyatt was left in the silence of the house, which was worse than anything he could have imagined.

Chapter Seventeen

Molly had shoveled the last bit of dirt onto her brother's grave, tears streaming from her big golden eyes. The last of her family had been taken from her. She didn't care about anyone else. She didn't mind the crowd of kids who had surrounded her as she worked. Derek had approached her, asking if he could help in any way, but she just shot him a look that clearly sent a message for him to back away and leave her to tend to Desmond's body alone.

Alex had returned from the cornfield the night before, babbling and crying about some kind of monster among the stalks, and how it had gotten to Molly's brother. She remembers how heavy her heart felt, and the anxiety that gripped at her all night. Derek had decided to check the field once again that morning after Chloe texted from the Farmer Burnett's farmhouse where she and Wyatt had sought refuge. After Desmond's body was found, Molly

228

couldn't handle it. She lost her temper and her sanity. Wyatt had taken Desmond along on that rescue mission for a missing teenager she didn't even know, so Molly had made the decision long before she even knew for sure her brother was dead, that *this was Wyatt's fault*!

It had taken her nearly all day to clean the blood from the wound in his back, then dig the hole in the valley in between the church and the forest. Once she was done filling in the grave, Derek approached again and placed a hand on her shoulder as she gazed at the dirt.

"He was a good guy, your brother." He stated.

She wiped her face on her sleeve as a gust of wind blew her hair back from her shoulder, revealing the dirt that had collected on parts of her face from the work. She stayed planted where she was as children came by one at a time, gently grazing their hands across the wooden cross she had constructed out of a couple of sticks tied together with twine. Teenagers from both West Side and Lyonside mourned the loss. Alex and Chloe comforted Molly for a while out of respect for her brother, a beautiful soul and a willful protector. Her lower lip began quivering, but she took control quickly, swallowing the lump in her throat. Once the crowd dispersed from the field, she knelt on the grass to visit with him one last time.

"You were too good of a person, you know that?" She sniffled out along with a slight smile. "You did everything for the people around you and not for yourself. That's what got you killed. You were just like Dad. I love you. I always will, big bro."

She heard the grass move behind her as she slowly turned to see Wyatt, standing and staring at the ground below him. He walked up carefully, his steps sinking in mud as he approached. His face was solemn and lacked its natural color. He placed a hand on the cross.

"I'm....I'm sorry." He stuttered, his voice quaking with sorrow.

Molly shook her head as she stood, moving her eyes over to him. "No, you don't get to be sorry. You don't get that privilege." She spoke with a calm firmness towards him.

He nodded in understanding. After pulling the hood of his red jacket over his head, he shoved his hands in his pocket, and walked away with his head down.

When she was finally sure she was alone, Molly wept.

****

TAKEN BY THE NIGHT

Once the news had spread of Dez's death, it was clear to Derek and the people of Lyonside that this situation was serious. Someone had to do something. Two kids had gone missing and two were dead. Whatever was happening, they couldn't handle this alone. After all, Desmond had said it best: they are all just kids.

"Can you remind me of why you're leaving?" Alex asked, swooping her hair out of her eyes as she followed both him and Wyatt down the sidewalk.

Derek shut the tailgate of his truck after loading the last bag. "Wyatt and I are going to get help. We can't contact anyone with our phones. We need the army or the navy...or something like that! We need adults. This is bigger than us. What happened to Dez made me realize this..." He looked down, then back at her. At the mention of what happened that night, Alex felt a chill move down her spine. She was still trying to repress those memories. She gripped the handle of the gun in her waistband.

"Remember," Derek said. "Hand out rations every morning. Make sure everyone is in bed at a decent hour, meaning no one running off to make out or anything stupid. Most importantly, do not let anyone go near the cornfield."

Alex sighed. "Don't worry. The girls and I can handle it."

They were abruptly interrupted by the sound of the truck's horn going off. Wyatt was leaning out of the driver-side window, his cocky grin curling at both corners of his lips.

"You sure, sweetheart? I mean, if you need a man to do the dirty work I can always stay!"

"You're such a misogynist!" Alex responded back, kicking a discarded soda can in his direction, the aluminum clattering next to the tire.

"Don't I need a license to do that?"

Alex stuck out her tongue, to which Wyatt returned with the same gesture. Derek laughed. The two of them suddenly locked eyes, both waiting for the other to say something more.

Derek suddenly hugged her, to which she embraced him. After a moment, the sounds of Wyatt's dramatic dry heaves could be heard.

"Alright, alright, I'm coming, you clown!" Derek let go of Alex and gave her a wave as he walked towards the driver side door.

"No, no, don't let our life-saving mission interrupt!" Wyatt shot back jokingly.

Alex felt like part of her was walking away with him. This was not a romantic feeling, but of stress. She acted calm, collected and in-control on the surface, but deep down she was shrieking in terror. Derek was the only person that held this town together. Lyonside was a million-piece puzzle, and he was the glue. Now with him leaving, it felt like they were just trying to hold everything together with peanut butter. That's what she was, Alex was peanut butter. Like a puzzle held together with peanut butter that's smashed against a table, it would only take one event, one incident or death and everything would come apart.

Alex gripped her gun even tighter.

She walked into town with an anxiousness in her step. She was waiting for someone to have a problem. It seemed like it was every day that Derek was being flooded by requests and demands. Ever since Dez died, things were even more hectic. She didn't know how he handled being in charge so well. She didn't know how *she* would handle things at all!

Dez would have been a much better choice to lead while Derek was gone. Even Wyatt would have been better, despite his obvious flaws. The kid was annoying and immature, but he was clever. He found a missing child in one day and outsmarted one of those creatures. Because of him, they now knew there were other things out there besides Smiling Man, the silhouette monster that was haunting them and was suspected to be behind the disappearances, including the parents. Smiling Man is what the little ones had started calling him. No doubt this was because of his hideous grin. It wasn't exactly the most threatening name, but this thing was not to be underestimated. It had claimed the lives of two people, Carlos and Jesse. Wyatt had suspected there was more to what happened to poor Jesse, however. Maybe he saw something the others didn't, or maybe he just felt guilty because of what happened between those two before his death.

"Hi, Alex," Chloe had approached her, looking completely different from how she normally appeared. She wasn't flashy, wearing a bland black shirt and jeans. Her cheeks were flushed. Her hair seemed less blonde, as if it had contracted the melancholy that infected her attitude after that fateful night in the cornfield. It had a dark brown tint to its color.

"How are you feeling, Chloe?"

"I'm brilliant," she responded, running a hand down her face in exhaustion. "Have you seen Wyatt? I haven't talked to him since...well you know."

Alex stopped walking and turned her head to Chloe. "He didn't tell you? He and Derek are going on a little road trip to find some help. I'm in charge until they get back."

Chloe displayed disappointment on her face. "No, he didn't say anything to me."

Alex scoffed. "I'm not surprised, to be honest." They started walking again, heading deeper into town.

"I swear, I don't know what to do about him!" Chloe vented. "I like him and all, but it seems like every time I attempt to get to know him better, he trails off on a different topic or ignores me!"

"He's probably just stressed. Give him some time," Alex lied. She truly suspected Wyatt was just afraid of getting too close to anyone. That may have been why he responds so crudely to people. She thought it would be better to tell her something more positive, though. They all needed a better outlook on life after everything they had been through.

"I guess," Chloe responded, not sounding very convinced. "Did they say how long they would be gone? I remember riding the bus into town for the game. It was a long way from any civilization. There's nothing but empty fields for miles and miles until the first highway."

"Yeah, welcome to Lyonside, sister!"

****

Derek and Wyatt had reached the city limit and were now driving down the eerily empty road that lead out of town. Even in broad daylight, they both were tense from a suspicion of being watched. Once they reached the end of the forest, Derek pressed firmly on the gas as the sounds of his engine roared through the trees like a lion.

Wyatt had elected to bring along Dez's book. He wanted to study every page. He wanted to memorize every word written, just like his football plays. If any more disturbing events were to occur, he wanted to know every exploitable weakness possible. He flipped the pages nonchalantly until his eyes caught something that made his blood run cold. It felt like his heart was in his throat, making it hard to swallow. He scanned the words repeatedly.

The Scarecrow

The story of the scarecrow is a classic tale discussed around campfires on foggy nights for over a century. This urban legend tells of a young girl who visits her grandparents farm during the summer, only to discover a horrifying fact. Many different

TAKEN BY THE NIGHT

versions of this story exist, but the documented entry below is the
most commonly known.

"I remember in the middle of the night, I would hear rustling in
my grandfather's cornfield outside of my bedroom window. I had
just assumed it was either him working into the wee hours of the
night, or an animal of some sort. I questioned him, asking what
the sound was, and he always responded with a shrug. 'Must be
the wind' he would say. I would help him pick the corn from his
fields in the daylight, but my eyes were always studying his
scarecrow. It seemed like every day something was different
about it. His head would be turned in a different direction or his
legs would hang loosely instead of tied to the stake, then the next
day it would be bound again. I once more assumed this was my
grandfather's doing, until he had told me that morning that it
had been nearly twenty years since he last messed with the thing.
He said he left it there to rot with no real purpose. He then
mentioned something about wanted to take it down before winter.
After I had gone home for the fall semester of school, I had
received gruesome news. My grandfather had gone missing one
night, and my grandmother was found dead in the kitchen. She

had fallen into cardiac arrest. I was heartbroken and wanted to

visit the farm once again, until I received news that sent a chill

down my spine. Along with my grandfather, the scarecrow was

missing as well."

No other details available.

Wyatt slammed the book shut as he thought about the night Dez

died. Alex had witnessed the murder, but she was to terrified right

after the incident, that all she would say was "Desmond" She

hadn't offered any information about what happened since. Wyatt

remembered that Chloe had mentioned that night before she

blacked out, that the scarecrow was missing from its post in the

field. Is this also what he saw when he had the…episode… after

returning from the town sleep-in? *Was it the scarecrow?* If so,

what did it want with him? Wyatt wondered what could have

brought this curse on. Sure, he could be less than pleasant to deal

with at times, but he genuinely did not know what he had done, if

anything, to bring this upon himself. Maybe these urban legends

premeditate their attacks and choose their targets accordingly. He

wasn't exactly a helpless kid, what with a shotgun always slung

across his back and by his bedside every night. However, it was evident he had become a thorn in these monsters' sides. Maybe they thought if they got him out of the way, they would be able to take the town with ease...

He rolled down the window and slid his hand into the wind, letting the breeze speed past his fingers. He kept his eyes on the sky, until something strange occurred to him as the blue color started revealing pink streaks, as if it were dusk.

"Derek?" He asked, pulling his arm from the window, but keeping it rolled down. He had to raise his voice to overlap the whistle of the wind.

"Yeah?" Derek replied, not taking his eyes off the road ahead.

"What time did we leave?"

Derek was silent for a moment. "Probably around lunch time. Why?"

Wyatt ignored the question and averted his eyes from the sky to the digital clock on the truck's radio. 1:00 p.m.

Wyatt's eyes widened slightly, then shifted his view back to the now orange-colored sky.

"Stop the truck."

"What?"

"Stop the truck!" Wyatt repeated in a frustrated tone. Derek pressed his foot gradually onto the brake pedal until the truck came to a stop. They were surrounded by endless green forest with nothing else in sight. Wyatt stepped out of the truck, followed by Derek.

"Wyatt, what's wrong?" Derek slammed the truck door unintentionally, then he walked around the passenger side. Wyatt stood like a sentinel, staring upwards.

"Notice anything?" He pointed.

Derek tilted his head upwards, placing his hands on his hips. As he realized exactly what Wyatt was implying, his stomach started churning. Derek could feel the staleness in the air, which now felt thick like soup on his lungs as he inhaled slowly.

"It's getting dark," Wyatt stated, not sure if Derek realized.

Derek gulped, forcing his Adam's apple up and down in his throat.

"We need to hurry, something bad is about to happen."

They hopped back in the truck, speeding down the empty road with much more haste than before. The air around them felt tense. They both knew Lyonside was going to be in deep trouble when the sun went down.

TAKEN BY THE NIGHT

Chapter Eighteen

Alex grabbed each sandwich bag and placed them on the table in front of her. They were stacked into different columns next to a box of chip bags so that each child could grab and go. She felt it was a better system than what Derek had concocted, which was to personally hand each kid the same thing. He was lucky none of the children had peanut allergies, or else they would have a lot of children having dangerous reactions.

The walkie talkie on her hip crackled to life, meaning Derek was trying to contact her. She slipped it off its clip, still organizing with her left hand.

"Derek, you there?" She breathed out as she wiped her forehead on her sleeve.

The transmitter was eerily silent.

"Derek?"

Finally, a burst of static, then a voice.

"Yes."

Alex sighed. "I don't know how you do this all day. I guess only some were born for leading, huh?" She let out a small chuckle.

"Yes" was the response from the radio.

She stopped. His voice sounded different. It seemed to crack more, a contrasting difference to his normally smooth tone.

"...You guys okay?" She asked.

"You are all in danger!" The voice sprung to life, almost with an echoing undertone.

Alex dropped a sandwich on the table as her eyes widened. "What?!? What's going on, Derek?!?"

Suddenly, a strange and frightening sound rang through the speaker. It was an echoing mixture of choking and gurgling. After a moment of silence, Derek's warped voice returned.

"Bring the children into the forest."

Alex felt nauseated as these words entered her ears. She was confused, since they had agreed to stay away from both the cornfield and the forest. Tears burned hot behind her eyes.

"W-what?"

"Take the children into the forest." The voice returned, this time she could tell something was wrong. This voice sounded different as it croaked once again. This was not Derek. She knew how to determine this.

"Derek, how's Chloe? She's with you, right?"

The transmitter went silent, before it croaked to life once again.

"Yes. She is okay."

Alex's hands started to shake, as she dropped her transmitter. It shattered onto the floor, the batteries spewing out like little rockets across the concrete.

Chloe approached her from behind, causing her to jump.

"You okay?" She said. "You're pale, like you've seen a ghost or something?"

****

The afternoon sun was chased away by a premature moon as the darkness of the night sky swallowed up the blue above them. Both boys were begging internally for more time, just a little more time is all they needed. As the pitch blackness suffocated the little sunlight left that guided their path, they had to face the harsh reality. Derek reluctantly turned the knob on the stick of his truck, turning on the bright headlights to show the way.

244

"What are we going to do?" Wyatt asked, an uncharacteristic paranoia in his tone. He was gnawing on his thumbnail as he stared at the nothingness beyond the passenger window, hoping that nothing was staring back at him.

"We're going to keep driving. Find some help." Derek glanced down at his speedometer, then back at the road ahead. "Continue as planned."

Wyatt stopped chewing on his nail and turned to look at the dashboard. His eyes caught a glance at the clock. 2:00 p.m. No sign of light outside. Wyatt buried his face in his hands. There was no waking from this nightmare. They were in Hell. At some point, during the eerie darkness of what should have been a sunny afternoon, he was abruptly punched by Derek in the arm.

"Wake up, moron!" He said. Wyatt had not realized he had fallen asleep. "There's a gas station!"

Wyatt pulled himself out of his slouch, popping his back before rubbing his eyes. He fixed his view on the road ahead, catching in the distance the dim beam of a streetlight casting on a lonely building with gas pumps in its lot. It wasn't much really, but to the boys, it was a cure to a disease, water in a drought.

"People?!?" Wyatt began to grow excited, his heart jump-starting.

Derek squinted. "I don't know, man. I don't see any other cars."

"Maybe they're parked where we can't see them."

"Yeah, that's probably it."

Derek cautiously drove by the beam of light before stopping the truck right in the middle of the two-lane road. The inside looked barely lit, and it was hard to determine if this was an internal source or the streetlight next to them casting its bright beam through its dirt covered windows.

"So, how do you want to handle this?" He asked, a shakiness to his voice.

Wyatt didn't answer him. He just scanned the darkness around them, waiting for the inevitable.

"Wy."

For the first time since Derek had met Wyatt, the boy was speechless. They sat quiet, only the idle sounds of the truck's engine and their breathing filling the air.

"Bro, I need your help with thi--"

"I don't know, Derek!" he suddenly popped back. "I don't freaking know, alright?!?" He slammed his hand on the dash during his rant, causing it to rattle along with his voice. His palm started to throb, but he ignored the feeling.

Derek sighed, then looked passed his friend and at the station once again. His eyes drifted back to Wyatt, who had his arms crossed and was staring straight ahead, lost within his own thoughts. He needed Wyatt to concentrate. Derek wasn't confident that he could do this alone.

"I need you to calm down and focus for a second, Wy."

Wyatt shook his head. "Don't tell me to calm down, it just pisses me off even more."

"What are you even pissed off about?" Derek asked, a frustrated growl growing in his voice.

"Nothing, man…nothing." Wyatt brought his tone down to a hoarse whisper. He turned away from his friend and stared out the side window at the gas station. After the adults disappeared, he had felt okay. Despite missing his parents, he could even admit that he felt content. After seeing Jesse's body, he could feel it start to take effect. A sense of dread burdened him; the fact that he was a mortal and essentially powerless against such beings burrowed into his brain. On the football field, he was a quarterback. He was never hit too hard during practices, and he was rarely touched during

247

games because of how quick his feet could move. His motor mouth was a by-product of this sense of invincibility he always had. After Desmond, someone he considered a friend, had died, the anxiety had been scratching against the walls of his mind. The scarecrow that had killed him was now locked in on Wyatt,

"Alright then, I'm going in. Stay here."

"You're going in alone?" Wyatt scoffed. "Yeah, and I'm the crazy one."

Derek held his hands out, showing his lack of options. "You have any better ideas? You've clearly been affected by this whole thing, and I don't need you getting paranoid in the dark and accidentally shooting off your foot."

Wyatt held up his middle finger as he continued staring out of his window. Derek hesitated a moment, then proceeded to step out of his truck.

"Lock the doors. If I don't come back in five minutes, I might need help. Honk the horn a couple of times to let me know you're coming in. You got that?"

Wyatt stayed staring straight ahead, refusing to acknowledge his friend.

Derek shook his head, then slammed the door. He pulled the pistol out of his waistband, his fingers wrapped around the cold grip. This was a bad time to remember he had never fired a gun before. Pointing it ahead of him towards the door, his hands were shaking as he expected some type of hideous beast at any moment to come barreling out after him. His black boots clicked on the concrete. The night was silent, with the only sound coming from his truck engine; the steady yet unnerving hum only increased his anxiousness. His heart pounded against his rib cage as he opened the door, then progressed inside.

****

Wyatt stared down at his phone screen, typing vigorously. He kept his eye on the clock. Three minutes had gone by since Derek had entered the station looking for any sign of adults. He was trying to stay away from glaring into the darkness surrounding him, so he elected to check in on Chloe.

WYATT: Hey

CHLOE: Hey

Wyatt glanced up at the clock, then back at his phone as it buzzed in his hands.

CHLOE: Is it dark where you are, because it's pitch black here. It's only 3 pm.

WYATT: Ya. Crazy.

He felt a shiver down his spine, accentuated by the sensation that he was being watched. He brushed it off, as he always felt this way since the parents were taken.

Something jostled the truck, causing it to creak and bounce on its suspension. It felt as if someone was in the bed, bouncing like it was a trampoline. He realized he was sweating profusely, even though it was cool out, as he silently begged for the jostling of the truck to stop. The pure terror that gripped him brought him to the brink of tears. He dared not to look in the rear-view mirror, horrified he would see those horrendous eyes and that terrible smile.

The bouncing ceased.

Wyatt worked up enough courage to turn around and point his gun towards the back window.

Nothing.

He breathed a sigh of relief, then let out a slight chuckle.

SCREEEEEEK!!

TAKEN BY THE NIGHT

His thoughts were interrupted by a scratching sound on his passenger-side window. Someone was taking a sharp instrument to the glass and sliding it down its length repeatedly. He didn't want to turn his head.

The radio suddenly flickered on, springing to life and belting out the instantly recognizable, static-filled version of the opening tune of "I Ran". The fact that it had been a favorite of his dad was like a punch in the gut to Wyatt, and he struggled to keep his emotions under control. He was shaking uncontrollably, refusing to look at whatever terrifying being with hideously gnarly nails might be looking at him. This really was Hell. After what felt like an eternity, the sound ceased, leaving nothing to hear but Wyatt's breathing. It was shaky and labored as he turned to the window slowly, only to be greeted by nothing but the dim glow of the streetlight. He continued to scan the area, his eyes catching movement at the station. The door was closing, as if someone, or something, had just entered.

Chapter Nineteen

Alex could feel the tension in her shoulders. The children of Lyonside were going insane as nighttime fell upon them unexpectedly in the early afternoon. The sun had disappeared from the sky, and the midnight moon stood triumphantly over them, waiting for its creatures to pounce on the little town. Flashlights had been in short supply, so they were distributed to the older teens. Glow sticks were given to the smaller kids, mainly as a momentary distraction from the chaos around them. Now, half of them lay abandoned in the street. If you didn't know any better, you would think there had been a massive rock concert in the streets of Lyonside, and this was the aftermath.

"Alex, something doesn't feel right." Molly ascertained; her face drained of its natural color.

TAKEN BY THE NIGHT

Chloe was sitting on the concrete curb looking at the abandoned trash in the street, her toes pointing inward and her head in her hands. She could feel it, too. The stillness of the night caused uneasiness to spread like the flu, and everyone was sick. The wind was calm, and the ordinary night noises had silenced.

Somehow, it seemed the girls knew something was about to happen. A blood-curdling scream echoed through the night, a sound they were all too familiar with. Alex shuddered, and jerked her head in different directions, desperately searching for the source. The children in the street were in a panic, running for the safety of the bookstore. Alex squinted, trying to see what they were so terrified of. She heard a little girl yell amongst the chaos, just as a figure came into view.

"Smiling man! Smiling man!"

Alex was petrified as several figures appeared behind the first. More and more became visible as they slowly grew closer.

Smiling men.

****

His flashlight beam flickered as Derek scanned the backroom, looking for any signs of life other than the occasional rat that scurried by his feet. He felt uneasy as a wave of nausea struck him.

He slowly opened the door to a supply room, the creaking of its hinges cutting through the silence. There was nothing except boxes of beer cans and soda bottles. Derek sighed in frustration. *We should have just driven past this stupid place! Maybe they would be out of this nightmare if they had just kept driving until they reached civilization.* He searched the wall for a light switch, his palm sliding over the drywall.

A ringing entered his ears just as his fingertips found the switch, the sound causing him to freeze in the inky darkness. He turned and looked out of the backroom hallway, his eyes straining for a sliver of light. He recognized the ringing of the bell above the door at the front of the station.

Someone had walked in.

His mind raced, until he remembered Wyatt was out at the truck. That had to be him. Derek smiled at his childishness, then started walking down the hallway.

"Wy, I thought you were going to stay in the truck and honk the--" He stopped dead in his tracks.

His eyes widened as they focused on the figure in the darkness. It was too tall to be Wyatt, way too tall. From what the dim light revealed, he wore a bloody apron that was too small allowing his

254

large belly to hang out beneath it, and a hook was sloppily sewn to his wrist where another grimy hand should have been. He had broad shoulders, massive legs, and his eyes were bloodshot to the point where the whites were crimson. His hair was greasy and matted to his head. As the man stepped forward, Derek swore he felt the Earth shake.

The sound of Derek's breathing, and the pounding of his heart in his ears was interrupted by the roar of an engine and tires squealing down the road.

His truck. *Wyatt.*

"No," He whispered to himself, his eyes never leaving the giant of a man in front of him.

The man let out a deep, long gargling sound, and then what could have been perceived as a chuckle. It knew Derek had nowhere to go. He was at its mercy.

****

Wyatt drove. He just drove. His foot was smashed onto the gas pedal, and he was gripping the wheel to the point his knuckles were turning white. He was crying. No, he was bawling. He had finally snapped. The nonchalant, carefree attitude that made him refuse to take anything serious, no matter the gravity of the situation, was gone. It had caused him to take unnecessary risk at times, like in his search for Lucy, or when he ran like a madman after Jesse when he was snatched, or in searching the dreaded cornfield for Carlos. It was all gone, and all that was left was pure fear and dread. Everything that had occurred over the last week was catching up to him and searing into his brain like a cattle brand. His parents were gone. Carlos was gone. *God, Dez was gone!* He was gone because of Wyatt. He had gone to help, even though Dez had never cared for Wyatt, he still went into the cornfield to help. Dez was dead because of him. Chloe was scarred mentally because of him. Alex had a mental breakdown because of him, and now, Derek was alone and left to the mercy of whatever had followed him into the service station....

because of him.

He blew through his mouth, exhaling forcefully, and punched the wheel in a rage. He wanted to stop and just throw a fit. He wanted to smash the windows in rage, but he couldn't stop. There were monsters out there, and if he stopped, he would be at their mercy like Derek. *God, Derek! My best friend!*

He pulled at his hair with one hand in frustration. *What have I done?*

TAKEN BY THE NIGHT

He revved the engine more, until the roar drowned out his cries.

****

"Everyone, follow me!" Alex ran down the road towards the school. The children behind her were terrified. Scared, and pumped full of adrenaline, the football players began helping Alex herd the children towards the school. It was a strange sight for her. She had never seen a six-foot-two, 290-pound high school boy look so genuinely terrified. Chloe tried shooting at the smiling men, but the bullets did nothing to the mere shadows. Not a thing. It went straight through their narrow torsos as if they were inky black butter. Hordes of the creatures were running from the woods and surrounding the town. The kids who attempted to fight back were simply overwhelmed by the flood. They came from all directions. Alex could only think of the school gym. It was the only place big enough to hold the kids, and sturdy enough to even have a chance of holding back the smiling men. Chloe followed, her hand on her pistol if only for the false sense of security. They could hear the stomping of the hundreds, maybe thousands of feet heading for them. Alex had to maintain her composure, but it was so dark outside she could be leading them right into more of those things and not even realize it. They couldn't just sit there though, waiting to be snuffed out by the army of shadows overtaking them from the darkness. The beams of a few flashlights lit the dirt road, shaking in the unsteady hands clutching them. The children whimpered and screamed as the group moved steadily, ever so closer to the school. They were almost there.

"Wait!" A boy from the crowd yelled out.

No one stopped moving until he yelled even louder.

"Wait, guys! Wait!"

Alex stopped, thinking maybe he had fallen behind until she distinctly heard him close behind her. She snapped her head around suddenly, her eyes searching the crowd behind her, until they locked on the small boy.

"Do you hear that?!?" He yelled directly at her; his voice shaky in the darkness.

It was hard to hear exactly what he said, let alone exactly what sound he was referring to. After all, there were hundreds of creatures marching towards them and the many wails originating from the terrified young ones. She focused on her hearing and could barely make out something else.

An engine. Derek and Wyatt?

She nearly jumped for joy, knowing that Derek would have the wisdom to lead them to safety. However, her celebration was premature, as a horde was heading straight for them from the other direction and were mere yards away. Alex ran to the other end of the crowd of children behind her, bumping through teenagers and kids alike.

"Hold on and stay calm!" she yelled above the noise.

No one could hear her over the screaming, as a shadow creature approached, yanking at a football players jacket. The boy screamed, then flailed around in a state of panic, his flashlight being thrown around wildly. The beam crossed the face of one of the shadows, creating a crackling sound like bacon on a fryer, but smelled much worse. It was as if someone had scorched a rubber tire. The shadow's head splattered like it had been hit by a powerful laser beam of some kind, leaving nothing but a limp black body and a wickedly crooked smile.

The light! Even though it was just a simple flashlight, the concentrated blast of energy in proximity of the creature had somehow been enough to destroy it! This must be how you stop them! Alex's hand was shaking as she pulled her flashlight from her waistband, turning to face the next charging creature. Pushing with one hand on its chest to hold it back, she jammed the flashlight underneath its chin and turned it on. The sudden blast of light blew the top of its head open, sending an icky warm goop splattering in all directions. She booted its limp body backwards.

"It's the light! The light!" She screamed. Chloe mimicked her friend as she pressed her flashlight to the chest of another, sending it flying backwards with a shot of white light.

The sound of the truck approaching had been drowned out by the chaos around Alex. Eventually she saw Derek's truck rumbling towards them like a starving lion pouncing on its kill. She could see the dim headlights as they collided full speed into a group of the creatures, sending them sprawling forward. The window rolled down, and Wyatt leaned his head out in confusion of what he had plowed into.

"The brights! Turn on the high beams!" Chloe yelled to him.

He reached over with his free hand and turned the knob. The headlights grew brighter, shining on a crippled pile of the monsters that evaporated with a sickening shriek. He began to understand what Chloe was yelling about as another creature leaped at the window, only to be met with a shotgun blast across the neck.

TAKEN BY THE NIGHT

Wyatt stomped his foot down on the gas and jerked the wheel causing the tires to spin through the gravel turning the vehicle in donuts. The headlights spun round and round with the truck shining on anything within range. He had it moving fast in a tight radius, and as one of the wheels ramped off a fallen smiling man, the truck rolled on its side from the momentum, sliding across the dirt road through the main horde. The engine ceased, and metal creaked as what seemed like a thousand smiling men began climbing the turned over truck. The distraction gave Molly time to lead the kids to the school only yards away.

"Alex, come on!" She yelled back, shining her light at straying shadows while the children began pouring into the entrance.

Chloe was racing towards the mass of darkness surrounding the truck in the street., yelling at the teens who were shining their lights wildly.

"We need to help Wyatt!" "Shine at the truck!" She turned to Alex in a panic. "Help me! He's still in there!"

"I don't care!" Molly yelled back as she slammed the gym door, "Let him rot!"

Alex had already taken off for the road, lighting up the advancing shadows.

****

Derek ducked down an aisle in a state of panic. Silence had coated the dark room. The only thing he could hear was his own heartbeat, and he prayed that the hook man could not hear it.

He licked his chapped lips and tried to slow his shaky breathing, but to no avail. He was trying to think about whether Wyatt had abandoned him or not. *No, he wouldn't do that!* Wyatt was his friend. He would never do that, never. In recent weeks, he had risked his life to save people he didn't even know, and even faced certain death to try and save that jerk Jesse!

Wyatt had lost a lot in recent weeks though. Dez. Carlos. He had grown distant from Chloe since that night in the cornfield and had seemed really stressed in the truck earlier.

But why? Why would he leave me?

His thoughts were interrupted by a thumping that suddenly grew closer at a lightning fast pace. Something suddenly smashed into the shelves behind him, sending them, him, and bags of chips flying forward. He slammed into the cold metal of the shelf in front of him, sending candy bars raining down on top of him.

"Come on out, boy!" A sickening voice croaked through the silence.

TAKEN BY THE NIGHT

Derek whimpered like a puppy as he struggled to climb to his feet. He had to get out somehow, but where would he go? If he escaped, the psycho would just chase him into the forest. He believed he was better off in here rather than in the hands of whatever lay waiting for him within the trees. No, he had to kill the man. Derek reached for his pistol only to find an empty holster. He remembered he had pulled the pistol before seeing the bloated being in the doorway and must have dropped it in his panic to dive out of sight. He searched through the bags of chips around him as he could hear more metal shelves being ripped apart, imagining the damage the sharp hook would do to him once he was found. A chill shot down his spine just as his hands bumped the barrel of his gun. *Yes*! He nearly cried out for joy as his shaking hands checked the chamber for a round. His knuckles turned white as he gripped the butt of the gun tightly. Suddenly, the remaining shelves around him opened, and standing there was the hook man, his grotesquely bloated body hovering over Derek. Drops of a black goop and warm sweat splattered against Derek's head. The psychopath had a sickening smile spread across his face, before letting out a horrific scream as he swung his hook towards Derek's chest. Derek yelled in a fit of terror and rage, lifting his pistol and aiming directly for the hideous man's belly.

BANG! BANG! BANG! BANG!

He squeezed the trigger as fast as he could, squeezing his eyes shut as his eardrums rang from the noise. Every ounce of fear and pain drained from him as he riddled the monstrous man with bullets. He had no idea if it was enough, but he wouldn't stop trying. He would never stop trying.

The gun clicked, then the silence took over.

He opened his eyes, finally letting himself breathe. Just breathe. The only sight his eyes caught was a crimson red blood splatter on the ceiling, with bullet holes spread across the tiles. His nerves finally caught up to him, and the nausea hit like a freight train. He puked while still laying down and began choking on his vomit. He quickly snapped out of his trance and turned over, coughing out his stomach contents violently. Derek scanned the room, still on his hands and knees.

The man was gone. No dead body. Nothing.

He let out a rage-filled yell, his face growing red from the intensity. The sound bounced from the walls of the chaotic room and traveled back to his ears. The smell of blood and vomit filled his nose as he breathed in, then out. He had just noticed how cold the room was. The darkness seemed tangible as the silence surrounded him, and the fear that had nearly driven him to the point of insanity began to slowly subside. His adrenaline levels began to drop, and exhaustion set in. All he wanted now was to sleep.

Chapter Twenty

Wyatt's head was foggy, and his vision was blurry. He hadn't been buckled in, so as soon as the truck turned over, he went flying out of his seat and smacked against the passenger side dashboard, his head cracking against the window. He didn't know how long he had been out, but he could see a mass of shadow men standing on top of the driver side window, trying desperately to get inside. They snarled and snapped their teeth, letting out rabid screeches while they jumped and punched the glass that now lay above him to no prevail. His vision began to clear, just as a crackling sound began to fill his ears. Those things would be on him if the glass gave way.

He reached behind his back for the shotgun, but it was gone.

TAKEN BY THE NIGHT

"Craaaaaaaaap," He let out, silently. He had thrown his shotgun onto the seat next to him while trying to maneuver the truck. There's no telling where it went when the truck flipped.

He scanned the cab, searching for the weapon to defend himself. He had figured out what Chloe was screaming at him earlier, about the light being the only thing that could hurt these beasts, and the flash from the end of the shotguns barrel when he fired was enough to work like a charm.

He leaned around the back of the front seat and peered into the backseat. There it was, under the backseat where it had become wedged when the truck was rolling over, exposed by a shimmer of moonlight shining through the driver side window that was now above his head.

Wyatt reached over the seat trying to grab the barrel. If it was a little bit longer, it would have not been a problem, but the barrel was cut down. He gripped the headrest and the dashboard, trying to pull himself up to stand. When he put pressure on his right leg to balance himself, a blast of pain erupted from just above his knee.

He screeched from the agony grasping at his leg as he cursed under his breath, inhaling and exhaling at a rapid pace trying desperately not to panic. He fell on his back against the passenger window. All he could think to do was try again once he regained his composure.

He clenched his teeth in determination as he pulled himself up again, this time knowing the pain would come. It shot through his knee and up his body feeling like a red-hot blade was jammed in the back of his thigh. He propped himself up on the seat, then swung his arm over, stretching, trying to grab the gun again. He breathed carefully, inching his fingers ever so close to the shotgun. Another crackle from the glass above him made Wyatt rush himself, putting all his body weight on his leg just as he grasped the barrel.

"Agh!" He cried out, falling back onto the window violently.

He checked the chamber and let out a curse as two used shotgun shells shot out. Empty. He hadn't had the chance to reload before the truck rolled.

He couldn't do it. He just couldn't. For the first time in his life, Wyatt Richards was accepting defeat. *Is this how it would end? After everything he had done to survive, would it all end here? Would he die by drowning in the wave of monsters banging on the glass above him?*

TAKEN BY THE NIGHT

No. No, no, no. There had to be some way to beat this. There always is. There's always a way to survive.

He threw the now useless gun aside, then looked around the passenger door, which was now the floorboard, in hopes of finding something, anything he could use as a weapon. He felt around blindly, touching something wet and sticky, praying silently that it wasn't blood, and if it was, it wasn't his.

He dug frantically through water bottles and fast food trash until his hand bumped against something cold and metallic.

"Oh, yes! A flashlight!" he exclaimed aloud, remembering again what Chloe had said about how to kill these creatures. He grabbed the slender instrument and fumbled around with it in his hands. He clicked the button on one end, nothing. *No, no, no! Please don't tell me this!* He banged the light against his other hand, clicking the on and off button as he did so. Still nothing. The batteries were dead. Suddenly he remembered his dad used to put the batteries backwards in his flashlights to keep them from draining down while not being used. Driven by sheer panic he quickly began unscrewing the end of the flashlight to access the batteries, hoping Derek had the same idea as Wyatt's father.

Careful not to drop anything in the dark, he removed the end and felt for the batteries, holding his breath.

"YES!" He shouted aloud. The batteries were in backwards! He quickly installed them correctly, twisted the end back on and BOOM! *Halle-freaking-lujah*! It wasn't the brightest, but nevertheless, it was light.

Wyatt turned it off, conserving what battery was left for when the window broke. The light was weak, so if he kept it on, he risked it going out. He would have to time it just as the glass shattered and the creatures fell in. If he waited too long, they would smother him before he had a chance to turn on the light.

He aimed the flashlight upwards, leaned his head back, and waited patiently with his thumb on the button, listening to the glass begin to give way. At the last moment, he smirked with as much confidence as he could muster.

Crackle....Crackle.... Bang!

****

Alex watched the flood of smiling men dropping into the vehicle after the window caved in. Only seconds later, a massive chain of explosions set in as inky blackness erupted from the window. It started out small, like popcorn, then grew into what seemed to be firecrackers going off.

"Wyatt!" A younger boy, who looked to be a Lyonside football player by the red letter jacket he was wearing, rushed over to the truck and finished off the last of the "smiling men". Chloe was right by his side, racing to assist their friend.

"There's no way he survived that. No way," Alex overheard a cheerleader from West Side, who was covered in dirt, mutter.

"Wyatt! Can you hear me?!?" Chloe yelled at the truck, searching for a way to get in.

A bigger teenage boy with red hair covering his head and jaw, on what seemed to be a naturally angry face, rumbled past Alex at the school and stomped his way towards the truck.

"Come on," He said unexpectedly gentle, but still firmly towards his teammates. With the Lyonside boys following, they reached the truck, then proceeded to rock it back and forth. Finally, after a chorus of grunts and groans from the players and the wrecked vehicle, the truck finally rolled onto its wheels with a loud thunk.

"Get the door open," a chorus of whispers said simultaneously as Chloe struggled to pull the handle of the dented metal.

"It's jammed!" She yelled, yanking with desperation.

They went around to the drivers door, realizing it was standing open from the explosions earlier and was barely hanging by its broken hinges. It looked like it would fall off and clang on the ground any second.

Once Alex caught a glimpse of the inside of the cab, she immediately began to gag. She hadn't realized just how bad the ooze from those shadow men really smelled. She knew it wasn't pleasant, but the whole cabin was soaked in the smell of scorched hair. The smell slugged her in the gut.

"Wy?" The younger boy looked inside, seemingly unaffected by the rancidness.

At first, they couldn't see anything except inky darkness, until something began to move within the ooze. Tony held up a pistol and aimed it inside as a precaution.

"Ay!" An all too familiar voice with a hint of hoarseness responded. "PBn'J! Where the heck have you been this whole time?!? You've missed some serious crap, my man!"

The boy laughed. "You're a freaking god for surviving that!"

"No," Wyatt coughed out as he wiped his face enough to reveal a smile. "But don't let that stop you from worshiping me."

Chloe reached a hand in to help him out. "Glad you're okay, moron."

He waved a hand in response, gritting his teeth as if he were in pain. "No can do. Busted my leg up pretty bad in the wreck. Can't move."

Tony, the big redhead, searched around, until he found something he had seen earlier when approaching the truck. He picked the object up, then offered it to Wyatt.

"Here, grab it and I'll yank you out!"

Wyatt's entire face was covered in the ooze, so he couldn't really see what he was grabbing. He felt his body sliding through the disgusting black on the leather seat, just before his injured leg smacked against the steering wheel.

"Ah!" He yelled in complete agony. He wanted to curse but had no idea if any of the young ones were outside and could hear him.

"F-F-Freakin' fartknocker!"

Someone laughed, but he didn't find it humorous. He fell out of the cab and onto the ground with another shot of pain. Someone lifted him up, taking whatever it was he had used to get out of the car, from his hand. He could barely see through the dripping ooze now, but his sight was clear enough to tell what it was.

Derek's crutch. It must have fallen out of the truck bed during the crash.

"I got you, man," A rough voice said.

Wyatt looked up, and through the one eye that didn't have goop covering it, he saw a glimpse of red hair.

"Is that you, Ninety?" He called the boy by his football number.

"Yeah, it's me."

The boy lifted him to his feet. With one arm around Wyatt's waist, and one of Wyatt's arms around the boy's neck, they hobbled forward, towards the school.

"I'm sorry I called you bigfoot the other day."

The redhead chuckled heartily. "You're not the first to call me that."

They trotted slowly, followed by the herd of teens behind them. Suddenly, they stopped.

"What's wrong?" Wyatt grunted.

There was a silence, before he reached up and cleared his face enough to see in front of him.

"You okay, loser?" Molly, who was standing a few feet away from him, said while keeping her eyes on the ground.

He remembered when she lost her mind after Dez died, blaming him for his death. He blamed himself for what happened to Dez.

"Yeah. I'm alri-" He was interrupted by her, as she ran up and hugged his neck, ignoring the stink that surrounded him.

"I'm sorry, Wy," She whimpered. He had never seen her like this.

Wyatt was startled by this reaction, as his eyes began to moisten, and there was a lump in his throat.

He slowly wrapped his arms around her, then buried his face in her neck and began to sob.

Chapter Twenty-One

It was only nine o'clock, so the sun had not returned to its natural place in the sky. They would have to wait until morning to see if they really were in as serious trouble as many of the children feared. Wyatt was resting, leaned up against the wall of the nurse's office, his eyes gazing into space as Molly sat down next to him. She crossed her legs as she cleaned the ooze off his face, searching for any serious cuts.

"Listen, Molly," He began to speak. "About Dez..."

She never looked up from the medical bag in her lap she was digging in. "He was my friend," He explained. "Even though we fought a lot, and he wanted to strangle me on more than one occasion, I considered him one of the few people here I could trust. Believe me, if I had known what would go down in that cornfield, I never would have gone in."

276

TAKEN BY THE NIGHT

She looked up from her medical bag then, revealing the wide golden eyes that reminded him of his late friend and her late brother. "Yeah, we've all wanted to strangle you on more than one occasion, Wy."

"Fair point," he said, leaning his head back against the wall.

"Look," She averted her eyes back to the bag. "He was my brother, Wyatt. He was my family. He helped my dad raise me. Now they're both gone, and it just hurts. That's all. I didn't mean to lose it on you. You've done more for these kids and this town than anyone else."

Wyatt began to say something, but she made a quiet motion. "No, shut up. Don't respond like a jerk and make me take back what I'm saying right now. Just be quiet."

He did as she ordered.

"Look, you're a good guy Wy, but that doesn't change the fact that Desmond is dead now, and I'm afraid to get close to anyone anymore. That's because of you, but you're still my friend, and I'm grateful for everything you've done for us."

She leaned up and kissed him on the cheek. Wyatt was flabbergasted, and the kiss took him by utter surprise.

"Uh...", he uttered; his eyes wide.

"Just don't say anything, or I might have to slap that stupid look off your face. By the way, you might want to take a razor to those whiskers, or else, no girl is ever going to want to do that again," She turned back to the bag as Wyatt ran his hand over the stiff hairs that aligned his jaw.

She pulled out a roll of gauze and a flask, Jesse's flask.

"Pull your pants down. I can't get to the wound to clean it by rolling up your pant leg. It's too high up on your leg and your jeans are stiff."

"Say what now?" Wyatt asked, still in shock from what she had told him earlier.

"Oh, relax, Romeo. I'm not going to grope you. It's not like you have anything down there, anyways."

Wyatt mimicked her mockingly as he yanked the belt out of the loop, then pulled his jeans down to his shins reluctantly, wincing as the material peeled away from the wound. A sharp piece of the dashboard from Derek's truck had come loose and lodged itself in the meat of his thigh right above his knee. He grabbed a towel from her bag, then placed it over his boxer shorts for modesty. A long period of silence took over the room before he spoke again.

"Where'd you get that flask?" He asked, eyeing the metal object in her hand.

"It was on Dez's body, in his back pocket." She responded.

"You saw his body?" Wyatt asked.

She eyed him, showing a hint of anger deep within her eyes. "I cleaned his wound."

Wyatt went silent, then decided to respond. "It wasn't his."

"I know, I was there when you gave it to him, remember?"

The room went silent again, with nothing but the ticking of the clock on the wall filling their ears.

"Where's Derek?" She asked, not taking her eyes off his injury.

"What?"

"Where's Derek, Wy?"

He thought about the question, his face growing cold and losing its color. He really didn't want to tell her how he had left his friend back at the gas station to fend for himself, and that he might be dead. Wyatt knew his actions were the total opposite of the nice things Molly had just said about him.

"That bad, huh?" She responded to his reaction as she wiped goop from his wound. "That'll kill Alex. Look, they asked me to tell them when they could come in and talk to you, so after I leave, they're going to come in and ask questions. Don't tell them the truth. I don't care how he died, let her down gently. Tell her he didn't suffer. That poor girl has been through enough after what happened with Carlos."

She poured the bourbon on his leg conservatively, but the burn of the alcohol on the opening in his leg was enough to make him scream in pain.

"Should have warned you. My bad." She looked unaffected, her face insincere and lacking emotion. "I'll count to three this time. One-"

She poured it out again, and Wyatt smacked the tile floor he sat on in rage.

"You're freakin' mean!" he said through clenched teeth.

She wrapped his leg up in the gauze, then packed up her medical pack without saying a word. As she stood to exit the room, Wyatt grabbed her hand firmly, causing her to snap her head around. He loosened his grip, running his hand down her palm and grasping her fingers gently. He noticed how cold her hands were.

"Listen to me, Molly." He begged. She could tell from the look in his eyes that this was one of the rare times he was serious.

"What?"

"I didn't turn around to come back," he blurted out.

"What are you talking about?" She didn't let go of his hand.

"I kept going, Molly." He let out, in disbelief himself of what he was saying. "After what happened to Derek, I didn't come back. I kept driving away from Lyonside."

Her expression grew cold, before she pulled her arm away. "Then how are you here?"

He looked down, deeply considering the situation at hand.

"I don't know."

****

Derek awoke from his slumber, a death grip on the gun in his right hand. He had locked himself in a back room and made a makeshift bed out of filled cardboard boxes. He used a large bag of chips as a pillow, before falling into a deep sleep. Startled awake by a dream, there was a moment of slight panic until he remembered where he was.

Dreams were clever. They had a way of making an unsuspecting person forget their problems and ailments, replacing them with a false reality. In his mind, he was back on the football field, getting ready to throw the ball, when he was hit by a truck. Not a player, a truck. His truck. It had been driven onto the field at an impossible speed and plowed into him. He tried to stand and scream for help, but his legs were broken, and his mouth taped shut underneath his helmet. He started to panic, looking around for anyone to help him. He quieted down after he saw the people in the stands, their skin rotten and their eyes rolled back in their heads. They trampled forward slowly, limping and inching their way towards him. He reached for the waistband of his football pants and pulled out his pistol, firing an endless number of bullets into the crowd. The crowd of his friends, Alex, Chloe, Molly, and even Dez marched towards him. They were zombies.

The truck roared over him as the back wheels dug into the turf and slung dirt up into the air. It halted in front of him, separating the crowd of the undead from him. Stepping out of the vehicle was Wyatt, or a twisted version of him. He looked like the crowd behind him, his skin a rotten blue and his eyes missing their green color. He had a gun in his hand, and that stupid cocky grin he always sported.

"You gotta do what you gotta do, Derek. You understand, right?" He said, crouching down in front of his distressed friend. Derek leveled the gun he didn't know he had in his hand at Wyatt's distorted face, pulling the trigger without hesitation. Of course, it was empty.

Wyatt made a clicking sound, as if scolding a child for reaching into the cookie jar. "Wow. I'm genuinely hurt, buddy. Ouch!"

He shrugged his shoulders, which had protruding bones and was oozing a green puss. He then leveled his shotgun at Derek's ghostly pale face, and smiled again, right before the blast went off.

That's when he woke up.

As Derek sat up from the boxes he been laying on, his mouth was dry and from the taste in it, felt like a cat had used it as a litter box. He wasn't sure what time it really was, although the clock in the storage room said nine, but he didn't know if it was morning or evening. The fact that no light was shining through the blinds on the window would usually signify the latter, but after what happened before with the odd disappearance of the sun, there was no way he could be sure. All he knew was that he was starving, and it was a good thing he was surrounded by food that wasn't rationed.

A sudden surge of excitement brought him to his feet, and he marched towards the door into the main room. When it opened, he could feel a cool rush of air from the freezers with shattered doors brush across his skin, causing goosebumps to form.

"Oh, yes." He muttered as he made his way to the snacks section, then opened a small corn chips bag by squeezing it tightly, waiting for that popping sound.

Pop.

That was a technique he learned in kindergarten, along with every other child. Oh, how he missed those days.

He dumped the contents of the bag into his mouth, letting chips scatter on the already littered floor. He was the organized type, but he wasn't bothered by the chaos around him. That was one of the things that made him a phenomenal quarterback. He could lead a team no matter what was put in front of him. He could lead Lyonside no matter the chaos. It didn't matter if he had been pressured in the pocket, Derek could still launch the football and "thread the needle" into the arms of one of his receivers. At least he used to, until he broke his leg and Wyatt took over. He had still been leading Lyonside in the fight for survival off the football field, until Wyatt stepped in and abandoned him.

Screw him.

Derek crumpled up the empty chip bag and flung it across the room, then he bolted for the busted door of a freezer. He reached through the opening left by the shattered glass that lay on the tile floor and grabbed a bottle of cold, refreshing soda. He let it burn down his throat and finished it in one long chug. He flung the bottle across the room, before it clunked against one of the fallen shelves. The sound was loud but was quickly overtaken by the deafening silence right after. He had to get out of there, but how? Walking outside was suicide right now, and he didn't know when the sun would return, or if it would at all.

Derek laid back down, the feeling of hunger finally subsiding. He counted the tiles on the ceiling as he began to drift off to sleep once again.

****

Molly was right about the group becoming curious concerning Derek's whereabouts, as Wyatt soon learned. She was a smart girl, and in his opinion, she was very attractive. Molly, however, was different from all the other girls. Nobody messed with her if they wanted to keep their teeth in their head.

Wyatt contemplated on this. He was not one to back down in an altercation and neither was she. However, that was also where they differed. Unless Wyatt was really backed into a corner and felt like he had to come out swinging, he would usually just fire back with something clever to embarrass the opposition. Molly, on the other hand, was scrappy and would shove her foot somewhere unpleasant at the drop of a hat if you challenged her. He liked that about her. Wyatt felt something when she kissed his cheek, a feeling that quickly returned as he thought about her.

He quickly shook it, thinking it was stupid to contemplate on feelings when there were monsters among them.

Alex and Chloe had approached him as he made his way out of the nurse's office after sliding up his soggy black jeans. He hobbled over through the doorway to avoid putting pressure on his right leg. The pain had let up, but there was a warmth surrounding the area. He bumped into them as he entered the main hall.

"Hey," Alex said, still sporting the dirt and grime from the venture before. "You okay? You gave us a scare out there."

Wyatt looked at her, then turned to Chloe, studying their serious expressions.

"I'm fine. Thanks." He hobbled forward, until he reached one of the classroom doors.

"Wyatt, where's Derek? Why did you turn around and come back?"

He stopped himself as he reached for the door handle, closing his eyes as he processed how to answer the question. He knew that question would come, just as Molly had known. How could it not? Alex and Derek were close, and he had been the only thing keeping the town from plunging into chaos. He contemplated how Molly had told him to lie, to let Alex down easy and to save face. After Molly had lost it on Wyatt, openly blaming him for her brother's death, a lot of kids in town who didn't know him that well, probably were suspicious of him. If he told the truth, they would crucify him. He sounded like a murderer. Two teenage boys were dead, and he was responsible for both.

"He's gone, Alex," He said, genuine tears building up in his green eyes. "I tried to stop them. We were just...overwhelmed." He sighed, followed by a cough.

Alex was in shock, her face revealing all the emotions she was feeling. Chloe just shook her head in denial.

"God help us," She whispered to herself as she covered her mouth, eyes wide with shock.

"He went quickly." Wyatt refused to look them in the eye. He wasn't one to shy away from a fib or two when he was younger, and he had gotten away with most of them with a straight face. Not this one. His face was scrunched up as he tried to hold back tears.

"I...I have to go lay down," Alex muttered, her eyes still wide as she left the two of them in the dark hallway alone.

Wyatt turned to Chloe; his eyes bloodshot.

"You look tired," She pointed out. She followed his eyes over to Alex, watching as she walked away. "She'll be ok, hopefully." After watching Alex walk out of sight, she turned back to Wyatt. "Are you?" "Ok, I mean?" "I know he was your best friend."

Wyatt shook his head as he sniffled, then wiped his face on his arm. "I'm okay. Just need to clean myself up in the gym shower. Do you know where I can get some soap or something?"

She nodded. "Yeah. It's all in the gym in big baskets by the wall." "Hey," She said reaching over to touch his jaw, gently moving his head from one side to the other.

"Don't shave. I kind of like it like that. Wash that hair, though." She smiled playfully, then turned and walked towards the big doors that lead into the gym. Wyatt watched her walk away.

****

TAKEN BY THE NIGHT

Molly was leaning against the gym wall, right next to her bed. She clicked her black boots together as she took another swig of the wine bottle in her hand. It wasn't the hard liquor that usually got confiscated since the disaster that stranded her in Lyonside, but it was still frowned upon by the "leaders" like Derek and Dez, when they were still alive. Derek had instructed that any form of alcohol would be collected and kept in the grocery store in buggies. She didn't want to make a fool of herself, but she needed something to take the edge off, so she had grabbed a bottle of red wine when no one was around the store earlier that day. She dared anyone to say anything to her. She wouldn't mind beating someone's head in if she had to.

A boy around her age approached from the crowd of kids, his pink button-up shirt ironed, and his jet-black hair slicked back with a truck load of hair gel. His stark white shorts lacked any stain or wrinkle. He was clean shaven, revealing a strong jawline and narrow cheekbones. His only noticeable flaw was the long nose jutting outwards. Molly had always been told how gorgeous her eyes were, but his were much more noticeable. They were an extremely bright, light blue. She could have sworn there were traces of silver in them.

"Hello there. You're Molly, right?" He had an unnatural charm in his smile and a southern accent so thick, you would swear you could see it dripping from him. She could sense he was up to no good. She had always had the uncanny ability to tell when she was being manipulated, and right now, she felt his tongue held more silver than the color of his eyes.

"Yeah. Why do you care?" She said, gulping down another swallow of wine, the red color staining her lips. She was already on the defense.

The boy smiled, causing her to feel uneasy. "Oh, just curious. I want to help the town any way I can, and I figured I need to get to know as many people as possible." He stretched out a hand. She could see the veins underneath his skin. "I'm Ruttledge."

Molly refused to move from where she stood, and she sure wasn't going to shake this creep's hand.

"Oh, come on," He chuckled. "You don't hate me already, do you?"

Molly's eyes scanned him from head to toe.

Her grandfather, who had endured extreme prejudice as a young black man, instilled in her father at a young age that it was never okay to judge someone by the way they looked, especially their skin color. She and her brother had been the recipient of the same lessons from her father many times throughout their childhood, until it became a part of who they were. Prejudice was something she had never had to deal with, partially because her mom was white, and Molly's skin was a lighter shade than the men on her father's side of the family. People often didn't even know she was half African American.

Something else her father had taught her was how to spot a con.

"I'm still deciding." She took another swig of the bottle. She was already a suspicious person, but this guy was putting off a bad vibe that she sensed the moment he approached. He cleared his throat, then pulled his hand back.

"Well, if you ever need help with anything, I'm sleeping in the chemistry room." He laughed. "Never thought I'd say that."

She smirked, then flipped the hair out of her face.

"How come I don't recognize you? Most of these faces I can at least recall seeing during class. Why can't I place yours?"

Ruttledge flashed that smile again. "I don't go to your high school, although, I am surprised we haven't seen each other around town at least."

"Are you from West Side?"

"Oh no, no. I was born and raised here in Lyonside. This is my home," He ran a hand over his perfectly-aligned hair. "No, I was homeschooled."

Molly nodded, then took another swig of her wine.

"I thought drinking wasn't allowed," He said, his voice soft and without condemnation.

"Well," she responded. "Most of our leaders are out of commission right now." She turned the bottle up once more, took another long pull, then swallowed with a sigh.

"Hm," The boy let out, running his hand over his over-greased hair. "Yeah, I heard about Desmond, and Derek's nowhere to be found since taking off with that Wyatt guy. Say, do you reckon he was involved in what happened to both of those boys? I mean, it's commonly known around town that he was in the cornfield the night Desmond died."

Molly sucked on her teeth, trying to hold in the anger that had begun building inside her. This guy was overstepping every boundary and trespassing on dangerous territory.

"Yep. I've decided." She nodded. "I don't like you."

The boy's expression changed, as his eyebrows arched.

"You need to back away right now." She pushed herself away from the wall and moved towards him, the heels of her boots thumping on the gym floor. She held up the bottle, swirling around the little bit of wine left at the bottom. "I'm going to finish this, because God knows I need every bit of it, but if you're still standing here when I'm done, I'm going to shove this bottle somewhere very unpleasant." Her voice never changed, and neither did the expression on her face.

He received the message loud and clear, as he puckered his lips and stared at the ground. He nodded his head as he slowly backed away.

"Okay, okay. See you later, Molly."

He disappeared into the crowd, leaving behind an uncomfortable feeling that she could not shake.

Chapter Twenty-Two

Derek woke up, temporarily disoriented by his surroundings as the morning light made its way through the window blinds. A headache had set in, and his body was sore, but he had felt worse in the past. Before he was a quarterback, before he met Wyatt, he played the linebacker position. As a quarterback he was protected from hits during practice to keep him healthy. Playing linebacker, it was always smash mouth football, practice or not, and he was the one delivering the hits, resulting in bruises up and down his body. He would wake up the mornings after, unable to move his legs from how sore they were. He missed those days now. Rolling off his cot, he stretched thinking he needed a plan for the day.

Walking out of the dim station, the sunlight blinded him until his eyes made the adjustment. It felt like forever since the last time he felt its warmth on his face, and he would never take it for granted again. He walked over to an abandoned dark red sedan parked in front of one of the pumps. It seemed incredibly old with its chipped paint and rusted areas. One of its side-view mirrors was hanging off the door by the wires. He tried to pull the door open, but it was locked.

Of course it is.

Earlier, he had found a wooden baseball bat propped up in a corner in the backroom that the station owners probably had for self-defense, in case of a robbery. Now, Derek clenched it tightly in his fist, and swung it with intent towards the center of the window glass. He couldn't help but imagine Wyatt's head being on the receiving end of his swing.

The glass shattered, the pieces scattering everywhere. Reaching in, he opened the door, then plopped down on the dirty, stained seat and began searching every nook and cranny for the keys, with no success. The gas station clerk probably had it on him when he disappeared. Since hot wiring a car was a skill he never thought he would need, he had never learned how to do it, so that was out of the question.

The old car probably doesn't run anyway.

Derek got out of the car, then gripped the bat as rage filled him. Everything he was feeling suddenly became loose. He swung the wood down on to the windshield, sending a vicious crack down the center. He swung again. It all started when he broke his leg. If he hadn't gone out skateboarding with Wyatt, he would've been playing in that playoff game. He would have never seen that hideous creature that still haunts him.

He swung again.

He had two options. He could walk back to Lyonside or keep going to look for help. It had taken he and Wyatt a few hours to get to where he was now by truck, so it would probably take him a couple of days to walk back on the road. However, the many uncertainties of continuing further away from Lyonside to look for help made him apprehensive about continuing, to say the least. Either way he went, there was a chance of being stranded outside at night, but he did remember something from the day before, during their drive out there. The road they had driven away from Lyonside on had curved almost directly East about an hour before they reached the station. The shortest distance between two points was a straight line. The only issue was that the straight line that lead back to town happened to lead him through the forest. The same forest that held the unknown horrors that had been terrorizing the town. He didn't know if he would make it back to the kids before dark, but he had to try. He decided it was worth the risk to take the straight shot through the forest, and hopefully, cut his travel time back to Lyonside in half. While shoving his pack full of snacks, bottles of sports drinks and water, Derek noticed the entire right arm of his shirt had been torn and was stained with blood. It took him a minute to realize it was from the "bloated man" that had attacked him the night before.

He tore the sleeve off, then tied it around his head to soak up any sweat that might sting his eyes, before loading up and walking to the tree line, his eyes searching the silent trees beyond him. He felt like everything that had happened before was a dream, but he knew better. He knew that the peaceful forest beyond him had claimed lives. Kids, adults, it didn't care. The beast was merciless and hungry, and he was about to jump down its throat.

Chapter Twenty-Three

Wyatt hobbled down the sidewalk towards his house, a bag of chips underneath his arm and a warm water bottle in his hand. As soon as the sun had come up, he left the school and the children, but some were already awake and getting ready to head back into town, including Molly. He wasn't sure that girl ever slept. Nobody really slept anymore, at least not a real night's sleep. It felt like those times when you spend the night away from your home, in a strange bed and you don't rest very well. The next morning your still tired, and your head is in a bit of a fog. That's how it is every day now, nobody is comfortable anymore.

Someone jogged up to him, somehow sweating in the cold November morning air.

"Hey, Wyatt!" His receiver, PBn'J., waved to him, smiling as if nothing had changed in Lyonside.

"What the heck are you doing, man?" Wyatt responded. He didn't know whether to laugh or not.

"Running! Gotta stay in shape for when the adults come back and off-season training starts," his long brown hair flopped in front of his glasses as he jogged in place, breathing through his nose and out of his mouth annoyingly. Wyatt laughed, but he didn't want to mention the doubt he had that the parents would be back anytime soon. He didn't want to decrease morale. It was all anyone had now. However, he would not let this go unpunished.

"Is it difficult being this gung-ho, or does it just come naturally?"

"Hey, man. If you're going to do something, do your best at it!" The boy said. Wyatt smirked as he looked at the ground below his feet.

"My dad used to say that a lot," He responded.

"He's a smart man, Wy." Seeing the opportunity to heckle Wyatt a little, he added with a grin. "How you ever were the product of him, I'll never know." Besides, maybe if you had tried a little harder, we would've won that game!" He said, unnaturally gleeful.

Wyatt smirked again. "Yeah, well I have five fingers. Guess which one's for you."

"I'm going to assume it isn't the pinky."

They parted ways as Wyatt continued to hobble down the street. The sun was out to the relief of the kids in town, but its sudden brightness caused his head to ache. It felt like a little bee was trapped inside and was stinging his brain relentlessly. Passing the bookstore, he remembered Dez seemed to spend days there looking at that stupid book. *Where was that thing, anyways?* It was in the truck with him before the gas station. Maybe he put it in the glove box when they stopped. He stopped and pulled out his phone, sending a text to Dez's phone, knowing who had it.

WYATT: Molly?

DEZ: Yeah, it's me. Don't text me on this number. Here's mine.

She sent hers to him.

WYATT: Hey.

MOLLY: What do you want?

WYATT: Dez's book is in the glove compartment of the truck. You should have it.

MOLLY: Thx

Something didn't seem right with her responses, but he put the phone back in his pocket then kept limping along. A lot of things entered his mind. He needed a new gun, since his old one was still in the truck, covered in the rancid smelling "smiling men" goop.

Need a new leg, too. He thought to himself.

He made it to his front door, dug the key out from under the mat, turned the lock, and stepped inside.

"Wyatt!" Isaac ran up and hugged him.

"Hey, Frodo. You and your sister okay?"

Isaac pulled back, then looked down at the goop on his hands in disgust.

"Yeah, I'll change. Give me a few minutes to get my thoughts together."

Isaac ran to his makeshift room. Wyatt had given Isaac his old room, and Lucy got his parent's master bedroom.

"Lucy, you good?!?" He yelled throughout the house.

There was no answer, until Isaac yelled back in response. "She's not here!"

"Where is she?"

"Out with her friends!" He announced.

Wyatt was taken aback by this answer. "Well, how long is she going to be out?"

"She's fourteen. She always tells me she can do what she wants, so I didn't ask!"

Wyatt remembered just two years earlier, when he was that age. He understood the need to be independent, so he didn't dig any further. If she was indoors before sundown and away from the cornfield, she would be okay.

"Alright, I'm going to get cleaned up some!" He began to make his way to the hallway bathroom where his hygiene supplies had been moved to.

"You look like a caveman!" Isaac yelled back from upstairs.

"Thanks, bud."

He made sure the door was locked behind him before he turned to the mirror, gasping in shock. He didn't know he looked as bad as he did. His skin was pale, and his eyes were bloodshot. It had been a while since his hair had been cut, and it was longer than he normally kept it. It was all over the place, dirty and matted, with strands hanging in front of his slightly swollen left eye. He felt the patches of whiskers that had grown along his jawline and around his chapped lips. A headache had set in earlier that morning, and it seemed stronger when the bathroom light had flickered on as he entered. He recognized it as a sign of a concussion that must have occurred during the wreck. He had never personally gotten one before, but he had watched many players suffer through one. The best medicine was painkillers and sleep.

He grabbed his razor, then began to apply the blade to his cheeks, then chin, then upper lip. He remembered when he first started growing facial hair. His dad took the time out of his day to teach him how to shave carefully and precisely. Wyatt had cut himself bad the first time, but he eventually got the hang of it. He could feel the familiar ache from the loss of his father as he reminisced.

He finished, rinsed himself off, then observed himself as he rubbed his fingers along his smoothed chin. He recalled how Chloe had liked his facial hair, while Molly had mentioned something negative about it when she was patching up his leg. Maybe, if he was a little more patient, he could grow one comparable to his father, who could grow a magnificent one, but Wyatt could never get over the itchy feeling. He never really liked the way his father looked with one anyway. He liked being able to see the way his jaw was structured, because Wyatt's own complexion was a perfect

303

match. It gave him hope that he could one day be like him. He didn't know where he got his copious amounts of sarcasm and crudeness. He remembered something about his grandpa getting into a lot of bar fights when he was younger, maybe that's where it came from. As he looked in the mirror in front of him, he could see his mother in his eyes, but he was his father in everything else physically. Shaving wasn't his way of choosing between girls, it was an attempt to be a better man in his own eyes, and he needed a fresh start.

****

Derek's whiskers scratched against the back of his hand as he wiped the sweat from his upper lip. The cold wind that whistled past his ears and down his neck made him shiver. The hair on his arms stood on end, and goosebumps rose across his skin. It was getting later into the year, and although it wasn't guaranteed to snow, there had been winters where Lyonside and the surrounding areas did get several inches of snow. He knew he didn't want to be caught in the forest in that kind of weather. He didn't want to be in the forest at all, for that matter. Judging by the location of the sun in the sky above him, he guessed that it was around noon. *How many miles have I walked?* It felt like he had been walking forever, and his feet hurt because his boots weren't really made for hiking. The only pleasant thing he could even remotely enjoy at that moment was the smell of the pine trees around him.

His thoughts were constantly being interrupted by the sounds around him. A twig broke to his left, and he jerked his head in the direction of the sound with his eyes narrowed. He would scan the trees on his left, before another sound would come from his right causing him to pivot around to look in that direction. It was maddening. This forest was actually driving him mad. He stopped to check the magazine in the pistol, already knowing there were only four bullets left, but hoping maybe he had overlooked some, or miscounted.

Yep, only four. Great.

He kept a hand gripped around the bat that hung loosely by his leg, and the other was on the pistol in his waistband as he continued walking.

Keep going straight, Derek. You're doing great. It's just like wind sprints. Just keep going. You'll be done before you know it.

There was a noise behind him, but he refused to turn around. He had come to the conclusion that the trees were messing with him, and his paranoia was making things worse than the situation really was. Another twig snapped behind him.

It's okay. It's okay. It's just a squirrel.

He stopped, then everything went silent. It was almost as if the trees had held their breath. He kept going but stopped again after hearing something heavy hitting the brush and leaves on the ground.

Don't turn around. Don't turn around.

He kept walking a normal pace, until he noticed something on the path in front of him. The forest around him was illuminated by the afternoon sun, but a phenomenally tall shadow was cast in front of him, one that he was not nearly tall enough to create.

He heard another thunk, and his mind screamed for him to run, but his body was frozen with fear and would not cooperate. He tried to avoid thinking about how it sounded like footsteps.

He exhaled shakily, then heard another footstep come from behind him. Derek could feel something warm brush against his neck. Something warm and wet. He tried to keep his mind straight, but his thoughts were spiraling into the chaos of fear. He again was faced with options. He could continue walking at the pace he was going, and potentially be a sitting duck for whatever was behind him, or he could run. He could just run like never before. His eyes locked on a stump not too far ahead of him.

It's just a wind sprint. Just go.

No. That's how you end up dead, with your body dismembered. He had seen enough horror movies to know not to do anything stupid like that, and even though this was no movie, he knew whatever it was would catch him, and he would just die tired from the run.

How do you survive this? Who has survived anything like this?

He knew of only one person, the boy who had abandoned him. The question kept racing in his head.

What would Wyatt Richards do?

He sighed, gripping his pistol.

Time to do something stupid.

Chapter Twenty-Four

Chloe asked to borrow Molly's earbuds so she could listen to music while she cleaned up around the house, and Molly was more than happy to let her use them. From the look in her eyes, Chloe could tell her friend was dealing with the aftereffects of all the wine she had the night before in the gym. It was obvious, Molly would have done anything to keep the noise down in the empty hallways. She dug them out of her pack, then handed them over, tangled into knots.

"Here. I'm going to go lay down," She muttered as she scratched at her head.

"Molly, we can't afford to have you like this. She put her hands on her hips, much like a mother scolding her child. She noticed how condemning her tone had become, then spoke softer. "You're the only one in town who even remotely knows anything about medicine. We need you to have a clear head in case anything bad goes down."

Molly shut her eyes while simultaneously waving a hand in front of her face in irritation. It reminded Chloe of that scene in *Star Wars* when Ben Kenobi used his mind trick.

Wow. She thought. *I have been hanging out with Wyatt way too much!*

"Easy, Queen Elizabeth," Molly let out. If she had said it with more anger in her tone, then Chloe might have taken offense, but she seemed tired as she let out a chuckle and brushed a strand of hair out of her eyes. "I had a bit of wine last night, but I didn't get wasted. I'm just a bit dehydrated and may have a slight hangover from it."

She brushed past her blonde friend and shuffled into her room. The door was open, and Chloe watched her plop down on her messy sheets.

As she finished cleaning up what little mess there was around the house, she thought she heard something and removed one of her earbuds. The front door thudded a couple of times before she heard Molly yelling from down the hall.

"Chloooooooooooeeeeeee! Get the door!"

"I'm getting it!" She responded as she moved away from the kitchen and into the foyer. She grasped the cold nob before unlatching the door and pulled it open. She was met with a bright smile from an unfamiliar face.

"Hi! You're Chloe? One of the football players said I could find you here." His voice was smooth and enduring. She enjoyed the sound and wanted him to keep talking. She smiled back as she studied him. He appeared preppy, his skin smooth and lacking any blemishes, and his hair was slicked back to reveal a marvelous pair of bright blue eyes.

"Yeah, that's me," She brushed a strand of hair behind her ear as she leaned on the door frame. He was very attractive. "Can I help you with something?"

He flashed a smile that tickled her stomach. "Yeah. I was told that Molly lived with you. I wanted to tell her I'm sorry about last night. I said something that was kind of insensitive about Desmond, and I had no idea that he was her brother. Is she here?"

Chloe turned her head to look inside. It was deathly quiet, but her eyes caught a glimpse of movement in the hallway.

"Uh, yeah," she responded, turning back to look into those eyes. It hurt her to lie to him because he seemed so innocent. "She's sleeping though. She has insomnia so I don't want to wake her up."

"Ah," The boy responded, shoving his hands into his pockets. "Well, let her know I'm sorry."

He stopped talking, then just stared at her with that radiant smile on his face. It reminded her of the face that Wyatt makes when he said something he thought was amusing, except this smile seemed kinder and stayed longer.

"I'm sorry, but you are simply gorgeous!" He suddenly blurted out. "Would you mind going to get some ice cream with me later?" He asked, causing her to blush.

"That sounds fun and all, but I don't even know who you are!" Chloe said with a smile.

He chuckled hardily, putting a hand to his ribs. "I'm so sorry. How rude of me not to introduce myself. I'm Ruttledge."

Ruttledge. What a unique name, she thought.

"Hello Ruttledge, nice to meet you."

"Were you one of the girls who ran into the cornfield?" he asked.

Her eyes narrowed and her head tilted slightly. "Yeah. How'd you know about that?"

He chuckled pleasantly before replying. "Everyone's famous in a small town, Chloe." He nodded his head in farewell. "Well, I'll leave you alone. Let's meet at the creamery in town at, let's say seven?"

She was about to respond, but he had already made his way down the porch steps, his boat shoes slapping on the wood before he joyfully leapt onto the sidewalk with his hands in his pockets.

She shut the door and closed her eyes, contemplating about the boy. He was clean cut, unbelievably so, in-fact. The only thing about him that seemed to bother her was his nose. She knew it was shallow to think this way when his personality was flawless, but she couldn't help herself. Her thoughts were interrupted by a stern voice that came from behind her.

"I see we now have a mutual friend. Did you get the same vibe from him that I did?"

Chloe turned and looked Molly in her eyes as she leaned on the front door, smiling. "Yeah, actually. He seems awesome!"

"What?!?" Molly had her arms crossed and her cheeks were flushed. "No!"

"What do you mean? He seems perfectly fine to me."

Molly threw her head back in a laugh mockingly. "You're just as crazy as him if you think he's normal!" She walked towards her friend, hands on her hips.

"What's not to like about Ruttledge, Molly?"

"Nothing. There's nothing not to like about him, and that's exactly the problem. That guy gives me the chills, Chlo!"

"Have you actually met him?"

"Yeah. In the gym last night, he approached me with that stupid grin. He had an unnatural interest in Wyatt. I don't like him."

Chloe threw an arm out accusingly. "And were you drunk before or after this happened?"

Molly scoffed as she shook her head, then turned to stomp into the kitchen. "I don't need a lecture right now. I already said I wasn't drunk, princess! Even if I was, who are you to judge? I lost my dad! I cleaned the blood off of my dead brothers' body and buried him!" A single tear ran down the side of her nose, and she wiped it away with the inside of her shirt sleeve.

Chloe wasn't buying the martyr act, as she moved towards Molly. "We've all lost people! We've all watched our parents disappear. We're all on our own!" She slapped the counter in frustration. "So, don't act like you're so special!"

Molly laughed mockingly and shook her head in denial. "No, Chloe. Your parents are better off than ours right now."

She was taken aback by this response. "Yeah, and how do you know that?"

"Because," Molly leaned up off the wall and crossed her arms. She abruptly stopped speaking, almost as if she had caught herself from saying something important.

"What? Molly if you know something about the parents..."

Molly averted her eyes from the ground to her friend that stood a few feet away. "I... I don't know for sure, but..." She shook her head. "Wyatt talked to me after he got back last night and told me everything that happened. He said that after Derek's death, he didn't turn around to come back. It was nighttime and apparently they were already a few hours away, so he kept driving, away from Lyonside! "

"Then, how did he get back here?"

"That's what I asked." Molly responded. "He said he didn't know. Chloe, I think whatever is happening, is only happening here. That's why I think your parents are okay. Lyonside is isolated from the rest of the world. According to Wyatt, he left at the south end of town and came back in the north! This place is stuck in like a loop or something! There's no way out, and I have a hunch that we're the only ones being affected by this since there have been no attempts to help from anyone on the outside."

"We're trapped here?" Chloe said, her voice cracking from the gloomy feeling that overwhelmed them.

"I think so. I'd bet my house that you can head east out of town but end up coming back into town from the west."

Chloe ran a hand over her face, feeling distressed. "So, the parents are taken, we start being attacked by things that shouldn't even exist, time apparently doesn't apply here, given that we don't know when the moon will decide to come out, and now, we are stuck in a loop!" "It's as if we are being targeted for some reason."

"You think it's all connected?" Chloe sat down on the kitchen counter by the sink.

Molly reached into the fridge and pulled out a can of soda. She pulled the tab and took a long drink before answering Chloe's question. "Either that or Lyonside is a hot spot for coincidentally-timed unnatural phenomena."

****

It was elongated. Derek had noticed that at first glance. The thing that had been stalking him through the woods was insanely tall but looked like a person. The facial structure looked like a human, but the skin was like a mask that was stretched tight over the face. It was pale, with clothes that were way too small that clung to its bony, narrow body. Its physical structure reminded him of a giraffe. What really chilled him to the core was the eyes. They were white, lacking a pupil or an iris, with red veins running in every direction. It smiled at him showing nothing but gums and its tongue sticking out.

Derek pulled the pistol firing many times before turning to run further into the forest, his breath coming in gasps as he jumped over fallen logs and tree limbs. He wasn't sure how many times he had fired, or what the bullets might have done to the thing because he had turned so quickly. The crunch of leaves beneath his feet seemed extremely loud and he was afraid the noise would drown out the sound of the creature if it was following him, waiting for him to stop. He kept his legs pumping, his hips growing numb and his stomach burning. He wouldn't stop. This wasn't an end of practice conditioning sprint that he could slack up on because he was the quarterback, this was life or death. He wasn't sure of what would happen if he let up at all, but he had a feeling it wouldn't be good. There was a ditch below the base of a tree up ahead to his right. *Just a few more steps...*

Turning towards the tree, he slid into the ditch, plopping down on his butt suddenly as the impact jarred his body. A wave of nausea overtook him, and he leaned over onto his hands and knees puking up chips and soda until his stomach emptied. He fell on his elbows in exhaustion, huffing and puffing as he spit into the dirt.

Sweat was stinging his eyes, his chest was sore from sucking in the cold air, and his legs felt like rubber, but he was still alive. All he could hear was his own breathing in the still forest surrounding him.

Focus, Derek. Get your thoughts together, stay alert! You're no good to anyone if you're dead.

He looked at the pistol that he had momentarily forgotten was in his hands, his knuckles white from clenching it so tightly. The slide was locked back, indicating that it was out of bullets. He released it with a sharp clink and shoved the now useless weapon into his backpack, then pulled out the bat. He ran a hand along the smooth wood before clenching the handle tightly.

He could smell something foul, like stagnant water. Carefully standing to look around, he saw the light reflecting off something between the trees to his left. Adjusting his position to see better, he could tell it was a large body of water with moss floating on the surface.

That doesn't make sense.

He remembered many times in class where they had to look at maps of Lyonside, and the closest body of water that size was miles north of town.

This shouldn't be here!

****

It was early in the afternoon and Wyatt, hobbling towards the school with Isaac not far behind, was expecting the sun to disappear any second like it had done the night before.

"Where are we going, Wyatt?" Isaac asked.

"I want you to learn how to defend yourself, kiddo. The way luck tends to avoid me, I won't be around for long." He thought about the scarecrow, and how it had a vendetta against him. He still didn't know why, and he didn't know how long until it would come after him again. He may not survive the next encounter.

"You mean like Mr. Miyagi taught Daniel? I watched *Karate Kid* like you told me!"

"Good job, Isaac son," Wyatt responded in a playful manner. "But not quite like that. I'm going to show you how to shoot a gun."

"But I'm only nine, Wyatt."

He smirked. "Yeah, well that's life now. Those monster things don't care how old you are!"

There was silence for a while as they walked down the dirt road towards the school, then Isaac spoke up again.

"How old was Dez when he died?"

Wyatt was caught off guard by the question. He cleared his throat, then kicked a rock as he walked past it. "Seventeen, I think."

Another moment of silence.

"What about Derek?"

"Look," Wyatt peered over his shoulder. "Can we *not* talk about my dead friends?" He said rather harshly.

"Why not?" Isaac asked in an innocent manner as he studied his own tennis shoes.

"Because..." Wyatt resisted the urge to get angry, as he slowly exhaled. "It...it makes me sad."

"Okay. Can we talk about your friends that are still alive?"

"Sure, buddy. Like who?"

"How about that scary girl? The one with the pretty yellow eyes!"

Wyatt laughed. "Molly? What about her?"

"Well...is she your lobster?"

Wyatt laughed as he threw his head back. "My what?"

"You know! Is she your girlfriend!"

"Oh, okay. First off," Wyatt turned to him, then looked down with a smile spreading across his face. He grabbed a hold of the strap that held the hunting rifle to his back to keep it from sliding off his arm. "Stay out of my *Friends* collection. Second, why would you ask that question? Not every girl a guy is friends with is his girlfriend." He ruffled Isaac's black hair, which earned him a chuckle.

"I know," the kid brushed the hair from his eyes. "But when you were taking a nap earlier, you said her name in your sleep. My dad always used to say that a guy likes a girl when he can't stop thinking about her."

The smile left his face, as an eyebrow raised. "Uh huh. Well...lets, uh, keep walking. We're almost to the high school." They began moving again and had walked a bit further before Wyatt attempted to change the subject.

"So, you're afraid of Molly, huh?"

"Not really," His little friend responded with a shrug. "She just isn't afraid to hurt people. I don't like hurting people."

"Are you afraid of me?" Wyatt asked sincerely.

"No," Isaac responded. "But the other kids are."

"What? Why?"

Isaac hesitated before he responded accordingly. "They just heard some big kids talking about how you were there when two people died and probably did something to them. Something about you being the 'common designator'."

"Do you mean denominator?"

"Yeah, that."

Wyatt grunted as he thought about this. "Yeah, well..." He stopped and shook his head as he contemplated. *God, I'm scaring kids now!*

"Don't worry about it, Wyatt! Little kids are jerks."

"Thanks, man."

They approached the school parking lot, and instead of coming across a deserted facility like they had anticipated, it was a beehive of activity in and out of the buildings. At the front doors were two West Side football players all padded up in Lyonside gear, helmets strapped to their heads, standing guard with shotguns. A girl was arguing her case in front of them with a voice that he recognized to be Alex.

"What is going on here?!? All of our supplies are in there, you tools! Let me in! I want to talk to whoever is in charge! I swear, I'm walking in there! You'll have to shoot me!" She heard the two boys approaching, then turned to them with anger on her face that didn't match her personality.

"What's happening?" Wyatt asked, his hand resting on the rifle sling.

"Woah, hey! He's got a gun! Go get the boss!" One of the football players leveled his weapon at Wyatt's head. The other rushed inside, before locking the door behind him.

"Stand down, sir!" The kid said, attempting to be professional and threatening.

Wyatt rolled his eyes. "Sir? Are you serious? Is that thing even loaded?"

The kid kept the barrel steady. "You'll never know!"

"Maybe, but what I do know is..." He pulled a pistol from his waistband and chambered a round out onto the ground, the brass clinking against the gravel. "..that this one is." He brandished the weapon in front of the guy. "Now go get whoever set this up before I show you if there's anymore, huh?"

The kid took off inside, as Wyatt attempted to follow before Alex grabbed his arm.

"No," she said. "Just wait."

Wyatt nodded in agreement, then turned and looked down at Isaac. "I need you to go back to the house. Go get your sister and go home, Isaac."

"What? Why?" He asked him.

"I don't know how ugly this is going to get, kid. I'm sorry. Remember what you said about little kids earlier?"

"Yeah."

"Well, big kids are jerks, too."

Isaac nodded in understanding, before taking off back down the dirt road towards the town center. Wyatt turned and offered the gun to Alex, who gladly accepted.

"Thanks. I left mine at the house." She inspected it, then kept it leveled at the ground. Wyatt nodded again, then unslung the rifle off his shoulder and aimed in the same direction. It had a scope, but it was useless this close, so he kept it at his hip. The two boys returned, their helmets clunking as they held the two doors open, letting out a rush of warm air. They stood at attention, with a sort of amateur seriousness about them, as a boy who seemed to be around Wyatt's height walked out. He was much better kept, clean-shaven along with a suave, slicked back hairstyle. His shirt and pants were well ironed, and his boat shoes slapped against the concrete as he exited the building.

"May I help you?" He said, his voice smooth and steady.

Alex spoke up first. "I'm Alex. This is Wyatt," she said, nodding in Wyatt's direction. "And you have all of our supplies in that gym!"

The boy stared at Wyatt, his piercing blue eyes scanning him from head to toe. "Wyatt Richards! We finally meet! My name is Ruttledge! I've heard so much about you!" He spoke ecstatically, offering a hand to shake.

Wyatt seemed uninterested. With an eyebrow raised, he stared the boy in his eyes, trying to figure out what his game was. "I suggest you listen to the girl, Rutt."

The boy's expression changed as his eyes narrowed and his face hardened. "Don't call me Rutt."

He turned to look at Alex, with his hands behind his back. "Please, continue. That was rather rude of me."

Alex crossed her arms, gun still in hand. "You are holding our supplies? Why?"

"Why, sweetie, this is my camp!" He threw his arms up, marveling at the school behind him.

"Your camp?" She asked, lowering the barrel of the gun towards the ground as tensions eased. "What do you mean by that? Why would you set up camp here?"

"Well," Ruttledge kept his eyes locked on the school, before his eyes scanned over to the gym.

"Well, you said it yourself, Alex. This is where the supplies are!" He let out a laugh as if someone had told him a joke. "It isn't a bad place to stay during the apocalypse!"

"The apocalypse?" Wyatt entered the conversation. "You mean the end of the world?"

"Is there any other kind?" The well-dressed boy walked towards him.

"You can't stay here, and this isn't the apocalypse!" Alex spoke again. "You can't keep our stuff hostage. We have little kids depending on that stuff!"

"*The great dragon was hurled down – that ancient serpent called the devil, who leads the world astray. He was hurled to earth, and his angels with him.*" Ruttledge said, with his eyes wide and in a loud voice, almost as if he were a street preacher here to save them all. "Revelation 12:9, doll-face." He turned to her, before smirking cockily. "And don't pretend you people care about the little ones. When Derek was still alive, he passed that responsibility on to you. And now that he's gone and you've taken over, where are they now? In the same houses as rebellious teenagers with deadly weapons?"

"It's the safest bet," Wyatt said as he clutched the rifle tighter in his hands.

"Is that right, Wyatt Earp?" He turned to him, eyes narrowed again and finger pointing accusingly. "So, it was your idea?" He scoffed. "Well what a piss poor job at planning that was, cowboy!

Tell me, since this was all put into place, how many people have died?"

Wyatt took the time to process what he said, before looking at him in his steel blue eyes and commenting.

"Neither of them died because of the guns, you half-wit. Desmond died because of one of those monsters. And Derek..." He paused, turning to look at Alex in her big brown eyes as he tried to avoid a guilty expression.

"Aw, what?" Ruttledge tilted his head to the side curiously. "Oh, that's right! No one knows what happened to him...except you, right? I think you've got a little bit of explaining to do. Meanwhile," He turned to head back inside, before stopping and backtracking. "I'll be here. It was nice to meet you, Wyatt. You people should really consider bringing the children. There's a gate, food, and water here after all!" He stuck out a hand to shake again.

Wyatt held up his middle finger. "Up yours, Rutt."

The well-dressed boy shot Wyatt a look, before nodding towards Alex, bidding her farewell in a gentlemanly manner. He retreated inside, the two West Side boys followed along, shutting and locking the double doors behind them. Alex and Wyatt started walking back down the dirt road.

"What are you thinking?" She finally asked as they reached the bookstore. He turned to her as he ran a hand through his messy hair.

"I don't know," He responded. "That Rutt guy gives me the creeps."

"Yeah. He's too nice. After everything this town has been through, most people have turned sour. It's almost as if he's hiding something."

Wyatt nodded in agreement. "Did you notice how bipolar his disposition seemed? And he had a weird...feeling about him." Wyatt's face expressed a concerned look, before he turned to Alex.

"I don't know. What's the plan, boss?"

"Boss?" Alex asked as she studied him. This was unlike him. Wyatt seemed like the kind of person to only have one boss, and that was himself.

"Since when do you listen to anyone?"

Wyatt playfully scoffed. "I don't," He explained. His nostrils slightly flared for a split second. "But you took care of this town when no one else could or would. Plus, I'm coming to realize that I can't do everything alone."

Alex nodded, then puckered her lips and narrowed her eyes as she thought to herself. "Okay, then. Ruttledge seems like a guy with all bark and no bite. You were able to call his guard's bluff about the gun being loaded. We know he isn't lacking the ammunition, considering we keep it stocked in the cabinets of the chemistry lab."

"Hm," Wyatt grunted. "So, he's a coward, huh?"

Alex glared at him. "He probably just doesn't want to hurt anyone." She rationalized.

"Right. So, a coward, then." Wyatt shook his head, then began moving faster down the sidewalk as he gripped his gun. "We're going there tonight."

"For what reason?!?" She raised her voice to reach him as he gained distance

"To get our stuff back!" He yelled back over his shoulder as he kept walking. "I'm going to get some people who have a bark and a bite!"

****

Molly opened the door to find Wyatt and the tall, burly redhead that had helped him before. His name was Tony.

"What do you guys want?" She leaned against the doorway, a half-tired smile greeting them.

"Have you met a guy named Ruttledge? Well dressed? Snobby? Big nose? Bit of a god complex?" He described the boy using hand gestures.

Molly motioned with her head for them to come inside.

Once they were in the living room, she sat down on the edge of the sofa, while Wyatt leaned against the wall. "Sometime today, this tool was able to gather a whole bunch of Tony's boys from West Side," He nodded towards the redhead as he spoke. "And set up camp at the school. He has all our stuff. Not just ammo, either. He has our food and water rations. The spare medicine in the nurse's office, too. Kids are probably bugging Alex about that stuff as we speak!"

Molly thought about this as she scratched at her arm. "Why?"

"Cause he's a freaking nut job, why else?" Tony piped in.

"I ran into Tony on the way here," Wyatt explained. "He was looking for some of his players, who happen to now be under new authority."

"That's not the only reason for having a bone to pick with this guy," Tony spoke as he glanced over at the clock on the wall, cracking his knuckles. "It sounds like he's a psychological bully. He has basically blind-sided the entire town threatening our chances of survival. He has decided to play god when there are the lives of children on the line. Plus, I bet his face would be as much fun to punch as yours, Wyatt." He smirked.

Wyatt mocked his smile as he scrunched his nose. "Whatever you say, you overgrown leprechaun." He responded passively.

Molly studied the back of her hands as her mind raced for a solution. "Does Alex know?"

Wyatt nodded. "She was there during the confrontation. It seemed as if she was more pissed about it than anyone."

"Who else knows?"

"Right now? Just her and the group at the school as far as I know, but he could be sending guys out to bring in kids now. The streets seemed calmer than usual on my way here. Alex will probably try to keep them away from the little ones if she can."

"Yeah," Tony scratched at his red beard, "But keeping them away from the kids isn't going to do any good if we don't have the supplies. We might as well let them take the kids. They have everything we need to survive in there, remember?"

Wyatt closed his eyes and inhaled deeply through his nose, held it for half a second then exhaled deeply through his mouth as if doing meditation. "Great. So, we're screwed."

There was a long silence before Molly questioned him again with something she had desperately attempted to avoid bringing up until necessary. "You know Chloe is going on a date with this guy tonight, right?"

Wyatt's head snapped toward her.

"Wait, what?" His face showing utter shock at the news. She could see the sweat gleaming off his skin.

"Yeah," Molly stood and put her hands on her hips. "He showed up here looking for me so he could apologize for making me threaten him. He used his snake-like charm on her, and she fell right into his trap."

Wyatt, still stunned, leaned against the wall as Tony stood up to pace the floor. "This dude is looking like more trouble than he's worth."

Silence coated the room as the trio searched for a solution to their problem.

"Hey..." Tony stopped, then turned and paced. "What if this is a good thing?"

"How?" Wyatt inserted himself suddenly, a fire in his wide eyes. "How is this a good thing? You want to hop on into his crew too, Lucky Charms?"

"Hold on," Molly said, holding up a hand. "Maybe he's onto something." She walked towards the center of the room. "We can't do anything without supplies, right? If they're on a date, that means he's not at the school to monitor those idiot guards." She turned to Tony. "No offense."

Tony nodded passively. "Oh, no you're right. They're complete morons, but please continue."

She smirked mischievously. "We go there tonight while they're out, sneak in, and grab the supplies before they even know what hit them."

Tony snapped his fingers and pointed in triumph. "That's exactly what I was thinking!"

Wyatt stayed silent, the shock still setting in. "But what about Chloe? We don't know what this guy is like! He could...you know!"

Molly shrugged off his concerns. "I'm sorry, I told her I didn't like the guy and she didn't listen. We might as well use this opportunity to our advantage."

"Okay, well...." Wyatt stuttered. "We can't just run in guns blazing trying to kill kids, can we?"

"No, that's why we *sneak* in." Molly explained. "We wait for the sun to go down, then we find a way in."

"Woah, woah, woah, now!" Tony protested. "I am not stalking around looking for somewhere to get in during the pitch-black night knowing what's out there! Those things are just waiting for some suckers like us to do something stupid like that!"

Molly shot him her signature eyebrow raise, before turning her head to Wyatt. "During those school assemblies in the gymnasium, did you ever look up?"

Wyatt shrugged and shook his head. "I don't know. Maybe." He shifted his stance and pushed his hair back. "I know there are skylights up there."

"That's our way in. We climb the ladder to the roof, then drop down inside using some rope or something."

"Sounds like suicide," Wyatt laughed out.

"It's either that, starve out here, or give in, and from what I've gotten from your personality, you're not one to give up easily." Tony pointed out rather forcefully.

"You didn't let me finish," Wyatt had his classic punk grin. "It sounds like suicide...but I'm in. The only thing I regret is not being able to see that window-licker's face when he finds out the supplies are gone!"

"And his people," Molly interrupted. "The kids will go where the supplies are. Wyatt and I will head out before sunset to make sure our way in is easily accessible. Tony, we need you to go get Alex and fill her in. We'll need as many hands as possible to carry the supplies."

"Want me to get anyone else?"

"Considering everyone else I trusted in this town is now dead, no."

Wyatt clapped his hands together in excitement before he winked at her. "Okay. Time to have a little fun!"

****

Derek was perched in a tree with his eyes locked on the pond below. He wanted to keep going and get back home, but something about the mysterious water source beyond him left him feeling very uneasy. The water was covered in algae and moss and had a horrible smell. It didn't just smell like stagnant water, it stunk like something had died. He recognized it because not long ago his cat had been run over while he was at school and in the summer heat, it had decomposed quite quickly. The scent was gag-inducing. Part of him had wanted to get out of there fast and not look back, but his curiosity won out, so he had planted himself securely in the canopy of the tree.

The wind was chilly, but the direct light he was receiving from a diagonal sun provided enough heat that he had to remove his outer shirt. The nausea and vomiting earlier still made his stomach feel somewhat queasy. His eyes scanned the shore for any sign of movement, but his vision was slightly blurry, and his eyes stung from the sweat that poured from his hair. Pushing his hair out of his face, he wiped his eyes and brow with his shirt, which he then wrapped around his waist. Tiny bugs hopped along the top of the water, sending ripples outward towards the muddy shore where overgrown grass dangled over the water, creating a ledge that reminded him of a small version of a canyon. A bird cawed in the distance, and Derek snapped himself out of the trance he was under reminding himself to stay focused and alert. This was where the "things" that haunted Lyonside had come from, among the trees, and right now, he was in the middle of them.

TAKEN BY THE NIGHT

He heard the crackle of leaves below him causing his heart to jump into his throat and he couldn't catch his breath. Squeezing his eyes shut to keep the tears from forming, he felt goosebumps on his skin, and his heart pounding out of control. Something moved below him, and he somehow managed to hold back the sheer panic that was trying to take over him.

C'mon, Derek. You're okay. You're okay.

He slowly turned his head downward and focused his tired eyes on the ground below, the setting sun illuminating the grass in an orange glow as a light-colored rabbit hopped below him, unaware of the frightened human in the tree above it. It gnawed on a blade of grass, then pawed at its nose. Derek sighed in relief and let out a chuckle. He was losing his mind! Shaking his head, he attempted to clear his thoughts and focus on survival. He was hungry and something besides chips and candy bars from the station sounded good. He checked his pistol for ammunition, contemplating a shot at the rabbit.

Just as he had suspected though, the gun was out of bullets from firing frantically at the creature earlier that day, so Derek gripped the bat in his bag and slid it out, the zipper grazing the wood gently. He kept his eyes locked on the furry creature, planning his descent onto the forest floor and his strike. The branch that he rested on was only about ten feet up, but if he jumped down, there was a possibility of spooking the bunny before he had time to pull back for a swing. Also, the worst-case scenario would be he could sprain an ankle or re-injure his recently healed broken leg, then he would be stuck out here alone, with no help. He decided he would tie the sleeves of his shirt and jacket together to make a crude rope, and then attach it to the branch above him. Using one hand, he would repel down until he was close enough to swing at the fur ball, hopefully with enough force to stun it. Derek had tightened the knot around the branch, gripped the cloth tightly and was about to begin his decent when something further down the shoreline caught his eye.

There it was, its eyes wide and lacking an iris, making them appear beady and creepy as it stared, not at him, but at his prey below. A few strands of greasy black hair dangled from its pale bald head. He wasn't sure whether it had seen him or not, so he remained as still as possible, slowly lowering the bat back to his waist.

The thing had locked onto the rabbit, and Derek felt a little sympathy for the innocent little creature that was unaware it was about to meet its demise. It was almost like a metaphor. The bunny was the children of Lyonside, and the creature represented its own kind.

It stalked, waiting to pounce without blinking or looking away for even a second. Derek's sympathy for the rabbit took over and he suddenly felt the urge to yell, to chase away the poor animal before the creature knew what was happening. What if when he scared away the rabbit, the thing would lock on him? He didn't know if he could fight this thing. He had bet his life on the fact that the thing didn't have the ability to climb and was even more sure that if the thing could indeed climb, he couldn't get down fast enough to avoid becoming its prey.

It bolted out from behind the tree, revealing its grotesque body. It looked like a naked human, but lacked any parts revealing its gender. Its bones were bent in the wrong direction. its spine arched upwards like a cat to where he could see the definition, and its arms and legs were bent backwards in a way that reminded him of how dog legs appear. It crawled on all four limbs with lightning quick speed, before leaping onto the rabbit before it could hop away. It was too fast for Derek to be able to identify any other features. The crunch of the thing biting down on the animal's neck

339

made Derek's stomach feel sick, and he tried to quietly control his breathing as he covered his mouth. Tears fell from his cheeks and he shook uncontrollably while listening to the creature smacking, as it fed just below him.

****

Wyatt rolled the arms of his shirt up as they walked, while Molly removed her hoodie. She tied it around her waist, revealing a t-shirt for some band he had never heard of. His head was killing him, and the sunlight hurt his eyes making him struggle to see. Suddenly, he wasn't sure of where he was or what he was doing.

"Molly?"

"What's up?"

He swallowed hard. "Where am I right now?"

She turned and looked at him with her eyebrow raised, then smirked. "Quit screwing around, moron. We don't have time for this."

He stopped walking as a wave of pain shot through his brain. "Oh, God." He whimpered as he bent down, hands on his knees. Although it only intensified the pain, he tried shaking his head violently to clear the fogginess. She stopped walking and bent over beside him.

"Hey, hey! Take it easy. Tell me what's wrong." There was a seriousness in her tone, like a mother caring for a child, trying to keep it calm.

He sniffled as he kept his eyelids shut. "My head is freaking killing me." He stood back up, blinking away the tears welling up in his eyes. "I smacked it hard in the wreck."

She ran a hand through his bird's nest looking hairstyle and looked him in the eyes, studying his pupils intently. He wasn't sure how he felt about that, Molly standing so close to him, looking him in the eyes so intently. It made him uneasy and his stomach flutter, so he tried to view it as a doctor consoling a patient.

"Must be a concussion. Your eyes are slightly dilated." She said softly, knowing that loud noises would make the symptoms worse.

He winced in pain again. "It hurts, Mol."

"I know." She responded in a whisper, moving her hands to his cheeks in order to feel for a fever of any sort. They were flushed.

"W-what are you doing?" He asked.

She put her hand to his forehead. "Making sure it isn't a neurogenic fever."

He raised an eyebrow. "A neuro-what?"

She rolled her eyes. "A brain infection." She removed her hands. "I want you to go back to your house, okay? I'm going to get the meds back."

Wyatt suddenly perked up as he remembered what they were supposed to be doing. "No way, sweetheart! You're crazy if you think that I'm not going with you!"

"And you're crazy if you think you can do this right now! You need to get out of the light! You're in pain! Go get some sleep, please!"

"No," He concentrated on her golden eyes, which shone in the sunlight, contrasting against her wavy black hair. "No way, sister. I'll be out of the light when the sun goes down, and I'll sleep when I'm dead." He grabbed her hands, then gently moved them away, a partial grin across his face. "You have something for the pain, right?"

She sighed in frustration with him. "Yeah. I have a couple of acetaminophen tablets in my pack."

"Look, if you don't have anything, just tell me! Don't make up words!"

She pulled the pack off her shoulder, then she glared at his face when his response registered in her head. Even in pain, he was cracking jokes.

"Shut up, you idiot."

She handed him two round red pills that reminded him of candy. Pulling out his water bottle, he popped them in his mouth and chugged them down.

"Okay," He kept one eye open, then let out a breath of air. "I'm good. Let's go."

They walked forward along the dirt road back towards the school where Ruttledge and his men had set up camp.

"Crap!" Molly suddenly let out. She turned to Wyatt anxiously. "Let me see your rifle, Wy."

He ducked out of the strap, then handed it over. She leveled it to her shoulder, keeping her fingers away from the trigger, and placed an eye against the scope. There was a long silence as Wyatt scanned the area around them. They were close to the spot where Jesse was killed and up ahead Wyatt thought he could see a dark area on the ground that was left by the blood.

She let out an exhausted grunt of rage. "They've got a man on the gym roof! We aren't getting anywhere near the ladder without being spotted!"

She handed the rifle over to him. As he focused into the scope, she couldn't help but study his face, hoping he wouldn't notice. He had shaved the night before, and she wondered if he did it for her, since she had mentioned getting rid of his scraggly looking beard.

Stop it, Marcella. She thought to herself. *He's the jerk-bag who got Desmond killed. Why should you care what he does? He's probably the crudest person in Lyonside and the most selfish. No, wait. He's not selfish. He may be all talk, but he has a good heart, that's clear. He's done so much for so many people and risked his life for everyone on more than one occasion.*

"Well, there's good news and bad news to this," He pulled away from the gun and slung it back over his shoulder. "Which do you want first?"

"Give me the good news," She responded, crossing her arms, curious to hear what he had to say.

He turned to her, a smirk she hadn't seen on his face in a while appearing from the left corner of his lips. "But I have to give you the bad news first because it emphasizes the good news."

344

"I'm going to punch you in the face."

He chuckled at her threat. "The bad news is you're absolutely right." He nodded in the direction of the school. "There's no way we're getting any closer than where we are now without that guy seeing us."

"And the good news?" She began to grow impatient.

"I know him." He laughed again in disbelief of what he said. "That little twerp in the glasses is one of my receivers!"

"Your what?"

"My receiver," He repeated. "I was a heck of a football player back in my day, sweet cheeks!"

Molly laughed, playing along. "Oh, yeah! We did have a football team didn't we!

Since the night the adults were taken, they had been so caught up in just surviving, the lives they had before that seemed like a long, long time ago.

Weren't they something stupid like the Lions? The Lyonside Lions?"

"Yeah. We were pretty good."

"Until you lost, right?" She laughed again. "In a small town, football is religion...."

Wyatt let out a sigh. "And losing is like blasphemy. Coach used to say that."

"So, did my dad. He kept track of the school's sports." She responded to him as she remembered her father. He watched as her face showed a hint of happiness.

Wyatt's wasn't sure what to do or say next. He felt the urge to hug her, to feel something besides the fear and despair they had all been living with for what seemed like forever. Everything outside of this situation had felt unreal.

His body did something without his mind realizing, and he reached out and hugged her tightly. At first, she was stiff, not expecting the sudden show of affection from someone like Wyatt. She loosened up and hugged him back.

"You okay, Wy?" She asked, still curious as to why he had embraced her.

The sweet lavender scent he could smell as her hair caressed his face made his head spin a little. Well, he really wasn't sure if it was the scent or her being so close to him that caused it.

Surrounded by monsters and this is what I'm scared of?!?

"I'm sorry." He finally said.

"It's okay."

346

"I just..." he struggled to find the words.

"Hey, we'll make it through this." She responded.

"I know we will." He responded.

Wyatt let go of her. As he pulled away, his eyes focused on her golden irises.

"Let's go see if we can blackmail or bribe this moron, huh?" She said.

He laughed.

They were swallowed by the shadows of the trees surrounding them, signifying the sun's descent as the night began to fall. Wyatt pulled out his phone, his thumbs moving lightning fast as he scrolled through his contacts. He tapped once, then held it up to his ear.

"PBn'J!" He said loudly after a minute causing Molly to jump.

"Jeez, Wy!" She whisper-shouted at him.

He placed a finger to his lips, shushing her so that he could hear his friend in peace. She mouthed something vulgar towards him.

"Hey, Wy!" He sounded enthusiastic through the speaker. He was obnoxiously loud. "Is something wrong?"

"Nope!" Wyatt responded; eyes shut as his head rung from the noise. "Why would you ask that?"

"Well, given the situation we're all in, what with all of the monsters roaming around!" Porter laughed before continuing. "And you don't ever call me unless it's for the team or something like that."

"Right, right." Wyatt tended to only contact the starting group back during the season, and even then, he had his own isolated group consisting of just Derek and Carlos. Those were his two best friends. They were the three musketeers. Now, he was just a lonely soul in a messed-up town trying not to end up like his deceased friends. "I need you to listen to me for a second, okay?"

"Can do, QB two!"

He rolled his eyes. "First, why are you on top of that roof?"

"What?" The boy's voice pierced the static.

Molly kicked him in the shin, causing Wyatt to hop around in pain.

"What the freakin'—" He doubled over and grabbed his leg. She was shaking her head, one hand on her hip and the other clutching her pistol.

"Don't let him know we're watching him!" She whispered back.

He shook his head before pressing his ear to the phone once again. "Uh, I mean...Where are you right now?"

There was a moment of silence before the sophomore responded. "I'm at the school. Some guys have set up camp here. They seem cool. Some dude named Ruttledge is the mastermind behind all of it!"

Wyatt had just met the guy not long ago and already wanted to strangle him. He wanted to erase that name from existence. "Right, we met. Look Porter, that guy is a bad dude."

"Why do you say that?"

Wyatt rubbed the back of his neck in frustration, "Because...Look, I'll explain later. Please, just trust me right now, okay? I'm your quarterback, remember?"

"Derek was my quarterback, Wy. You're the backup."

"You're a backup, too! You were a backup for the backups! And that's not the point, you turd!" He pulled away from the phone for a second, shooting Molly a look that begged her to shoot him and end his misery. "Port, please trust me on this!"

He took a second before responding. "Okay," His tone hardened through the speaker. "So, he's a bad dude. What do we do about it?"

Wyatt thought for a minute, his mind racing, searching through the fog in his head for answers. "Does he have you doing jobs? You know, like patrolling or keeping track of supplies?"

The phone went quiet once more, its screen generating heat against the skin of his cheek. "Yeah, yeah," his friend sounded enthusiastic again. "He's got me and some of the linemen working patrol. I'm on top of the gym and keeping an eye out towards the road. Can't really see much because of the trees, but I guess the monsters aren't going to come cruising up in a mini cooper, am I right?" He laughed at his own joke again.

"P. B., that's actually perfect for us," Wyatt nodded towards Molly, who was wrapped up in her hoodie, its hood covering her face. "We're going to sneak in and get our supplies he took from us. Is every door inside the school guarded?"

"You bet", came the response. "The other patrols on the roof of the school can see clearly all around the perimeter. Ole Rutt's as thorough as he is creepy."

Molly and Wyatt had expected this. That meant the only blind spot would be the back gate that lead to the rear of the gym, where the ladder was that went to the roof.

"Are you alone up there?"

"Yeah, at least until sundown, then someone else will be taking over."

"Crap, Porter." Wyatt let out in exhaustion.

"I can just ask him to let me have a couple of extra hours up here. I'll just say I like the view or something stupid like that!"

"A couple of hours is all we need. Is anyone usually in the gym?"

"Just this dude named Trae from West Side. That's his station at night. It's our entertainment center. There's a game system, a mini fridge, and a hockey table in there! Get this: The place is closed at night to everyone else except for him. How lame is that?" His friend excitingly pointed out.

Wyatt thought about this, running a hand through his hair and holding it up in a fist above his head. "Okay. Tonight, we need you to not be there, buddy."

"What? At my station?"

"Exactly," Wyatt smirked. "And leave the skylight unlocked for us!"

Chapter Twenty-Five

Chloe walked along the sidewalk, the fading sun casting an orange glow as it raced for the horizon. If it weren't for the trash left in the streets from kids who were left to themselves, the quirky small town of Lyonside would have struck her as beautiful in the light of the approaching moon. The few trees that were planted along the sidewalk in isolated beds were shedding their coats of orange, yellow, and red leaves. A winter breeze blew, whipping her hair and the scarf that was wrapped around her neck. It was so comforting. For the first time in a long time, she felt something. She could feel the shiver-inducing air that surrounded her. December was right around the corner, and they had to celebrate Christmas, if only to give the little ones a semblance of normality. Hopefully, the parents would be back by then. She didn't know how much longer this isolated town of kids would survive on their own. She didn't know how much left they had in them. Most of the teens were exhausted, and the rest were dead. Molly had started drinking, that much was clear to Chloe, no matter how much her friend protested, and Alex was stressed out of her mind. She wasn't even sure where Wyatt was. She hadn't seen him since the night before in the gym when he had delivered the news to them that Derek, the town's fearless leader, had been taken by the night also. He seemed as if he was a mess with his bloody leg bandaged and his eyes glazed over. That night, the boy she thought could never yield, mentally or spiritually, seemed broken. That was the one reason why she had agreed to a date with the mysterious boy named Ruttledge. She didn't really care for him that much, its just after all she had been through, and seeing Wyatt like that, she wanted to feel normal again, like nothing had changed. Ruttledge seemed above the reality they were all facing, like it couldn't touch him.

A scent reached her nose that reminded her of Thanksgiving. It smelled like sweet potato pie and cinnamon.

She turned a corner as she made her way towards the town center, she was surprised to find it deserted, and clean. All she could hear was the wind.

"Chloe?" A familiar voice called from behind her. She had been in such a trance that she had completely missed the ice cream shop they were supposed to meet at. Ruttledge was leaning out of the doorway, holding it open and revealing the source of the smell.

"Hi!" She greeted him with a smile as she slightly squinted and pushed her hair from her face. The wind was growing stronger.

"Hey." He laughed, motioning for her to come inside. She didn't realize it was possible, but this boy had cleaned himself up even more than earlier, even though he was wearing the same clothes. His skin seemed clear of any signs of blemishes or sweat, his teeth were pearly, and his lips had a silky shine to them. *Was that lip balm?*

"Where is everyone?"

"At my camp. Haven't you heard? Me and a few other guys have our own place set up at the school. The kids love it! Many of them have decided to stay there tonight and see how they feel about it."

"Oh," She responded after a moment of consideration. "Do the others know? Alex, Molly, and Wyatt? They've been the ones leading the town so far and I think the town really trusts them with those sorts of decisions."

Ruttledge laughed, causing Chloe to become suspicious. "They know. As a matter of fact, they trusted me with holding the supplies in the school! Don't worry about that!"

Chloe stared into his silver blue eyes. They reminded her of her godmother's Siberian Husky.

"Okay," She responded with a grin, not sure if she believed him. The streetlights came on, presenting a glow along the street as the sun was setting above.

****

It was quiet out, as Alex looked at the stars noticing how the sky wasn't black at night, like she had always thought, but rather a deep shade of blue in comparison. Anxiety and anticipation over what was about to happen was eating away at her. She was camped with the others behind a hill of overgrown weeds that lay between the gym and the forest. Molly said she was certain no one could see them in the dark in their current position, but they still stayed crouched down. Tony was behind them, watching for any creatures who might take advantage of the opportunity and attack them. He was armed with a pistol and a flashlight, which was only to be turned on in an emergency, lest it give away their position. Alex and Tony had met up with Molly and Wyatt earlier to stake out the school in hopes of an opportunity to secure their much-needed supplies. Molly was peering at the school through binoculars, trying to make sure that their plan would go as smooth as possible. Wyatt was laying down in the grass next to her with large red headphones on, his head slowly bobbing back and forth to his music. He was cradling a rifle, his soft tapping on the wood stock creating the only sound between the four of them. The cold wind reminded Alex of how much colder it could be without the rays of the sun to warm her. She had on just a plain old blue hoodie, and Molly had on one that was similar, but it was plaid and the hood part that now covered her head from view was gray. Wyatt was wrapped in a butt-ugly multicolored windbreaker while Tony had on a simple crimson red long sleeve shirt, but he showed no signs of being cold.

"Alright," Molly croaked through a dry throat before clearing it. Her tone became measured. "We need to move soon. Wy, when is your friend supposed to leave?"

She received no answer, so she leaned over and nudged him with her sneaker. He removed the headphones and glared up at her. His music was blaring. Every word of Aerosmith's "Dream On" was easily decipherable.

"You shouldn't be listening to music right now, or else your head isn't going to heal."

Wyatt shrugged. "Can't screw it up any more than it already is." He attempted to put the headphones back on, before Molly reached down and yanked them away.

"When is your friend supposed to leave?"

He sat up from the ground. "He said the other kid who is going to take the night shift is supposed to show, then he will ask for more time up there. We can move in after that. Have you seen any other kids go up?"

"No," Molly responded as she pressed her eyes to her binoculars again. "Just your friend sitting there picking his nose."

"Nice," Alex inserted.

"Wait. He's picking up his phone."

It took a moment before it occurred to Wyatt that his phone was ringing, the chorus of Michael Jackson's "Bad" echoing through the silence of the night. Molly panicked, whisper-shouting at him to turn it off. He fumbled through his pockets, then answered.

"Yo."

"Hey, Wyatt!" Pbn'J spoke, his tone excitable and his voice loud as usual. "So, Walt didn't show up for his shift. I think he's sick or something!" Wyatt heard a crunch and smacking come through the receiver. He covered the screen with his palm and leaned over to Molly who was still surveying the school.

"What's he eating?"

"An apple," She responded.

He turned back to the phone. "Okay. So, we're good to go, then?"

"Roger that, QB two! The door out is locked from the inside! So, when you're done, you can just walk right out!"

"Great. We'll be there faster than you can finish that apple!"

He hung up the phone, then stuffed it into his back pocket. Molly chuckled as she watched the boy look around in confusion, now realizing that they were watching him.

They shuffled through the grass in the field, slicing through the darkness until they reached the back of the building illuminated by a dim light. Wyatt limped along, the pain in his leg mild in comparison to the pain in his head. Tony had taken the lead, sprinting ahead to open the gate to the ladder for them.

"Oh, what a gentleman," Wyatt joked as he passed him.

"Ladies first, Richards," The redhead teased.

"Whoever smelt it dealt it." The girls passed them both and began heading up the ladder. Tony looked at Wyatt, amazed at the stupidity of the response.

"That doesn't even make sense."

"Neither does your face."

Wyatt let Tony go first. If his bum leg were to go out on him, he didn't want to fall on anyone on the way down. He could hear his friends as they climbed the ladder, a faint ping occasionally as something brushed against the metal. Hesitating a moment before starting up the ladder, he had the eerie feeling that they were being watched. It felt as if eyes were burrowing into the back of his skull and he was tempted to turn around and face whatever was watching him. Instead he hurried up the ladder, unsure if whatever it was would follow him up. Once he reached the top, he caught his breath, then forced himself to look down.

Nothing.

He continued to peer out into the darkness, unable to shake the feeling.

"You good, Wyatt?" The enthusiastic Pbn'J asked. "You don't look too hot."

"Yeah, well you're no Brad Pitt yourself, Porter." He was bent over, hands on his knees.

"He has a concussion," Molly answered for him.

"Oh, crap, bro!" The boy responded unnecessarily loud. "I'm sorry. They suck. I had one that time we played Central. I got knocked out cold! I thought I was at school!"

Wyatt kept shaking his head, attempting to focus. "Yeah, that's great, bud." He passively moved the conversation to the objective ahead. "You guys ready?"

Molly's eyes scanned the roof for anything sturdy enough to tie a rope to. The ladder they had accessed the roof with was too far from their point of access to use as an anchor point. The only thing she could see close enough was an air conditioning unit, but if they wrapped the rope around the entire structure, most of the length would be used up. She wasn't so sure it wouldn't slip from the top when they put some weight on it anyway, and it was a straight fall downward onto the cold, hard basketball court below.

"Oh, no."

"What's wrong?" Alex asked, concerned.

TAKEN BY THE NIGHT

Molly pulled her hood down. "We don't have anything to tie the rope to, and there's no way we're going to jump down into the gym without breaking our legs."

"Yeah," Wyatt interrupted. "I'd rather not do that again, thank you. Any other ideas? Can we get through one of the doors?"

"You can try, but it won't work", Pbn'J answered. Given that I now have night shift, I'm not supposed to go inside until daylight. The doors will stay locked until then, or at least until Ruttledge comes back from whatever he's doing. Unless you guys just want to wait until he gets back..."

"No way," Tony spoke. "I've got a bad feeling about that guy. He's too smart for his own good. I think he'll catch onto us pretty quickly." He ran a hand over his face. "It's now or never."

He grabbed the rope from Molly, then proceeded to tie one end around his waist. "I'll stay up here. You guys rappel down."

"Will that work?" Alex asked, approaching slowly.

"It should. I weigh around two-fifty. You two girls and Slim Jim here shouldn't be an issue," He nodded at Porter. "I just hope I can keep myself planted while lowering Wyatt down."

Molly took the time to think about this before giving her answer. "Alright. Let's do it."

Tony nodded as he tied the rope tightly around his hips. "I've never done this before, but I have a bad feeling that this is going to hurt."

Pbn'J lifted the skylight slowly as the warm air from inside swept over him. "When we get inside, I'll take off for my sleeping quarters while you guys do what you need to do. If Ruttledge asks tomorrow why I wasn't there, I'll say it was a communication error between me and Walt about the shift."

Wyatt placed a hand on the small boy's bony shoulder. It was a wonder how he didn't break it during hitting drills with the team back during the fall. "You sure you don't want to help us get some supplies out? We need as many hands as possible now that Tony will be stranded up here."

Porter shook his head. "Nah. No offense, but if you get caught, I don't want my punishment to be in the hands of that creep."

"Punishment?" Molly interrupted, clicking the strap on her backpack across her chest. "What do you mean? How does he punish kids?"

Pbn'J sighed, then took a serious tone not often heard from Porter. "He has this...set of rules that he wrote on the white board in Mrs. Taylor's math class. If you break any of these 'commandments', as he calls them, you risk receiving punishment. They're pretty bad. I'm talking stone age justice system here! If you get caught stealing anything from rations, it doesn't matter if it's just a pack of crackers, the common punishment for that is exile."

"Exile?" Tony asked, a concerned look growing across his freckled face. "You mean from the facility?"

"No. I mean from Lyonside." Porter finally explained. "He makes them walk into the forest and never come back."

****

Derek awoke from his slumber, straddling a branch with his back against the trunk of the tree. The sick feeling in his stomach from earlier had subsided, and now he was famished. Still, he preferred hunger over nausea any day. Shivering from the cold, he reached for his shirt and jacket, untied them from the branch then slipped them on. Huddled against the wind with his arms around himself trying to get some warmth back into his body, he heard water splashing, like people in a pool.

The pond. Something was in the pond. No, wait. It sounded like something was leaving the pond. He couldn't see, but he could hear the water in the pond being disturbed and then water splashing on the ground. It didn't sound like one thing, however, it sounded like many. It kept repeating, the water would be disturbed, then splashing on the ground. Derek was becoming unnerved, while his brain was trying to logically explain this. His attempt to rationalize what was happening kept bringing him back to one thing, this is where they were coming from!

They were climbing out of the depths of the stagnant water. This pond was the originator of all the incredible evil that had captivated his beloved town.

"God help us," He whispered to himself. The sound of his hoarse whisper slicing through the silence of the night that surrounded him. Derek suddenly realized his mistake. He hadn't noticed until then that the forest itself lacked any sound after the moment the pond came alive. It was like nature was holding its breath in horror at the monstrosities it was awakening. Slowly turning his head, hoping he had not been heard, his eyes met the green eyes of something unnatural. Glowing, they stared him down, and he knew that this thing was big and hungry. It was so close that he could smell the stench of its breath. He gripped his bat ever so tightly as an idea sprang into his head. The plan was stupid, but it gave him a chance. He was sure he was going to die at the hands of this thing, anyways. He had always heard the saying from those military movies describing sniper targets. 'Don't run. You'll just die tired.'

Forget that. He thought to himself. If he was going to die, he was going to go down swinging, literally.

He remembered a pinecone that was further down the branch, and he felt around with his foot until he touched it. Still locked on the glowing emerald eyes before him, he kicked the pinecone off, causing it to snap into pieces on the forest floor. It wasn't much, but it was enough for the eyes of the giant to shift downward. Derek used this opportunity to sit up and pull back with his bat, and as the eyes shifted back to him, he swung forward with all his might. The bat landed, the wood vibrating in his hands. It felt no different than when he was playing softball with the team in the summer. A sickening *crack* echoed in waves through the trees. The creature retracted backwards, roaring in pain. The force of its screech made Derek lose his balance as he fell backwards out of the tree. He smacked the ground violently, knocking the air of his lungs. He struggled to get his footing as he stood, dropping what was left of the bat in the grass below his feet.

A.P. JENNINGS

C'mon, Derek. Number twenty-two! You're on the football field and just took a helmet to the gut! You can breathe! You're okay! It's time to run! The end zone is right there! Go!

In a stumbling run, his breath coming in gasps, he sprinted for his life once again, this time through the unforgiving darkness.

Chapter Twenty-Six

"What?!?" Wyatt was shocked. "What?!? Are you freaking kidding me right now, Port?!?"

"I wish I was," The boy responded. "It hasn't happened yet, but given the severity of it, he explained to us the process and how it'll only be used as a last resort. He..." Pbn'J stopped as he processed what he was saying. "He will tie their hands behind their backs, then give them a pack with a knife and a flashlight."

"And everyone is just okay with this?!?" Alex blurted out with her own input. "Nobody is trying to stop this?"

"Like I said, it hasn't happened yet!"

Tony stepped forward, pointing towards the forest. "And when it does are people just going to sit by and watch as a freaking kid walks into that forest alone?!? This Ruttledge is just one big bully on a power trip, isn't he?!?"

367

Porter remained quiet for a second, before calmly responding. "Yeah, he is. I agree. It's way out of line. That's why I'm helping you guys. That's why you have to do this before anything like this happens."

Molly was standing back, her arms crossed as she processed the information. "The longer we stay up here, the more likely we get caught. Let's go."

Tony walked up slowly, then braced himself against the propped open lid of the skylight. He lowered the rope inside. "Let's get this over with," he muttered.

Molly went first. Once she suspended herself in the air and started shuffling downward, it took a second for Tony to plant himself and get used to the intense tug. He kept his face straight ahead, concentrating on the task at hand. Next was Alex, whose hands were shaking as she lowered herself down. Porter was next, and Wyatt watched as Tony tightened his grip on the skylight structure. Wyatt could tell from the look on his face that he was in extreme pain.

"You sure you got this, hoss?" Wyatt asked him.

"Yeah," Tony grunted out through bared teeth. "I got this. Don't worry about me."

TAKEN BY THE NIGHT

A sound came from across the roof, causing both boys to snap their heads around in shock. Part of a head appeared over the side where the ladder was, revealing far too many eyes for a human being. It reminded Wyatt of a spider, and he hated spiders. It glared at both boys with beady little black, soulless spheres. Its head was incredibly hairy, and it was generating a clicking sound that made Wyatt jittery.

Wyatt took a step backwards as he reached for the rifle slung across his shoulder, not paying attention to where he placed his feet. Losing his balance, he fell backwards, grabbing onto the rope in a desperate attempt to keep from falling to the gym floor below. The rope grew taught in his hands as the slack ran out, burning his flesh. Despite the pain, he kept a tight grip on the rope as he dangled twenty feet above the gymnasium floor. He heard a yell above him.

"Tony!" Alex shouted from the gym floor. The commotion was loud enough to awake the guard who slept on the couch a few feet from Molly.

"What the he--" The boy exclaimed before he was cut off with a smack across the face from Molly's flashlight. It wasn't hard enough to knock him out cold, however, so she had to swing again while the boy was on the ground, causing blood to splatter across his face.

"Jeez, Molly!" Alex exclaimed, only briefly taking her eyes off the predicament above her.

Wyatt looked up and saw Tony dangling from the roof, his hands clutching the edge to keep from falling, his legs were swinging limply as he tried to pull himself up.

"Tony!" Wyatt whisper yelled up towards him. "Are you okay?!?"

"I can't—" He sounded as if he was crying. "I can't move my legs! I think the rope dislocated something! Oh...Oh my god!" He let out.

Wyatt could hear the fear in his voice. "Stay calm, Tony! We'll get you fixed up!"

"I-I-It's not that, Wyatt! Something is touching my hand!"

For Wyatt, time seemed to slow down at that moment, and everything happened at once seemingly in slow motion. He watched as the big teenager was yanked through the opening, accompanied by a mixture of his screaming and an insanely loud clicking sound that pierced his ears. The rope was being pulled up suddenly, giving Wyatt no choice but to let go and fall. He fell, flailing through the air until he smashed against something hard that made a loud *crack* from the sudden amount of weight, breaking and tossing him off onto the ground. He watched as a crimson trail of Tony's blood trickled down the rope that hung through the opening, before it was finally pulled out of sight.

He tried to call for his friend, but it was no use. The impact had forced all the air out of his lungs, making them feel like they had been crushed in a compactor. He was struggling to inhale, like a fish out of water.

"Wyatt, calm down! Slow down! You just got the wind knocked out of you!" Molly raced over and knelt beside him, placing a hand on his back at the base of his neck. She opened his jacket, then began pressing along parts of his ribs, checking for any breaks. "Does this hurt?"

He frantically shook his head. She sat him up, making him lean over. She was trying to help relax his diaphragm. After a minute, he began to calm himself, though his head had begun hurting again.

"Thanks." He gasped as he sat up off the gymnasium floor. He noticed he had landed on a pool table, its two left legs snapped, and splintered apart from the impact

371

Molly nodded as she pulled away and stood, wiping her forehead with the back of her hand avoiding eye contact with him. Wyatt was still trying to catch his breath, his face flushed from the awkward encounter between them.

Alex and Porter ran up, clearly in a panic.

"What was that? What was that, man?!?" The bony boy asked as he ran his hand through his hair, eyes wide with panic.

Wyatt shook his head solemnly before looking up at the open skylight once more, where he could see the bright, beautiful moon in the night sky.

"Something was watching us up there. I stumbled through the hole and pulled Tony down, too. It grabbed him, whatever it was."

"Oh, Jesus help us!" Pbn'J let out as if he were out of breath. His hands were on his knees as he stared at the ground with wide unbelieving eyes. "What the heck, man?!? He was there! He was screaming! Then....he was.... what the heck, man!?!?"

The group went silent, partly out of shock, but mostly out of respect for their fallen friend. Molly finally spoke up again.

"We need to do this. Let's finish this for Tony." She spoke, trying to swallow the lump in her throat.

"I didn't even know his last name," Wyatt spoke, his eyes still locked on the roof above them. He stood up from where he lay hobbling on one foot, his knee and his head throbbing as if they were in competition with one another on which one could hurt the worse.

"Ah, crap." He turned to Molly. "Do you have any more painkillers?"

"We're going to get some right now," She responded softly, moving towards the door into the main building.

"Coach taught us to fight through pain on the field, right? Just fight through it, man." Pbn'J said.

Wyatt glared at him. "He was referring to a rolled ankle, not a freaking brain bruise, you schmuck."

Porter held up his hands defensively. "Just trying to help."

They cautiously began their journey out the door and through the hall. The lockers were stacked with now useless books, and boxes were lined up in rows along with metal chairs. Pbn'J walked ahead to where his room was.

"I'm going to go now. Take care, yeah?" He opened the classroom door slowly and silently, then he slipped inside.

"You too, bro." Wyatt responded, his eyes narrowed as he studied his friend's body language.

"What's wrong?" Alex asked him in a hushed tone.

"Something's up with him. He's keeping something from us."

Molly approached. "Can we trust him?"

"I honestly don't know." Wyatt responded, keeping his eyes locked on the door. He reached over and grabbed a metal chair, unfolded it, then placed it under the handle to keep the door from opening. He wasn't going to risk it. "We need to hurry."

****

He was crying. Derek could feel the icy wind pushing the tears down his cheeks. He never cried, but the amount of fear that had built up inside was too much to bear. He was just running and running without stopping to rest. He was scared because he could feel the ground move and the Earth shake beneath his feet. He could hear the roar of the creature he had royally pissed off right behind him, crashing its way through the forest brush, knocking down trees with an almighty strength. It stomped after him with a rage that made Derek push himself, running faster than he ever had before. He had only been sprinting for a few minutes, but it felt like hours. His legs grew numb long before he started running out of breath, the result of good conditioning his coaches had put him through. Oh, how he wished he was back in football camp right now with his coach barking orders at him. Stumbling through the brush, and almost falling a few times, he suddenly saw an opening in the trees and made a beeline for it. He couldn't tell what was beyond it.

Just a little bit longer, Derek! For the first time in what felt like an eternity, he could hear his mother's voice urging him to keep going. He had to push through. He couldn't feel the ground below him from the numbness in his joints.

He finally broke through the opening in the trees, like the forest was spitting him out of its grueling mouth. Falling to the ground in the grass exhausted and out of breath, he realized he could no longer hear the thumping of feet charging at him or feel the ground shake beneath him. It was gone, he had lost it. Through tears of joy that fell from his eyes, he could barely make out a long, white, wooden fence line separating a row of houses from the forest behind him.

He was home. He had made it to Lyonside.

****

375

They snuck their way through the darkness of the dimly lit hallway, moving down to the rooms that they knew held supplies. Wyatt was in front of the two girls, his pistol at the ready. Alex turned to Molly, who had a look on her face that would scare anyone with enough sense away.

"Hey, Mol?"

"Yeah?"

Alex watched Wyatt, checking for any signs that he was eavesdropping on them.

"You okay? You knocked the crap out of that kid back there."

"Just doing what needs to be done. He would have called the other guards and we wouldn't be able to do what we're doing now. The plan would have gone down the toilet. I had to knock him out."

"But still," Alex looked at the ground and watched her feet shuffle forward.

"Look," Molly kept her eyes trained forward as she addressed her friend. "Alex, you're really cool. You're definitely one of the only people I trust around here, but you have to realize what we're doing. This is survival. We have to do what we have to do.

Sometimes I think that guy there is the only one who realizes it."
She nodded forward towards Wyatt.

"Can I ask you another question?" Asked Alex. "I mean,
besides that one."

"Sure."

"Did he ever tell you exactly what happened to Derek? I
mean...I know it was pretty bad, and that's why he doesn't bring it
up around me."

Molly remained silent for a moment; her face emotionless. "No.
He didn't tell me."

"Oh."

Wyatt stopped walking once he reached a half-opened door.
The hallway further down had no lights illuminating what was
beyond the darkness. He pulled the door open and once inside,
they began rifling through boxes full of can goods, food, and water
bottles.

"Do you think this will work? What if the kids don't want to
leave?"

Wyatt opened a box up, then showed it to the girls. It was piled
to the top with chocolate bars.

"Oh, they'll go wherever this stuff is!" he chuckled as he dumped it into his backpack.

Molly emptied a crate of bottles of water and sodas into her bag as Alex stuffed hers full of ammunition from the cabinets overhead. She opened a cabinet and spotted many kinds of weapons, but one stood out to her.

"Wyatt isn't this yours?" She picked up a sawed-off shotgun that had obviously just been cleaned and shined back to its original condition.

"No way!" He responded ecstatically as he raced over to her. He cradled the gun in his hands as he studied the exterior for any signs of the inky, velvety goop from the exploding "smiling men" the night before. He nabbed a box of shells that Alex pointed out, opened the chamber, and loaded it with a satisfying click. "How did he get this so clean? It looks brand new!"

"Guys," Molly interrupted from across the room as she frantically moved through the boxes. She flung an empty one across the room in frustration. "The medicine isn't here."

"Take it easy," Alex said, holding out a hand to calm her. "It's probably in the nurse's office."

"You guys stay here, I'll go check." Wyatt said as he started to move out the door. He made his way through the hallway, the darkness swallowing him. The headache was only increasing, and he didn't know if he could remember where it was.

One step at a time, Wyatt. Around the corner, two doors passed the chemistry lab on the right.

The pain in his leg and his head made it agony to move. It quiet. The only sound was his dirty red sneakers squeaking on the recently cleaned floor. Halfway down the hall he reached the lab and peered inside, only to see at least ten kids sound asleep on mattresses that had been brought in, he assumed, from each of the houses. He recognized a few of them, but two in particular made his blood boil. He saw Lucy Letrail and Isaac together on a mattress in the corner of the room. He didn't know why or how, but they looked helpless and alone where they were. First opportunity he had he was going to bust Ruttledge in the mouth.

He ducked below the glass to avoid being spotted from anyone who might be awake and continued forward until he reached a glossy wooden door with a large red cross on it, signifying the nurses office.

The door was unlocked and creaked as he opened it, carefully stepping inside and scanning his surroundings. The glow from the streetlight one window was bright enough to illuminate the room through the blinds. Opening the cabinets, he began removing pill bottles and first aid kits, one at a time, trying to be as quiet as mouse. He almost cried with joy when he discovered a bottle of acetaminophen. He popped two tablets, swallowing them dry. The light suddenly came on, causing him to flinch as the pain in his head spiked. Squinting as he turned to the door, he was relieved to see Chloe standing in the doorway, her finger still on the light switch. She looked beautiful, but the expression on her face unnerved him.

"God, Chlo. You scared me to death!" He turned to her and stepped forward to embrace her. She held out a hand to stop him, her face growing serious as she stared him in his eyes.

"What do you think you're doing?" She asked with an accusing tone.

"What does it look like?" He responded as he turned to make sure the cabinet was empty. "We're taking off with these supplies that Ruttledge nabbed."

A look of confusion was on her face. "Nabbed? What do you mean? You guys approved of him taking care of this stuff and the kids!"

Wyatt stopped, turning to her as he laughed in unbelief. "Is that what the little rat told you?"

Her hand moved from the light switch over to a red square with a handle right next to it on the wall. It was the fire alarm. Wyatt's face grew white as he swallowed hard.

"Chloe, no! Don't!" He begged. "Please! I don't have time to explain! I need you to trust me on this!"

"You're endangering all of these kids just to prove a point? Just so the guy you don't like doesn't take charge?" Her face seemed innocent, willing to try and understand.

"Chloe! This dude manipulated his way to the top! Please, we're trying to take him down, but I need to get out of here!"

She stared into his eyes for a minute, considering her options. Then in a single moment, she had made her choice.

"I'm sorry. You can't do this." She pulled the alarm, the bell screaming in both of their heads as Wyatt covered his ears and recoiled in pain.

"Wyatt?!?" She yelled over the bells, curious as to what was wrong. It looked as if someone had stabbed him in the brain. His face so full of pain, made her regret her decision. She began panicking. "Are you okay?!?"

Something shoved her in the back and further into the room. She turned and saw Molly, who violently pinned her to the wall by her wrists. Alex had moved in behind her and tried to push the handle back into place to turn off the noise without success. She cursed.

"Alex, just go! I'll get Wyatt!" Molly yelled as she tossed Chloe to the ground, smacking against the tile floor. She wasn't thrown hard, but just enough for it to sting against her backside. Molly ran over to Wyatt, trying to get his attention.

"Wy! We need to go, now!"

Wyatt seemed to understand as he nodded before grabbing his backpack. He slung it over his shoulder, then raced out the door with one eye shut, as the pain was excruciating behind the left side of his head. The trio took off down the hallway, only to have Wyatt stop halfway down.

"Go!" He yelled towards them as he turned around and ran in the opposite direction. "I've got to get something!"

"Wyatt!" Alex yelled back for him.

"Go! I'll be fine!"

Chapter Twenty-Seven

The fire alarm had already awakened Isaac and Lucy by the time Wyatt made it back to them. With one eye closed, and in a panic they could barely make out his voice over the alarm.

"Come on!" He was yelling. "We're leaving!"

"Wyatt?" Isaac let out, still half asleep. His sister, however, was more alert than him.

"Where are we going?" She asked as they exited the room full of confused kids.

"Away from here!" They took off down the hall after Molly and Alex.

How did she plan on getting out of here??? He asked himself in panic as they sprinted, children and teens alike filing out of the classrooms in utter confusion.

They reached the main entrance and came across something that made Wyatt shout expletives in anger. Guards had both girls by the arms. Alex appeared to have lost all hope, while Molly was still fighting back as she struggled against them.

"Let go of me!" She yelled. One of them swung a fist, smacking her across the face and to the ground. Wyatt let all his rage go as he charged forward, barreling into the back of the boy who had hit her. He tackled him to the ground, removed his helmet, then started swinging ferociously until he saw blood. Another guard attempted to pull him off, only to be grabbed by his face mask and yanked down violently, his equipment thumping on the tile. Wyatt stood with lightning speed, then stomped on the second guard's sternum.

The alarm was turned off as Wyatt caught his breath, turning back to Isaac and his sister. Ruttledge stood behind them, along with a chorus of kids and guards.

"Wow!" The well-dressed boy clapped his hands along with a chuckle of unbelief. "Just...wow! You....you can fight! Remind me not to piss you off!"

Wyatt squeezed his hands into fists. "Yeah, it's a bit too late for that!"

Ruttledge grinned before turning to the group behind him with his arms held out wide.

"See, this is what I'm talking about!" He exclaimed. "Barbarianism! Plain and simple! We can't have this in our camp!"

Wyatt approached; his bloody hands held out. "I can't believe this! You want to talk about barbarianism? How about playing god? How about threatening to exile people into a place where we know they will die or suffer a fate even worse?!? You're not a leader! These kids don't respect you, Ruttledge! They fear you!"

The gentleman stared Wyatt in his eyes as silence took over. "Look at your own two hands, then tell me which one of us is really to be feared."

Wyatt looked down at the crimson that was splattered across his fingers. He then turned to the two guards he had beaten senseless, both groaning in agony. Regret flooded his heart, and he began to tear up.

Was I really the one to fear? Were my actions justifiable?

His eyes then fell on Molly, who was sitting up against the wall. The skin below her right eye had grown bright pink and swelled slightly. Wyatt crinkled his nose in anger, his eyes growing cold as the remorse was chased away by a rage that infiltrated his veins.

He began wiping his hands off on his jeans, shaking as the breath retreated from his lungs.

"You can't just wipe away your sins like--" Ruttledge began ranting as Wyatt rolled his eyes.

"Oh, would you please just shut up?!?" He let out, pointing his finger towards the boy. "I don't need a morality lesson from a pretentious little snob who threatens little kids!" He scanned the eyes of the many teenagers from West Side. "Your boy, Tony, is gone, by the way! Just thought you'd like to know that! He went out fighting, because he believed what this little twerp is doing is wrong!"

He saw their expressions change into fear and sorrow at the news of their friend's death. He turned back to Ruttledge with a fire inside of him. "You want to play god?!? Fine. I guess I'm the devil, then! So freakin' bring it!"

The room was soaked in a cloud of dead silence as Wyatt walked closer to Ruttledge with cruel intent in his eyes. A couple of his goons began moving for him but were stopped with a movement of the hand.

"No," Ruttledge said as he rolled up his sleeves. "Let him prove my point for me." He approached Wyatt, the mob of kids forming a circle around them.

The crowd had gone silent, apart from the occasional murmur. It wasn't like the movies where someone started to chant for them to fight. What was happening now scared everyone.

He held up fists the way an older boxer would, his stance swaying. It seemed a bit goofy to Wyatt as he eyed his opponent. It was clear that he had never been in a fight before.

"Wyatt, don't," Molly said as she stood on wobbly knees. "It's okay. We just need to go. This won't help anything."

"Maybe not," He responded. "But I'll sure feel better!"

A sudden blast of pain shot up his leg and he buckled to the floor, followed by a shot to his jaw. Ruttledge stood over him, a fist balled up and held out as if it were a weapon itself. Wyatt could taste the blood on his tongue as he licked his lips.

"My grandma hits harder," he responded. Wyatt turned over onto his back, then kicked upward towards Rutt's groin. The boy was swift enough to move just as Wyatt's foot caught the inside of his leg, causing him to stumble backwards. This opened an opportunity for Wyatt to roll backwards onto his feet. He limped around trying to keep his balance, putting most of his weight on his good leg as his brain thumped against his skull at the rhythm of his racing heartbeat. For a minute, that was all he could hear. The adrenaline helped kill most of the pain, but he still groaned in agony. He kept one eye squeezed shut as he attempted to focus his other on his opponent. The blurry vision quickly subsided as the bright colors of Ruttledge's clothes raced towards him as the boy charged forward. Wyatt quickly sidestepped, pulling his bad leg over as he screeched in pain. He heard Rutt's boat shoes slap the ground going past him and the thudding sound of his face meeting the glass door behind Wyatt. The sound echoed through the building, causing the crowd to recoil in horror. Wyatt turned and watched the boy attempt to stand back up as he wiped blood from his nose. It was splattered all over him and the door he had run into.

Wyatt raced forward. He was in such a rush of rage that he neglected to bend into the tackling form he was taught, and he doubted that his throbbing leg would let him anyways. The two boys collided chaotically in a mass of limbs and screaming as Ruttledge fell backwards against the silver push bar of the door, causing it to swing wide open. A rush of cold winter air stung against their raw faces, but neither cared as they raced to see who could obtain the advantage. Wyatt swung a wild haymaker against an already struggling Ruttledge, who took the slug across the face and fell back on the outdoor mat that lay on the concrete just outside. It was no stalemate, and Wyatt made sure that statement was clear as he lifted the boy by the back of his collar and threw him forward into the dark parking lot and out of the visibility of the streetlight above them. Someone grappled at Wyatt's shoulder, then stood in front of him. He recognized the eyes.

"Wyatt, calm down before you do something you'll regret later!" Molly asked him. "Just wait a second and think about this! Little kids are watching you! A-and..." She struggled to find the words. She wanted nothing more than to let him at the little twerp and give him what he deserved, but she was seeing something in the teenage boy before her. She was seeing glimpses of the monster he was becoming. This was Wyatt Richards: the joker, the prankster, and the jester. She would never expect him to become this way. She knew deep down inside her own mind that she couldn't let him do this to himself, but she also couldn't explain it. Her voice nearly caught in her throat. "A-and you're hurt! You need to stop before you kill yourself! He's not worth it!"

TAKEN BY THE NIGHT

Wyatt stopped as he stared into the golden rings of her eyes. He just breathed. That's all he could do was breathe as she hugged his neck tightly. He couldn't raise his arms to embrace her back. His whole body had gone numb.

"Come on!" Ruttledge begged from beyond the darkness. His figure was barely noticeable in the night that surrounded him. "Finish it, Richards! Just like you did to Desmond! Just like with Derek! You freak! Keep going! You're not done, cause I'm still breathing!"

Wyatt closed his eyes as the pain approached him in waves.

"Fine, then!" Ruttledge emerged from the darkness, holding his ribs. His face was bloody, bruised, and beaten. His right eye had gone purple, along with the whole right side of his lip and the bridge of his nose. Blood drenched his lower jaw. He struggled to spit out the next words. "Boys throw them in one of the classrooms until I figure out what to do with them! Every single one of them!"

Wyatt kept focusing on his shaky breathing and the warmth of Molly's touch as the guards approached, their shoes clacking on the concrete behind them through the murmurs of the crowd.

"On your knees!" They ordered. Wyatt did as they asked, his head getting drowsy before he fainted in her arms.

A.P. JENNINGS

Chapter Twenty-Eight

Molly awoke, her eyes staring at the classroom ceiling above. She didn't know how long she was out, so there was uncertainty of how long she had left Wyatt unsupervised. He hadn't woken up since fainting in the parking lot after his brawl with Ruttledge, and she feared that his arrogance had caused even more damage to his head. She had examined his wounds when the guards locked them and Alex in a classroom. His leg had been re-injured and was plagued with swollen purple skin that surrounded the area she had treated before, but that was the least of her worries. The symptoms that he experienced from the concussion had her on edge. All of them were red flags for something far more serious. His fainting in her arms did not ease her stress. She felt an intense sense of helplessness because she had no way of knowing the extent of his injury. All she could do was comfort him and give him pills when the pain hit. She had been attempting to stay awake and alert to make sure he hadn't fallen into a coma or a seizure, severe conditions caused by bleeding in the brain. However, she had failed because of falling asleep. When Molly's eyes had begun to flicker open, a panic had taken over, and she could feel an uneasiness in her stomach. She stood up from the hard linoleum floor she had slept on. None of the guards were allowed to bring in any mattresses, so the three were condemned to sleeping on the hard floor. She had used her hoodie as a pillow. Wyatt was passed out on the teacher's desk, his rainbow jacket removed and used to prop up his head in case he was to start convulsing in his sleep.

The morning light of the rising sun casted its bright yellow color into the dark room through the blinds of the window, illuminating Alex's face as she rested on the sill staring outside, deep in thought. Molly could tell her mind was working vigorously. Silence covered the room, their breathing creating a whispered chorus between the three teenagers.

"You okay?"

"Why did Chloe pull the alarm?" Alex asked, her hair swooping from her face as it shimmered in the sunlight. Molly truly didn't have an answer to that, and it wasn't her place to do so.

"Why don't you ask her when we get out?" She responded.

"You mean *if* we get out, right?" Alex stood from the window, her sneakers squeaking as they hit the floor. She crossed her arms as she shot a glance at Wyatt. "What he did would be punishable even if the town wasn't ruled by a sociopath. He beat the living crap out of those kids."

Molly thought about this for a second. "That's exactly how I know we'll get out of here soon. Ruttledge seems like the type to be extremely prideful, but Wyatt did a number on that pretty face of his and the guards he attacked. They probably just dealt with a night full of aches and pains. He'll learn that I'm the only medically sensible person around. He'll send someone to come get me to treat him."

Alex scoffed. "Yeah, then what? He'll just lock you back in here when you're done."

Molly walked over to the door, peering through the narrow glass window into the hallway. It struck her suddenly how normal everything looked. Kids roamed the halls, trying to get to their next assigned chore. It reminded her of not too long ago, when these same kids were trotting to their next class. They shot her glances, as if she was some sort of criminal behind the bars of a cold, unforgiving cell.

"I don't know, Alex. I really don't know. I'll see if I can find Chloe, maybe hatch up a different plan to get you two out of here."

Alex looked at her with an eyebrow raised as she crossed her arms. "I don't think she likes us at the moment, considering you threw her to the ground and McFly over there turned her boyfriend black and blue."

A rustling came from the table Wyatt was laying on as he sat up, his eyes struggling to adjust as he blinked rapidly. Molly walked over to him, bringing her face down to his to inspect his eyes.

"If you want a good morning kiss, all you have to do is ask!" He said as he stretched into a yawn.

"Shove it, Richards." She kept her eyes focused on his, searching for any signs of abnormality in the dilation.

"What are you even doing?" Alex asked, her tone exhausted and weak.

"The only thing I know to look for. I'm not exactly a neurosurgeon. All I know about a concussion is that the pupils either dilate or are uneven in size. His are still not looking normal."

Wyatt hopped up from the table. "I'm not hurting that bad right now."

Molly stared at him for a minute, struggling to believe what he said. The fact that he made a joke did not convince her. She thought that she understood how Wyatt's brain worked. He used humor to defuse stressful situations and to deal with pain. He smiled at her cockily as he always did. She didn't smile back as her eyebrow arched.

"Don't lie to me, Wy, or I swear I'll break your other leg."

"I'm not. How's your eye?"

She instinctively felt her upper cheek, then recoiled as the pain struck. She shook it off, then focused back on him. "I'll live."
A noise interrupted, a knock from the door behind her. Two guards stepped inside. One of them kept his rifle trained on Wyatt as another approached with his hands behind his back.

"It's time."

Alex crossed her arms as she flipped her bangs from her eyes. "Time for what?"

"Your punishment." The other guard answered.

Molly acted surprised, as if she didn't expect this was coming. She knew good and well that they wouldn't get away that easily with what they had done. She pointed towards Wyatt as she leaned towards the guards and asked, "Does he look like he needs any more punishment?"

She turned her head slightly, catching a glimpse of Wyatt leaning up against a table. He had apparently understood the guilt card she was attempting to play, because he began grasping at his knee as if in extreme pain. A guard laughed.

"Oh, don't play stupid, girly. We both know who had the advantage in that fight! Now, hurry up. I won't ask again." He walked over to Wyatt, then bound his wrists with a white zip tie. The guard offered a shoulder to lean on, to which was greeted with a vicious shove from the limping boy.

"I'm fine. Get away from me!"

The guard did as he was told, turning to Molly. "Your boyfriend is a real charmer there."

Molly scoffed so hard it hurt her throat. She responded with no emotion displayed across her face. "He's not my boyfriend."

Wyatt winked at her playfully, to which she narrowed her eyes in a snooty manner, gifting him with the same expression she had first greeted him with that day in the bookstore. He began to limp forward with both of Ruttledge's geared-up boys on either side of him.

"If that were true, why have you been trying to keep me alive for this long?" He said over his shoulder.

"Because I'm a decent human being, Richards."

Wyatt nodded solemnly. "That you are, doc. That you are."

****

Derek had fallen asleep once again, but for the first time in what felt like an eternity, he wasn't afraid. Fear no longer enslaved his every waking moment. He had been trapped in that forest for over twenty-four painful, anguish-filled hours. He had found his house, but the group of kids he had assigned himself to watch were nowhere to be found. He was tempted to search the town for them, but the call of his warm bed was too much to resist.

Once the sunlight reached into his room through the window, Derek knew he had a job to finish. The bed was unbelievably comfortable, the soft mattress sinking like a cloud beneath him. He had to find the others as soon as possible. He had to find Alex and let her know he was okay. He had to make sure everyone was safe. He sat up reluctantly, then made his way to his bathroom. As his dirty, wet socks met the tile, his eyes caught of glimpse of himself in the mirror across the room. He cursed to himself, humorously.

A nasty figure stared back at him, his eyes bloodshot and his hair a greasy mess that hung in his face and partially stuck out in several random places. A weak attempt at a makeshift bandana had fallen from his head and hung from his neck pitifully. His skin was covered with a thick layer of black dirt. Specks of bark and leaf particles were sprinkled down his arms. One of his shirt sleeves was torn off, revealing a cut that ran down his bicep. He didn't even know where that had come from. His shoes and the legs of his jeans below his knees were covered in muck. He breathed in. He did it. He survived. He lived. He was breathing. His heart was beating. He was alive.

Derek stripped out of his clothes; a whiff of his own stench made him gag. It sent a wave of sudden nostalgia, making him long for the days of reeking football pads and rotten gym socks that spread all over their locker room. He hopped into his shower, welcoming the warm spray as it struck his face. It burned at first, but the sensation soon was replaced with pleasure. It felt amazing to his tired, stiff body.

He dried himself off, then put on a set of clean clothes he pulled from his drawer. After getting dressed, he stepped outside, his gun now fully loaded with bullets from the house and held out in front of him cautiously. God only knew what had happened to Lyonside while he was gone. He prayed for the best but was prepared for the worst.

His eyes scanned the abandoned houses. Even after the adults were taken, the town was constantly moving with kids attempting to enjoy their everyday lives. The silence that hung in the air was bone chilling and terrified him more than he had ever been in the forest, but he had firmly decided to pursue on in order to find answers. He turned a corner into the town center, then peered into the bookstore as he took a bite from a granola bar. It was empty and the books were still scattered across the floor, almost the same way as before he had left. He stepped inside, his black leather boots finding their place on the soft, dark red carpet.

"Holy crap."

He heard a voice behind him as he snapped to attention, turning at lightning speed and pointing his gun towards the doorway where what looked like a football player stood. The boy had on all the Lyonside Lions equipment, all the way down to the padded red pants, though Derek did not recognize him as one of his former teammates. He cradled a rifle on his shoulder. When he caught a glimpse of Derek's weapon, his eyes widened.

"You're Derek Hoff, aren't you?" The boy spoke softly in unbelief. "But...you're...."

"I'm what?"

The guard pulled out his phone, averting his eyes down to the screen. Derek just watched in curiosity. Someone answered.

"Quint! Go get Ru--"

Something took over Derek, and he watched himself aim for the teenager's leg and pull the trigger. The bullet narrowly missed, but the sound echoed through the room, its boom bouncing off the walls. His ears rung, but he was too shocked at what he had done to notice. He had just tried to shoot another human being. He watched the boy fall over in shock to the concrete, screaming endlessly. For every second that Derek heard the screams, more regret began to burn at his heart. He wanted to cry along with the boy, but whatever it was inside him that made him pull the trigger, wasn't done. With anger building, he marched forward with his gun at the ready, leaned over and picked the kid up by the front of his shirt.

"I'm what?!?" He spat into the face of the crying boy, who hiccupped as he tried to catch his breath.

"Y-you're supposed to be dead!"

Derek's face drained of its color. "What? Who told you that!"

"Richards! That quarterback!"

All at once, it was as if he couldn't control himself. He was flooded with an unimaginable anger. An inner rage let loose as he screamed at the top of his lungs, his voice echoing through the empty street.

****

Wyatt whistled as they walked down the hallway full of kids. Molly recognized the tune as "Everybody Wants to Rule the World" by Tears for Fears. It wasn't a particularly depressing song, but at the speed he was whistling it, along with the dread of what was to come, Molly couldn't help but feel hopeless for him. It was a dead man's tune.

He finished his melancholy melody as they stepped out of the front door and into the morning light that caused him to recoil in pain. He squinted his eyes as he attempted to focus on the crowd of kids in front of them. He recognized many faces as his former teammates, but he noticed Ruttledge and Chloe standing in the front. Ruttledge's face was badly beaten, swollen, and purple. However, Ruttledge kept his composure as he crossed his arms and stared at the weakened, bound boy before him.

"Without order," He spoke, his tone obviously strained from withholding anger. "There's chaos. You, Wyatt Richards, you are the definition of chaos. That makes me order."

"Is that right, frog-face? Shock me. Say something intelligent." Wyatt responded.

A couple of giggles arose from the crowd. Ruttledge did not find this funny as he approached slowly with his hands behind his back. Wyatt had really done a number on his face, but most of the purple color was in his nose, and Wyatt never punched him there. He had gotten in a lot of jaw and cheek shots, which were swollen. However, the broken nose had to be from when Rutt plowed into the glass door. He croaked out.

"Don't insult me!"

"I'm not insulting, I'm describing."

"Everything's just one big joke to you, isn't it?"

Wyatt shrugged. "No. Not everything. Just the funny stuff, like the way you look, because I screwed you up, dude! Then again, you had the perfect face for radio before. In that sense, I guess I helped."

Another laugh came from somewhere in the circle of kids surrounding them.

"You want to know what I think, Wyatt?" Ruttledge got closer, his eyes squinted to keep his composure and hide any sign of hatred.

"No," Wyatt responded honestly. "But you're going to tell me, anyways. Right, philosophical Frank?"

"You're afraid. You are so immensely scared of something," Ruttledge grinned as he explained, as if he was coming to realize the information as he spoke it. "You're not scared of me, or anyone with a gun to your head. No... but you're terrified of something. That's why you are the way you are. Your jokes, sarcasm, and every other little quirk you have are all an agenda to hide the fact that Wyatt Richards is scared. Stop me if I'm wrong, but don't lie to me."

Wyatt inhaled sharply; his eyes locked on Ruttledge's sharp blues. Taking a moment to think, his eyes fell to the concrete. He was scared, Ruttledge was right. He was horrified. The feeling didn't just start when the parents disappeared. He had been in this state all his life, ever since he began developing his own personality. He didn't care about people. Empathy was a stranger to him, and sympathy was nonexistent from a very young age. His father, however, was one of the most caring men he had ever known. Wyatt could remember him stopping by a homeless man holding up a sign on the side of the road to give him change, something he did often. He didn't care if he was getting scammed. It was built into him to be good to people, and Wyatt didn't have that. Yet, this was something he longed for since he understood exactly what it was. He desired love for others, and his father seemed as if he had an endless supply in his heart. That's what he feared. He feared that he would never be able to feel things for others. That's what pushed him to want to save others. That's why he idolized his dad. He wanted his heart.

Wyatt swallowed the lump in his throat as his eyes shot back up to Ruttledge, the fire burning within them. "You're full of it. Don't quit your day job, Dr. Phil."

He was angry, Wyatt could see a shade of red rising beneath the swollen purple on Rutt's skin as he turned to the crowd among them.

"What do we do to people who steal?!? Huh?!?" He yelled into the silent air, his voice croaking and cracking. "I wrote it on the white board, didn't I? Not to mention assaulting me! Attempted murder!"

Wyatt scoffed. "I wasn't going to kill--"

"Shut up! Shut up, Richards!" He turned and pointed at him, his voice quaking in anger.

"Shove it, Napoleon!" Wyatt continued yelling. "Come off your high horse! This isn't a kingdom, and you aren't a king! We're just kids, man! Just kids trying to survive!"

Ruttledge shook his head as he sucked on his teeth. "You still don't get it, and I'm done trying to make you understand how things work now!"

"So, what?" Molly intervened, her hair flowing in the morning wind. "You're going to exile him? That's sadistic!" She turned to look at Wyatt, who had that confident grin on his face he always had when he knew he had a situation under control. She knew he was banking on being exiled. If there was one thing she had learned about him over the past few days, it was that he was a survivor.

"Oh, no. Not him. That won't get the message across. Plus, as we all know, Wyatt has a way of getting out of sticky situations. I would be accomplishing nothing by sending him out into the forest." Ruttledge paced, but kept his eyes locked onto Wyatt, as if he expected him to pull out a weapon and start firing. "That's why I'm sending out someone else. Two someone's."

****

Derek was perched in a tree in the forest once again, but this time with an objective. He could clearly see into the parking lot of the school, where a mass of children and teenagers had collected. They surrounded people that he knew. Molly, Alex, and Wyatt were all there. Wyatt was bounded by something he couldn't make out. A boy, who seemed to be extremely well dressed and his face bruised up, stood in front of them. He was yelling at Wyatt, then Wyatt would fire back at him. They went back and forth, screaming at each other. He could only make out a few words. One of them was exile. He squinted, trying to study his friend's emotions.

Exile? He thought to himself. *What does he mean by that? As in sending someone away forever? Was Wyatt being exiled from the town by this kid? Was he the new leader?*

****

"You can't do that!" Molly protested with her death stare locked onto Ruttledge. She could see Chloe amongst the crowd behind him making her way to the front to speak up.

"Ruttledge, no! That's not right!" The crowd murmured behind her as she joined in. Molly nodded but was reluctant to trust her again. It would take a lot more for redemption. Maybe she wasn't even looking for such. Maybe she was just feeling guilt in knowing she enabled such treatment. Ruttledge turned to her.

"Chloe, sweetie, I'm actually going easy on him! He has committed double the crime, so I'm sending two people out to equal his punishment. Two people who deserve the exile anyways. I'm killing two birds with one stone!"

"No, what you're doing is condemning two kids to death!" She argued; her face contorted to beg for mercy. She looked as if she was about to cry, as her eyes glossed over.

"I'm not arguing this anymore!" He held up a hand to shush the crowd. "I let everyone know how things work now, and people broke the rules. We need to follow rules in order to function as a society! Without rules, there's chaos!"

The wind whistled a tune of sorrow as a silence once again fell over the gathering. Molly stepped in front of Wyatt, like a protective mother dog shielding her puppy.

"Send me out there, then!"

Wyatt shoved by, his shoulder bumping against her. His quick movement causing the guards to raise their guns and aim at him. He was livid.

"No, forget that, Molly! Forget this crap! Forget this town, man! I'm going! Nobody else needs to do this!"

Ruttledge shook his head intently. "No. I'm not as stupid as you think I am. Sending her out would be a death sentence for everyone here, considering she is the only medically savvy person in Lyonside." He turned and pointed at Alex. "Miss Egan, can you please come here."

Alex approached him, her big brown eyes burning with hatred for him.

"Porter!" He yelled into the crowd. "Porter Bancroft Jenkins!"

The skinny boy emerged from the sea of teenagers, his eyes carrying a worry that gave Molly a hint of anxiety for what Ruttledge was planning.

"Hands above your head. Both of you. Guards bring me the bags."

Two suited-up boys pulled away from the crowd. They set their guns down, then unslung two army green colored packs from their shoulders.

"Any supplies you need for the next few days are in here. Water, painkillers, food, things like that." Ruttledge said as they handed them to Alex and Porter. Alex's face was twisted into a tearful rage, while Porter was filled with an innocent confusion.

"Wait...you're sending me out? Why?!? I haven't hurt anyone!" Wyatt could hear the quiver in his voice as he tried to restrict the urge to cry.

Ruttledge walked closer to him. "How did they get inside the facility, Porter?" His steel eyes locked on the boys whimpering face.

"I don't know, man! They just got in!"

"The skylight on the roof to the gym was open! That was your area to watch, Porter! Don't lie to me."

Porter couldn't keep his gaze as tears began to burn hot. He turned away before they could fall to his cheeks. Molly trotted forward. A single tear fell down the swollen area beneath her eye as she marched forward before one of the guards could grab her arm.

"You're going to burn in Hell for this!" She yelled as she struggled.

Wyatt stared blankly, lacking any emotion. Ruttledge noticed his silence as he approached.

"This is all because of you. I don't want to do this, but I have to." He grew even closer to his ear, then brought his voice to an almost whispered tone.

"When this is all finished, I will need a formal apology from you to everyone for what you did to me and what you had attempted to do. Do you understand?"

Wyatt stayed staring past him for a second, seemingly comprehending his request, until he laughed, and his signature smirk grew across the right side of his face.

"I hope you understand exactly what I'm going to do. As soon as they disappear into the forest, I'm going to break free. Then, I'm going to come after you."

Ruttledge's eyebrow arched in curiosity. "Yeah? And how are you going to do that? Are you going to kill me?"

TAKEN BY THE NIGHT

"I don't know yet, and no, I'm not. I'm not a monster. I'm not you." Wyatt locked his eyes back onto Ruttledge, who recognized the fire that burned in them. It was the look he saw before he was beaten the night before. "But you can bet on one thing: you're sure going to wish I'd kill you."

Ruttledge chuckled slightly revealing his uneasiness as he backed away. Alex and Porter had their packs on. Alex stared into the forest beyond the parking lot, whimpering to herself, before inhaling sharply. Porter had broken into a bawl, snot and tears running down his reddened skin. He was crying so hard, begging for mercy as he hiccupped into untranslatable blabber. They began to walk together, slowly moving towards the tree line. She grabbed his hands to comfort the both of them, calming the chaotic feelings within them before disappearing into the terror of the forest.

****

Derek watched Alex and his former teammate, Pbn'J, shuffle into the forest hand-in-hand. Their path led directly underneath him. He watched as they carefully moved to their position below the branch he sat on, scanning the area around them for any sign of a horrid creature just waiting to pounce. He could hear them whisper.

"You're squeezing my hand too tight."

"I'm sorry. I'm just scared." He heard Porter whimper a little, before letting go of her hand.

"It's okay. We'll make it. We'll make it." She spoke again, struggling against the shaking of her voice.

Derek dropped down onto the ground next to them, a loud thump announcing his landing to them both. Leaves scattered in the air as they both screamed in horror.

"Sh, sh, sh, sh!" Derek hurriedly held his finger to his lips to silence them. Porter struggled to catch his breath as Alex stayed still, paralyzed in a state of shock as her eyes found his.

"...Oh my God...." She whispered out, as if she struggled to find the words.

"Derek!" Porter jumped forward, a wave of relief slicing the tension between the three of them. He held his hands out in disbelief as a smile grew across his face. "Yo! Holy crap! We thought you were dead, man!"

Derek stood from his crouched position, peering from the tree and towards the parking lot. He squinted, struggling to get a more defined view of what went on at that moment.

"Yeah, I heard. Rumors of my death were--"

Alex interrupted him with a bear hug as she jumped forward, burying her tired face into his neck.

"...greatly exaggerated."

Alex pulled away from him, and Derek pulled the slide back on his pistol to make sure a round was in the chamber. A look of determination spread across his face as he turned to face the direction they had come from and aimed toward the school.

****

The scream echoed from the darkness beyond the tree line, sending chills down Wyatt's spine. He was filled with so much sorrow and disbelief. *He killed them. Both of them. He sent them in there to die, just so he could send a message to him. Sick freak.*

"You sadistic little.... I'll freaking kill you!" A rush of rage had exploded from his lungs as he spit out a vicious string of expletives towards Ruttledge, who stood with his hands behind his back and his eyes down.

Molly was sobbing, her head down and her hair hanging in front of her face. Chloe was in a state of disbelief, her mouth hanging agape in shock. She peered at Wyatt and Molly before her face turned cold. Suddenly, she pulled her revolver from the holster on her hip, pressing the barrel to the side of Ruttledge's head.

"Let them go. Now! We're going after them!"

Ruttledge put his hands in the air, scoffing as he turned around.

"Chloe, really?" He asked almost playfully, leaning backwards as a chuckle arose from his throat. "I sincerely cannot believe you people! I'm not the bad guy here, alright?!? Chloe, you know that! You have to realize what I'm doing is for the good of this to--"

His rant was interrupted by a loud bang erupting from the forest. All at once, his right shoulder shot forward as something tore through the skin and his shirt, blood projecting forward violently onto Chloe. He grasped at his shirt, a wave of pain taking control of his calm state. Panic overcame him as his voice caught in his throat. He croaked out a shrill scream that sent a chill down Molly's spine as she watched him collapse to the ground.

Chapter Twenty-Nine

He was still alive. She could hear him crying.

The crowd had dispersed into a hysterical stampede of screaming children struggling to get away from wherever the shot was fired. Molly could still see him attempting to stand up as he wailed in pain, pleading humbly for any sort of help. Blood and tears dripped out of him onto the black asphalt of the parking lot. She didn't know what possessed her to do what she did next. Maybe it was her brother or her dad speaking to her from beyond their graves. Maybe it was because she had caught a glimpse of a wild-eyed Wyatt, who had taken advantage of the chaos to take down one of the guards and steal his knife to cut himself free of his binds, and she knew he was planning to attack a vulnerable Ruttledge. Maybe it was because what she said earlier was true: she was a decent human being.

Molly scrambled forward, brushing passed a group of young boys attempting to flee in the opposite direction, she picked up Ruttledge's arm, her hands squishing against the blood-soaked shirt that he wore. She helped him to his feet, then assisted him in moving towards the school.

"W-why?" He managed to slur out of his quivering lips.

"Shut up and walk!" She said in between grunts as they quickly shuffled through the crowd. She could see Wyatt, a large knife in his hands as he scanned frantically over the heads for his target.

The kids were scattering like ants in all different directions, but they were slowly but surely moving towards the wide-open doors of the school, which seemed empty from where she was. A couple of minutes went by with her head being filled with screams from random kids and the occasional whimper from Ruttledge, who was barely holding onto consciousness.

Their feet finally met the green tile of the hallway. She could hear the blood dripping from him splat onto the shiny surface below.

She turned around, glaring at the empty opening back outside. Wyatt wasn't there.

Okay, okay. She thought to herself. *Just keep moving towards the nurse's office!*

Ruttledge groaned in her ear as they turned a corner. They reached the door and she slung it open violently. They limped inside, and she sat him down on the examining table, opening his shirt and exposing the wound.

She had never seen a bullet wound before, but it seemed the bullet had passed clean through, missing his heart and any arteries. He was bleeding a lot, however, and she had to act quickly.

"It's okay, Ruttledge! I'm going to get you patched up!"

She rushed over to the cabinet behind her, grasping at the first aid kit and pulled out a piece of thread and a needle. She returned to him, inserting the needle into the wound, then pulling it through the other side as he winced in pain. The exit hole closed easily, but the entrance was more difficult to get to as she struggled to turn him over on his back. She blazed through the process of closing the second and last wound.

Okay, okay, Marcella. Now patch him up!

She turned back around to the cabinet, only to have her breath catch in her lungs as she came face-to-face with Wyatt. His hair was wild, sticking out in all different directions. His skin was as white as snow, and his eyes were dilated. He clenched a large blade in his right hand.

She had gotten over her shock, but a fear still had an iron grip on her. She wasn't afraid for her life, but for Ruttledge. She could see the killer in her friend's eyes that she had seen the night before, but this wasn't her friend. Her friend was a narcissistic sarcastic jerk but had a lovable fire to him. This was something else. This scared her.

"W-Wyatt, listen to me for a second." She spoke calmly, her hands out in front of her.

He stared into her eyes as he spoke, clenching the handle of the knife until his knuckles turned white.

"Get out of my way," He responded firmly, his voice raspy and weak.

"You're in pain, Wy! You're not thinking straight! Don't do something you might regret!"

Wyatt inhaled sharply, then exhaled a shaky breath before he responded.

"What happens if I don't, Mol? What happens if he sends another innocent child to their horrific death again? That's something I don't ever want to regret."

420

Molly was careful with her words as she reached up cautiously, running her hand through his wild brown hair. She could see tears welling up in his eyes before he blinked them away.

"I'm so sorry you're in pain, Wy. I'm so sorry I haven't been able to stop it! "

He squeezed his eyes shut, goosebumps growing across the skin of his neck and arms from the feeling of her fingers sliding through his hair. His lips quivered as he struggled to hold back the urge to fall into her arms and cry. She was right. He was in so much pain. His brain was throbbing uncontrollably with every single heartbeat, and it was agonizing.

"I'm sorry.... I'm sorry....I have to, Molly. He'll kill more people." He whispered as if trying to convince himself.

"No, you don't! You don't! He won't, I'll make him swear! I'm saving his life right now! You have to let me, Wy!" She begged.

Wyatt opened his eyes weakly, but before he could respond, a voice rang from the doorway. A rage-filled yell with a familiarity that shook both of them. Wyatt turned around, his heart dropping as his eyes locked on his late best friend charging towards him.

"Richards!"

A red-faced Derek Hoff rushed forward, a scream like an injured animal erupting from his throat as he slammed into Wyatt, his hands wrapped around his neck. Wyatt stumbled backward from the impact, then collided with the windowpane behind him. They grunted and fought against each other as Wyatt dropped his knife, the metal of the blade clanging on the tile floor. Molly had stumbled and fallen trying to move out of the way as the two boys struggled for the upper hand.

"Der-Derek!" Wyatt struggled to talk as Derek pushed against his face.

"You're freaking dead, Richards!" He yelled, his raspy vocals echoing across the room.

"Der—Derek! Please!"

Molly scrambled to her feet, grasping at Derek's shoulders as she tried to pry him from Wyatt with all her strength. Wyatt was squirming underneath his choke hold, kicking frantically and burying his fingers in his friend's face. Derek launched backwards into her as she tumbled to the ground once again. He had grabbed a hold of Wyatt's wild hair as he moved backwards, pulling Wyatt forward, as he screamed in pain. Derek sidestepped, turning his body while simultaneously throwing Wyatt headfirst through the window, shattering the glass. Wyatt lay motionless on the grass outside.

"Derek, w-w-wait! Stop!"

He ignored his best friend's weak pleas as he grasped the knife on the ground, then climbed through the opening. He was oblivious to the sharp glass on the edge that sliced through his palms as blood trickled from his hands.

Wyatt's head thumped like a drum as he grasped at the blades of grass that were still wet from the morning dew. He lunged forward in attack mode as Derek sliced through the air with the blade in his hands, blood slinging through the air from his palm, Wyatt dodged to his left, jabbed a palm forward against his friend's throat. He gripped his windpipe violently as Derek stumbled backwards against the wall, dropping the knife in surprise. Wyatt gained leverage as Derek leaned against the empty windowsill, scratching at Wyatt's hand desperately. He gave up scratching and began throwing wild punches towards his face. Most missed in his panic, but he managed to connect a right hook with his cheek. Wyatt stumbled backwards from the punch, which made his brain throb even more, and he groaned as he grasped his head. Derek, taking advantage of the opportunity, charged forward and speared him in the gut. They collapsed to the ground in a mass of body parts before Derek planted his knee in Wyatt's chest. He threw a jab, connecting with Wyatt's right eye.

"Why?!?"

He threw another identical punch.

"Why would you do that to me?!? You abandoned me! You left me to die!"

Derek slammed a hammer fist down on his right eye as Wyatt whimpered underneath the brunt of Derek's rage.

"You were my best friend!"

Wyatt coughed weakly. His eye was swollen to the point where nothing but purple flesh could be seen. He let out a raspy croak in response.

"I-I-I-I'm sorry! I'm sorry! I am your best friend!" He cried. A sudden, awfully loud *pop* erupted in his ears. It sounded as if someone had fired a rifle an inch from his head, a constant ringing now prevalent as he struggled against the worst pain of his life.

Derek's rage came out in a stream of vulgarity before he spoke again, pulling back to swing once more. "No! You can't say that! You don't get to say that!"

He suddenly felt something sharp and cold against the back of his head. As he attempted to turn around, an agonizingly sharp pain erupted from the top of his ear down to the ear lobe. He could feel the cold air striking the raw, torn skin as he caught his breath. A gush of warm crimson flowed down his neck to soak his shirt.

He let out a scream as he cupped his hand around where his ear had once been. He collapsed to the ground, shrieking until his voice became hoarse. His tear-filled eyes began to focus on Molly, who grasped the knife in her hands. Her eyes were wide, and she exhaled a heavy, shaking breath. Blood was splattered across her pale face diagonally, and it was an astonishing realization that it was his own. Alex and Pbn'J had made their way over during the fight, and Chloe had witnessed from the nurse's office on the other side of the window opening.

"Holy crap! That's a lot of blood!" Porter said, his face growing cold and pale as his mouth hung agape in astonishment. Wyatt sat up off the ground, grasping his head with his one good eye closed. Molly dropped the knife, then knelt to look at the opening in Derek's head she had caused.

"Alex, get my medicine bag from the room we slept in! Porter, Chloe, help me get him inside!" She began spitting out orders as

425

she tried to lift him to his feet. He stood on wobbling knees, blood squirting and bubbling from between his fingers as he gripped the side of his head tightly.

"We have to stop the bleeding!" She removed her jacket, then held it to the wound as Derek sobbed while wincing in pain. It soaked through the fabric, the warmth of the crimson reaching her hand. Alex was underneath the other arm, helping their disoriented friend back through the window opening. Molly spoke over her shoulder as they moved.

"Wyatt, I need you to come with us! Go see if you can find any other medical supplies! I think we're out of stitches!"

Alex cleared out the glass from the window opening, climbed inside, then pulled Derek through. Molly received no response from Wyatt, so she called out once more.

"Wy!" She called. She turned her head to look for him, only to find his body on the ground and his face against the grass. His legs were kicking, and his arms flailed slightly.

"Wyatt?" She ran over, kneeling in the grass and pulling him over to see his beaten face. His skin was hot, yet pale. His one visible eye that was not swollen began to roll upwards, his muscles tightening and his back arching. A brown froth of stomach bile

426

erupted from his lips. Molly's worst fears about Wyatt's health had become a reality and she knew the seizure was a sign of internal bleeding of the brain. He was having an aneurysm.

****

"Chloe, please I need your help!" Molly said as she lifted Wyatt's neck and turned him over on his side to keep him from choking on the bile. He was kicking hard, his arms flailing about uncontrollably. This sight terrified her, and she could tell it was scarring Chloe as she began to tear up.

"Oh, God! I'm so sorry! I should never have pulled that alarm!" She paced back and forth, wringing her hands. Guilt was devouring her from the inside out.

Molly attempted to calm her down, but there wasn't much she could do without letting go of her friend's head, who was barely hanging on to his life. She held one hand out firmly.

"Chloe, don't! If you want to help fix this, go get a pillow and a book or something to support his head!"

Chloe's lips quivered as she wiped hot tears from her eyes, the cold wind striking her face as she turned to run inside. Molly averted her attention downward. The foam and saliva had begun trailing down the side of his cheek to the grass at her knees. His movements were slowing, and she was struggling to remember whether this was a good sign or not.

"You can't die now, Wy! You've done too much! You've survived too much to die now! We have to finish this! You have to see this through until the end!" Tears began streaming down her face.

"Here! Here!" Chloe came back in a huff, a pillow and a thick textbook under both arms. She placed it under the struggling boy's head, whose body was beginning to calm its spastic movements. His one eye closed shut as he nodded to the left with a strong exhale through his nose. She wiped the bile from his lips to clear the airway, then placed two fingers on his wrist to check for a pulse.

Nothing. Her heart caught in her chest as her face burned hot with a frustration. She placed her fingers underneath his neck, where she finally felt a faint, yet steady thump.

She let out a shaky expletive in relief, her tears pelting his unconscious face and streaming to the ground. She turned to Chloe, who had her head buried in her hands, crying.

"Chloe, please stay here and watch him for me. I have to stitch up Derek." She stood up rapidly as her friend nodded.

Chloe fell next to her friend, buried her face in his sweat and blood-soaked shirt, then sobbed uncontrollably.

****

Wyatt's one uninjured eye stared up at the ceiling. He was confused as to why his other eye wouldn't open. As he sat up, a torrent of pain overwhelmed him. He groaned, then looked around. He was in the nurse's office, and someone with a familiar face that was beaten to a pulp was propped up against the wall sitting on the nurse's table. A bandage was wrapped around his chest and a white patch was on his left shoulder.

"Look who's awake!" Ruttledge said enthusiastically. Wyatt stared him down from where he sat on the floor. He had a crick in his neck from the way his head had been positioned. Instead of responding in anger, he simply asked the question that he was desperate for an answer to.

"What....happened?" He asked calmly, his voice coming out slower than he wanted.

"You had a seizure. I was shot. Your girlfriend cut off your dead buddy's ear."

Wyatt rubbed his temples with shaking hands, wanting to sob from the pain and the haze his head was in. Suddenly, Ruttledge said something that caused a cold shiver to run down his spine.

"Listen, I know we've been at odds over the last couple of days we have known each other. I was hoping while we were here, we could make amends. I'd rather not have to live with the fact that I didn't bury the hatchet with a dying man, when I had the chance, you know?"

Wyatt swallowed the lump in his throat. "Wh-what did you say?"

He could tell from the look on Ruttledge's face that he had slipped something out that he knew he shouldn't have said. "I just said let's make amends, that's all."

Wyatt leaned forward, uttering a phrase that Ruttledge often used.

"Don't lie to me. Did you say that I'm....dying?"

Ruttledge ran a finger across the patch on his shoulder, which Wyatt assumed was the gunshot wound. "You...You had a seizure because.... that's what happens when you have an aneurysm."

"English please."

"It means your brain is bleeding, and there's no way to stop it without a professional surgeon."

Wyatt nodded slowly, suddenly cautious of all his movements. He gently grasped his hair, his fingers shaking as he slid them through to the back of his head. Every second now meant something to him.

He didn't care that he was losing his life. He just cared about his friends. He wanted to make sure they were safe. With him gone, an indirect threat was also gone.

But what about the scarecrow?

Silence spread across the room, before Ruttledge broke the awkward tension.

"That just means you won't be in this Hell anymore." He took a sip of something in his hand that Wyatt hadn't noticed before. It looked like a whiskey glass. "I apologize to you   for what happened between us. I'm sorry that our views conflicted each other."

Wyatt looked up at him from his hands. "How long do I have to live?"

Ruttledge turned his head and looked out the window. "To be completely honest with you.... I'm surprised you woke up in the first place. I'd expect it to happen.... before the sun goes down." A single tear had formed in Wyatt's eye, before it trickled down his nose. He sniffled. "You want to fix things between us?"

"Yes."

Wyatt licked his lips. "I'm going to need you to….to tell…to tell your boys to let me have a couple of weapons. Let me say my goodbyes.... then I need you to lock…lock Molly in one of the classrooms."

Ruttledge raised an eyebrow as he rubbed his chin, thinking. "That's a... uh...That's one strange final request there. Why on God's green earth would you want me to do that?"

Wyatt stood up slowly, his knees threatening to buckle from underneath him as he made his way to the door. "Because I've done…bad…a lot of bad to a lot of people. I don't want to go out like that. I want to go out remembered…. for good…for doing something good."

He turned the knob, letting himself out into the cold hallway.

****

Molly could hardly eat, but she knew that she needed to. After everything she had seen, the blood and destruction, there was no way she could possibly ever desire food. She had to eat, though. She had stitched up everyone who needed it. Ruttledge had been okay, after some squirming as she finished on the last wound. Derek had screamed more but was just as content with the job she had done mending the hole in his head she herself had caused. He looked at her with disgust the entire time as she did. Alex had caught this and scolded him about how she could have just let him sit there and bleed, but she wasn't, she was fixing him. He hadn't responded to this. He only stared at the wall until she finished. When it was over, he walked away from the school, leading a group of kids who were willing back to the town square.

She was alone at a table as she opened a small bag of chips, crunching away at them as her mind was racing. She could hear her Dad's faint voice, a depiction of what he would say, or rather what she *hoped* he would say to her if he could see what she had done.

I'm proud of you, Marcella.

I know, Dad. I've tried to do what you've always taught me. She responded to her imagination.

433

Take care of people, no matter who they are or what they've done. Treat others the way you want to be treated. That was your mother's philosophy.

Molly traced her fingers in a ring around the top of her cola can as she smiled. It had been a while since a happy thought like that had surfaced amongst the chaos around her that constantly called for her undivided attention.

She was alone in the cafeteria, when the sound of a knock on the two wooden doors behind her that led inside echoed off the walls. She turned to see Wyatt, and she almost began weeping. He looked as if he would fall over any second as he swayed back and forth. The one good eye looked downward, and his other remained swollen from his face being beaten in by Derek. She had no idea if the eye could be saved, and it wouldn't matter, anyways. Wyatt Richards was dying, despite her many efforts, but she didn't want him to know. She didn't know what she herself would do if she had the privilege of knowing which breaths would be her last, let alone someone with the unpredictable personality that he had.

"Hi," He spoke, his tone soft and caring. She stood from her seat and walked over to him, the only sound being the clicking of her boot heels on the tile floor as she stepped. She tenderly wrapped her arms around his neck in an embrace. He returned the gesture without hesitation. She could hear him crying.

"T-thank you for everything you've done for me," He said gasping at almost every word. He was bawling like a child, and she felt so horrible for him. His last moments were in pain, and she couldn't stop it.

"It's okay, Wy. If I could, I'd do it all again." She said as she held the back of his head, her fingers caressing his hair.

"I'm sorry for the way I am. I'm sorry I was so freaking stubborn. I'm sorry I got Desmond killed. I'm sorry.... I-I'm so sorry," He said gently as he pulled back to face her, wiping the tears from his eyes.

She shook her head slowly with a slight smile. "That wasn't on you, Wy. You are who you are. You shouldn't be sorry for that, no matter how annoying you might be," She hit him with a mixture of her eyebrow raise and a mock of his signature smirk. He smiled back.

"That's why…that's why I have to do this." He said.

Her curiosity about his statement was met with a rush of guards, who grabbed her arms softly, yet restricting her movements. She didn't resist, as she was too confused. She stared into his one, green eye.

"Your eyes are pretty.... I-I don't know if I ever told you that. I-I can't remember." He croaked out. The fact that it seemed like it was a struggle for him to make this statement, yet he made it anyways, hit her like a truck.

"Wy...what are you doing?" She stared into his eyes, tears swelling as he began backing through the door frame

He smiled at her one last time. In that moment, even with his head in a fog and his heart conflicted about the decision he was about to make, Wyatt was finally certain how he felt about her.

"I'm going to avenge your brother."

****

"Wyatt! You're okay!" Isaac dropped his portable game system on the mattress he sat on and bolted up from his bed, running towards the teenager and hugging his chest. "What happened? Who started shooting? Is everyone okay?"

Wyatt struggled to find the words he looked for. It was as if his brain was restarting frequently like a computer. "Hey…doofus." He forced a smile that soon faded once he finally registered the questions. Lucy had walked up behind him, her arms crossed in an attitude that resembled the look Molly had given him when they first met.

"Slow down, Loser. Let him talk." She said with a chuckle.

"Oh...yeah. I th-think everyone's alright." He said as he gave Isaac a weak attempt at a noogie.

"Awesome!" Isaac said enthusiastically. "Hey, do you think when we get back to the house that we can watch *Ghostbusters 2*? It's not too scary, I promise!"

"Sure...whatever...you want."

"Sweet!"

He ran back over to the mattress and plopped down, grabbing his system and resuming the game. Lucy brought her voice down to a whisper.

"Hey, I'm thinking about naming the baby Indy....after your favorite movie character!"

Wyatt shook his head to signal her to stop talking. "No, d-don't t-t-tell me...something that will get me e-emotionally...s-stirred up."

"Why not?"

"B-because," He struggled to let out. "I'm dying."

Her words caught in her throat as her eyes grew wide. "What?"

"I'll be g-gone soon. I.....I'm bleeding from the inside. N-n-no way to fix…"

There was a silence between them as Wyatt turned and looked at Isaac, who was too entranced in his game to hear them. "I can't tell him. I can't...Just know that i-i-if you e-ever need anything.... p-people here…p-people…will h-help you..."

Tears began to form in her eyes as she bolted forward and hugged him. He could hear her sniffling.

"Stay s-s-safe. D-d-don't go…don't…don't go…"

"Into the forest," She finished his thought as she pulled away and wiped her nose with her sleeve.

He nodded, then looked at Isaac one last time. Wyatt said goodbye, then walked out of the room.

Chapter Thirty

Derek sat down in the town bar. It wasn't a place well known to families in Lyonside since it wasn't a family-oriented place, and rebellious teenagers had all but given up trying to con their way in and had moved on to more accessible places. It was more of a dive bar, where the few singles that resided nearby, who had also evidently been taken with the rest of the adults, would often frequent to mingle with each other. It was still in order. The countertop shined, and the neon signs blinked in many different vibrant colors advertising various alcoholic drinks. Derek never really cared for the idea of drinking, but today was different. He had never had a drink before, but he was in the mood for any thing strong. He needed it after everything that had happened that morning.

He poured himself a few drops of what he thought was scotch from a fancy bottle with a name that was uninterpretable. He threw the brown liquor down, the sensation immediately burning the back of his tongue and his throat. He spit out the burning stuff onto the nice counter, gagging and coughing. He then considered starting with something that had less of a kick.

He poured himself a glass of beer from the tap and sat down at the dusty piano that made its home in the corner of the room. He could play. He couldn't play more than one thing, but he could still play. The first minutes of Bill Wither's "Lean on Me" was the only thing he had ever managed to pick out, so his fingers found their places on the white and black keys, moving back and forth to create the melody that almost made him cry. He needed to distract himself from the world with the most beautiful of techniques: music. The music was a much-needed distraction, although, it seemed slightly muffled behind the gauze that covered the right side of his head. Derek closed his eyes as his hands danced along, starting over once he had played all he knew. His mom was the one who taught him how to concentrate his gift of music. He was so entranced in his creation that his one good ear had refused to pick up the sound of the bar door opening. When he stopped to start the song over once more, a voice interrupted the tranquility of the moment.

"I d-didn't know you…you could p-p-lay like that." A distant sounding, hoarse Wyatt spoke to him from the front door, his hands shoved in his jacket pockets as his dirty, red shoes shuffled across the wooden floor. Derek turned in his seat and glared at him. Wyatt noticed the bandage Molly had used on his ear that stretched across his head.

"What do you want?" He asked to his friend in an unexpectedly calm manor, but the tone in his voice revealed more.

Wyatt tilted his head slightly, like a curious dog. "Jeez… S-she really…did a n-number on…on you, huh?" He spoke as his eyes focused on the blood-stained white bandage.

Derek lifted a hand and gently caressed the material with his fingertips. She had forever scarred him physically, and Wyatt had forever scarred him mentally. Derek glared at his former friend; eyes slightly squinted as he studied his injuries. Derek had beaten him until the whole right side of his face was black and blue, but only his eye was swollen. He had a revolver strapped to his waist on his belt, and his short, stubby sawed-off shotgun slung across his back.

Wyatt stared back. He approached his friend with a request, a plea. He knew it was unethical after everything they had done to each other, but he had no other choice.

"I n-n-need your...your help."

A smirk of disbelief grew as Derek scoffed and looked at the ground. He shook his head, wincing slightly at the throbbing in the side of his head from his wound. "After what you did to me...that's a ballsy thing to say, you know that?"

Wyatt nodded as he struggled to speak. "I k-k-know..."

Derek's smirk disappeared from his face, but he continued to stare at the floor. His hand was gripping the empty shot glass that rested on top of the piano. Wyatt wondered if his friend knew that he was running low on time, that he could fall any second and be gone forever. He decided not to mention his imminent demise.

"Derek...p-p-plea--" He attempted to ask again but was met with an explosion of anger as Derek threw the glass at him. He ducked his throbbing head as it shattered against the door behind him. He looked back up at Derek who met him with wide, angry eyes.

"Get out of my sight before I do something I might regret." He spoke firmly, pointed a finger towards the two doors behind him.

TAKEN BY THE NIGHT

Wyatt stood for a second, his instinct urging him to challenge his friend's authority, but the unbearable pain in his head forced him down as he slowly nodded. He turned around, his sneakers squeaking as he limped his way towards the door.

****

"Let me go! Please! He's going to get himself killed!" Molly begged as she beat on the door, tears burning hot as they streamed down her face. When the guards had thrown her inside the locker room, she began to realize what Wyatt had meant. He was going to the cornfield: the same place Desmond had been brutally murdered.

"I'm begging you!"

She couldn't lose another person to that God-forsaken scarecrow. She refused to let anyone else die. She reached and pulled the fire extinguisher from its wall holster.

"Let me go!" She smashed the object against the door handle with an echoing clang as the metal slammed together. It put a dent across the end of the silver handle but did nothing to the lock. She spewed out a string of curse words as she threw the red capsule onto the ground, frustrated and filled with sorrow. She screamed until her face turned ruby red as she grasped at her messy black hair that hung in front of her eyes. She balled into a sitting fetal position in a corner of the room, between the walls and the bright cherry lockers. She wrapped her arms around her knees and stared at the wall in front of her, eyes glazed with tears that were reluctant to fall.

Wy, what are you doing?!? She thought to herself. *He was going to go die in the cornfield. He was wise enough to know he couldn't do it alone!*

That's why he's doing it. She reasoned to herself. *He wants to die. He knows he's dying. He wants to go out with a bang. What else could be expected of someone like him?*

But how does he know? The only people who have such extensive knowledge of his condition are Alex, Ruttledge, and Chloe!

She heard the squeak of the door opening as it echoed across the room. She leapt to her feet, rushing over to where all three of them stood. Ruttledge had his hands behind his back in a gentlemanly manner.

"Wyatt's gone!" She blurted out. Alex and Chloe were startled by this revelation, while Molly stared at Ruttledge's emotionless face, waiting for some sort of reaction.

"What do you mean he's gone? Did....did he...?" Chloe's eyes began to tear up.

"No, but if somebody doesn't stop him, he will! He's going to the cornfield!"

This piece of information granted a puzzled look from Rutt, a look displaying a mind at work.

"What?!? Why would he do something so stupid?!?" Alex asked, her voice shaking as she held back panic.

"He has to know he's dying! Did any of you tell him about the aneurysm?"

Both girls shook their head, then slowly turned to the silent Ruttledge, who was picking at the bandage across his shoulder. He nodded.

"Yeah. I did. It accidentally came out while I was under the influence of your medication after Chloe shot me."

Chloe was taken aback by this comment, her face turning red as she began to defend herself. "I didn't shoot you! The barrel was at your temple! If I shot you, you'd be dead, not have a hole in your shoulder."

"You didn't lower the gun and shoot me?"

"No!"

Ruttledge shook his head, as if trying to pop something loose in his head. "I'm sorry. That was an....ignorant assumption."

Molly wanted to jump out of her skin from the buildup of anxiety inside her. "We need to find Wyatt! He may already be there right now! He needs help!"

Alex nodded, a controlled, firm face radiating a sense of calmness to her as she turned to Chloe.

"Chlo, get to the cornfield as fast as you can. Take the red sedan out front. It belongs to our principal. I'm going to get someone who might help."

Ruttledge fished a hand into his jean pockets, pulling out a single key that had a car company's logo on it. "Here, I found it in his desk."

Chloe snatched the key and took off out the door at full speed. Alex left right behind her. As Molly attempted to move through the doorway, Ruttledge held out an arm to stop her.

"No, Molly." He shook his head solemnly. "You're not going."

"Are you freaking insane?!?" She pushed his arm away violently.

"No. I'm just keeping a promise I made." He responded gruffly.

"I swear, Rutt, I'll--"

446

Ruttledge suddenly burst into a fit of rage that must have been pent up inside, a sign that he was feeling guilty about something. "You aren't going to do anything! You deck me, there's a line of football players behind this doorway I've ordered to keep you here."

Molly took a step back, her bottom lip quivering as her rage dissolved into helplessness. Tears streamed from her eyes.

"Fine! Please, go get him! Send some guys! Please!"

Ruttledge shook his head. "Wyatt wouldn't want anyone else sacrificing their lives for him. You know that!"

Molly gritted her teeth and arched her eyebrows. "You have no idea what he wants! You don't know anything about him!"

Ruttledge nodded in agreement as he ran a hand over his re-greased hair. "You're right. Maybe that's where I went wrong."

****

Wyatt Richards stood on the lonely dirt road, the music from his earbuds blasting through his head. He couldn't tell, though. He only heard a distant muffle. He had reached up to his ear before he put them in and felt something warm inside with his finger. It was blood. He could hardly see out of his one blurry eye and his balance was off. He barely made it to his destination with the canister of gasoline in one hand before the pain started once again, a headache that he couldn't believe was real. His phone fell from his hand and yanked his headphones out somewhere along the road, but he didn't care. The agony was the most intense he had ever felt in his life. Wyatt didn't want to stand anymore. He didn't want to walk anymore. He just wanted to lay down and let fate take its course.

C'mon, Richards. There's always a way to keep going. You're almost done!

He stared into the cornfield, the cold wind striking against his skin. He had a plan. He would pour a trail of the fuel around the perimeter of the field, then he would enter and light it. Was it a smart plan? Probably not. His mind didn't exactly work well enough at that moment to even form a sentence, let alone a complex plan to slay a monster. He just knew that he had flames and a lot of firepower by his side. A lot of destruction was all he needed. He didn't need to take precautions, because nobody was going to make it out alive. If he was going down, he was going to take this thing down with him.

Those things want us to scream. They want us to cry. I....I won't give them that satisfaction. He began justifying his actions to himself. *I'm going to.... I'm going to....I'm....I'll make fun of their stupid faces! If I die doing that...so be it! The others should just bury me six feet under and finish the punchline.*

He halfway expected resistance from the creature when he began pouring the gas along the outside layer of stalks. He wanted the thing to try and stop him. However, he received nothing as it took everything in him to finish the job.

He walked deep into the stalks, turned around, then dropped his open lighter onto the gas trail, sending a train of hot fury along the edge of the field.

"Checkmate, freak." He coughed out as he fought off the blurriness.

He waited for something, anything except the billowing fire that grew steadily nearby, the crackling of the burning leaves and corn around him. His eyes wandered around, until they locked on the top of Farmer Burnett's house, where a form sat on the roof, its legs dangling from the edge as it stared at Wyatt. He could make out a large hat on its head, and a long stick with a blade across his lap. The fire hadn't encircled him yet, so he had time to make his way to the farmhouse. The climb up the creaky stairs was brutal, as his legs threatened to give out on him any second.

449

Come on, Wyatt.

He reached the top, where he exited a window onto the roof, his legs begging to give up and slip out from under him. He could smell the rising smoke. The figure stayed sitting as it hummed a grotesque version of Rolling Stone's "Paint It, Black". Wyatt wondered how this thing knew what music he had been listening to during the walk there.

"Do you know who I am?" The scarecrow finally said, his head down, staring into the rising fire in the field below them.

Wyatt could barely put together the thought as the pain struck once again in a vicious wave.

You're the thing that killed my friend's brother.

"You....you..."

"What's wrong, Wyatt? Cat got your tongue?" The thing turned its head slightly to where Wyatt could see its green eyes. They were greener than his own, and his strawberry red hair poked out from beneath the hat in jumbles with bits of hay.

"I'm gonna.... I'm-I'm gonna...." Wyatt slurred his words as he reached for the revolver on his hip, leveling it at the creature's head with an unsteady aim.

TAKEN BY THE NIGHT

"My name is Robbie. Maybe you remember me from algebra class, without the terrifying look." He stood and faced Wyatt, who was instantly taken aback by his face. His complexion was grotesque, and he was hideously thin. From the neck up, his skin had the look of a burlap sack tied with a rope around his throat. His smile looked as if someone had cut a hole through the material to create a huge grin, filled with sharp, thin teeth. However, this isn't what made Wyatt feel uneasy. His left eye, along with the pasty freckled skin surrounding it, was human. The recognition hit him like a freight train as not terror, but guilt ate away at him.

The boy from the alley.

Chapter Thirty-One

Derek was laying down on the bar, his feet dangling on both sides. He had finished a few beers, the bottles scattered along the floor. He didn't think he was quite drunk, but he wasn't exactly sober. He heard the door sling open as Alex stomped in with a rage-filled expression spread across her face.

"Why didn't you answer my calls?!?" She near about yelled.

"Oh, I'm sorry. I didn't want to get blood on my phone," He pointed at his injured ear sarcastically. This infuriated her.

"I had to ask around to find you. Is that why you're in here? You're sulking? Feeling bad for yourself?" She kicked a bottle, the glass clinking as it rolled across the room and smacked against a chair leg.

"Oh, lay off, Princess!" He sat up, exploding at her. "Over the last few days, I've had my parents disappear, had a friend die, had another friend abandon me, *literally* walked through that Hell we call the forest, and I've had my ear chopped off like a slab of meat! I think I deserve a little bit of sulking!"

Alex crossed her arms and shook her head in disappointment. "You're unbelievable, you know that? Everyone here has lost something. Molly had to bury her brother! I've watched friends get taken by things that shouldn't exist! I lost you, Derek! And now your best friend, who would do anything for you, is out there dying! He's sacrificing himself to that thing in the cornfield because he thinks he has to make up for his past mistakes! You want to sit here and ridicule him, yet he's being braver than you've ever been!"

Derek's look displayed shock as he took in the information. "Wyatt's dying?"

"Yeah, and you aren't there for him. If we lose him, that's on you." She turned and started storming off towards the door. "Me and Chloe are going to try and help take the scarecrow down."

Derek shook his head solemnly. "You don't get it. He may still be here for a little while longer, but I lost Wyatt a long time ago when he left me to die. I'm returning the favor. He sacrificed everything for everyone else, but when I was going to die, guess what happened?!? He stepped on the gas and didn't look back!"

Alex shook her head as she turned back around, her face as red as a tomato and her eyes tearing up in anger. "Oh, get over it! So what?!? Maybe he just had a moment of weakness! Just like you're having right now! The town needs you now more than ever and you're throwing yourself a pity party!" Alex turned back around, her clenched fists shaking as she stomped out of the bar, her boots violently stomping on the hardwood flooring. She pushed open the double doors, leaving Derek to stew in his loathing.

His head was fuzzy as he stared down at his hands.

Alex was already getting into her car, when Derek ran out of the bar, waving his car keys in his hands.

****

The scarecrow began walking towards Wyatt, whose skin had turned pale. He was struggling to breathe, gasping for each breath as he stared into the eyes of his doom.

"I'm going to kill you." He closed his mutated eyes. "I just have one question: Why?"

"Why....what?" Wyatt let out.

TAKEN BY THE NIGHT

The scarecrow came uncomfortably close as he waited for an answer, but Wyatt wouldn't back down. He stood and stared into both eyes, one normal and the other beady with a red iris. It exhaled slowly, breathing a gut-wrenching stench into his face. Wyatt pressed the end of the barrel to the creature's soft chest.

"Rob....Robbie...I," He tried to speak once again, but nothing came out. He was trying so desperately to explain himself. He tried to say that it was fear. It was always fear, though he never admitted it. He was a coward, always looking out for himself. He had left everyone. He abandoned Robbie, as he did Derek, as he even did to Molly. He left her behind so he could come justify himself and do what? Save the town? Die a hero? No, he wasn't a hero. He would never be.

Robbie shook his head as his arm suddenly launched forward, wrapping his clawed hands around Wyatt's throat, causing him to drop his gun. He coughed and sputtered as he scratched at the creature's iron grip. He began choking and wheezing as Robbie lifted him from the ground with a supernatural strength he had only seen in movies. The only air that entered his lungs was the black cloud of smoke that had surrounded them during their conversation.

A viciously loud bang erupted from behind Wyatt as the scarecrow recoiled backwards, a hideous screech exploding from beyond its disgusting yellow teeth.

It dropped Wyatt, who collapsed on the roof, rolling towards the edge. They were a good two stories up in the air. A fall from that height wouldn't kill him, but he was sure it would knock the air out of him. He was able to stay on the tile as he looked up. Chloe had found him and climbed her way through the window, firing off a shot from her gun. The scarecrow's face now had a gaping hole in between the eyes as it regained its composure. The mixture of a monster and teenager chuckled.

"Oh, you *really* shouldn't have done that, sweetie." Robbie said as a twisted grin grew on his face.

Chloe fired off more rounds, the bullets soaring through his ragged, flannel shirt. The scarecrow bolted forward, swinging his scythe towards her. She dodged to her left and pressed the barrel of her pistol against him and pulled the trigger again. The noise rattled in Wyatt's brain, causing him to quickly shut his eyes from the pain. He could feel the heat of the fire around them rising. *Was it at the house?*

TAKEN BY THE NIGHT

He pulled his shotgun from its scabbard and aimed as he propped himself up on a knee. Chloe and the thing were now wrestling over the scythe. Wyatt knew he had to shoot, but the scatter of lead would be too wide, and the risk of accidentally hitting Chloe was too great.

He struggled to let out a loud grunt through dry lips and a hoarse voice in order to get her attention.

She must have understood what he was trying to do as she kicked at the thing's chest, sending it sprawling backwards. Wyatt pulled the trigger, putting all his strength into controlling the powerful recoil.

BLAM!

Wyatt screamed as the blast rung in his ears, the barrel kicking upwards as the buckshot scattered into the monster, causing it to fall out of sight off the other side of the building.

Wyatt dropped the shotgun in exhaustion, letting the steel barrel clink against the tile and slide off the edge of the roof.

"Is he...." She began to ask in between gasps to catch her breath.

Wyatt didn't even try to speak. He just nodded as he stood, every movement sending a wave of pain through him.

Something suddenly cawed next to them. Wyatt couldn't clearly see what it was, but some type of bird was hovering around Chloe. She swatted at it in surprise as more began to swarm around her blonde hair. Wyatt took a step back in shock as she began to scream, and she suddenly stumbled, falling off the edge of the roof in a panic.

Chloe!

A sickening *thud* came from below. He knelt to look over the edge. She was on the ground not far from the fire, frantically swinging her revolver in the air to ward off the crows that relentlessly harassed her. She fired off a couple of shots, finally scaring them away into a flutter of feathers.

Something suddenly yanked Wyatt's hair, slinging him onto his back. He wailed in agony. Robbie was back on top of the roof, the blade of his scythe ringing in the air as he swung it like a pendulum near his feet, back and forth as he snickered.

"You're going to have to do better than that." He spoke, a snake-like hiss in his tone.

Wyatt backed up on his hands before sliding out the revolver in his waistband, firing off as many shots as possible into the creature's chest.

TAKEN BY THE NIGHT

Bang! Bang! Bang! Bang! Bang!

Robbie recoiled slightly, but this did nothing but infuriate him. He backhanded the blade into the revolver, sending the gun flying off the roof in a spray of blood as the sharp end sliced open Wyatt's wrist.

Wyatt gasped in pain as Robbie curled his hand around his throat, sneering and cackling in his face like a psychopath. He suddenly slung Wyatt through the window frame of the room Chloe had emerged from earlier, his body crashing through the glass as he plummeted to the floor.

He struggled to keep his eyes open as he lifted himself up once again, the cuts on his back from the glass raw and stinging, his bloody hand leaving prints on the white rug. He could feel the intense heat of a nearing flame.

Is that the best you've got?!? He taunted internally, wobbling as he attempted to stand. He was certain the words were not coming out the way he wanted them to.

Robbie's tall, slender, frame barely fit through the opening into the bedroom. He had to slouch to stand. He smiled, a giddy expression on his horrific face. It reminded Wyatt of a child. It reminded him that the terror in front of him had once been just like himself.

"This is fun!" He growled.

****

"Will you slow down?!?" Alex begged Derek as she gripped her armrest, her nails digging into the leather lining. He had already almost taken a corner way too hard and nearly flipped the already beaten down truck.

"No time!" He slammed his foot on the accelerator.

"How buzzed are you?!?" She scolded with her eyes shut. She could smell the exhaust coming from the roaring engine. Opening her eyes, she studied the bandages that wrapped around Derek's head from his injury. Both him and his truck were scarred from what they both went through. They matched: red, damaged, but still running strong.

"Not enough for this." He responded gruffly, the sound of the tires throwing around gravel behind them.

He suddenly braked, slinging Alex into the dash and making her regret not buckling up.

"What?!? What is it?!?" She nearly shouted, agitated with his lack of care.

TAKEN BY THE NIGHT

He put the car in park, then kicked his door open and hopped out, running to the front of the truck and bending down out of sight. He quickly reappeared, running back to his seat and slamming the door. He tossed something in her direction. She caught it, then brought it up to her face to see.

It was a phone. She turned on the screen and was met with a picture of two football players, their helmets off and swinging from their hands. One player was holding up a peace sign, trying to act cool. The other was holding up two fingers, like bunny ears and pointing at the other player and sported a signature smirk that could be recognized anywhere. Wyatt Richards. A pair of earbuds were connected to the top, still playing what sounded like the final verse of some classic rock song.

"Is this Wyatt's?" She asked.

Derek didn't answer her. He just yanked the truck back into drive, then slammed his foot on the gas once again. The engine revved as loud as ever as they flew past the cornfield, its stalks engulfed in flames.

Derek let out an expletive before taking another hard right into Farmer Burnett's driveway, once again nearly tipping the truck over. The back end of the house was blackened from the encroaching fire. Two figures were struggling from on top of the roof, before the smaller one was thrown through the window, followed by the taller figure that resembled a scarecrow.

"We need to go help!" She cried. Her eyes focused on a figure approaching the car, passing by a tree trunk with a large fire ax sticking out of it, limping and hugging her chest as she coughed.

"Chloe!" Derek cried out as he opened the door.

"Water!" She coughed out. He could smell the smoke on her clothes, the stench radiating from her hair. She had been breathing in the thick, carbon monoxide-filled air.

He ran to his truck bed and fished out an old, half-filled water bottle and gave it to her. She chugged it down.

Derek looked up. "Alex, I need--"

She was gone. His head shot around, until his eyes focused on the missing ax in the lonely trunk.

"Alex, wait!" He looked back at Chloe, who had her hands on her knees.

"I'm fine!" She managed to say in between coughing fits. "Go find Wyatt!"

"No! I need to get you to Molly!"

"I'll be alright, Derek! Go! Please!"

TAKEN BY THE NIGHT

Derek hesitated, for a single moment, then took off back to his car and revved the engine once again.

****

Chills shivered down Wyatt's spine as he backed out of the room. His hands grasped on the counters for anything he could use as a weapon. He knocked down books and trophies as he kept his one open eye on the beast before him. His hand rested on a wooden handle. It was a baseball bat.

He lifted it as Robbie lunged forward, then brought the slugger down on the atrocity with all his remaining might. The end caught Robbie's cheek, making him stumble to the floor in surprise. His knee broke through the wood planking in the floor. He growled in frustration as he struggled to yank his leg out.

Wyatt slammed the bedroom door. He peered around the hall in a panic, then grabbed a chair and shoved the backrest underneath the knob.

He began making his way downstairs. His head began to scream with pain once again, causing him to lose his footing and stumble the rest of the way down. He groaned and whined. He couldn't think. He couldn't breathe.

He turned and faced the stairway, his eyes darting to the left as shock fell over his face. Alex Egan had her back against the wall, her hair wild and in her face and an ax that looked like it weighed twice as much as she did in her hands. She held up a finger to her lips.

Robbie didn't even struggle against the barricade. He trucked out of the room with a *crack*, wood splinters from the chair and the door scattering through the air.

Robbie snapped his head in Wyatt's direction, the gleeful smile now faded into a terrifying grimace. Wyatt held up his middle finger as his other hand found the bat again. Robbie gripped the staff of his scythe as he trotted down the stairs, each board creaking under his weight as he glared at the weakened teen that lay on the floor in front of him. He reached the bottom step. He swung the blade upward, then brought it down through the air with a vicious screech.

Wyatt pulled the bat up to his face, gripping the tip with his other hand. The wood blocked the blade with a rattling *clink*. Wyatt kicked the inside of the Scarecrow's knee, sending him into a stumble to regain his balance. Alex let out a vicious war cry that pierced Wyatt's weakened brain as she brought the ax down into Robbie's skull.

He cried out, the monster inside him howling and clawing at the split between the human side of him and the scarecrow.

His screams clawed away at the inside of Wyatt's skull. He yelled along with the monster, a chorus of pain and agony that rattled Alex to the core. Robbie recoiled away, the blade of the ax embedded in his forehead as he pulled the handle out of her hands. He wrapped his impossibly large claws around the wooden end, struggling desperately to pull the heavy object out of him. He fell to his knees, clawing at the steel in his head, his breathing raspy.

Wyatt had to end it. He had to. He was going to.

He stood on wobbly knees once again, trying to fester up his last remaining amount of strength. He lifted the bat above his head to bring it down in a last attempt to put down the monster.

Robbie suddenly turned around in a flash. He had grasped the blade of his scythe without Wyatt realizing, and was shooting upwards in Wyatt's direction. He couldn't react fast enough before the blade penetrated the skin of his side.

Wyatt gasped for air as Alex screamed in realization. He fell to the floor with a vicious *thud,* coughing and spitting blood from his lips and onto the oak wood floor.

A horn honked from behind Alex as she turned around. She quickly jumped into the kitchen and out of the main room to avoid what was coming.

An insanely loud crash commenced as Derek's truck plowed through the doorway and the surrounding wall, the tires splitting and snapping the floorboards as it smashed into Robbie's body. Straw and wooden splinters fluttered through the air before the truck came to a halt.

The flame was beginning to engulf the house as Derek stepped out of his truck and onto the broken floorboards. He offered Alex help up before rushing over to his best friend's side.

"Wyatt!"

The injured boy was attempting to stand yet again, an act his body should not have been able to perform in his physical state. He flashed Derek a look at the stab wound in his stomach. He couldn't speak, so he just nodded, every motion sending a surge of pain through his skull. He was covered in soot from the smoke. Still, he struggled to sport his grin. His chin was quivering as he tried not to cry or let his voice crack.

"Here," Derek helped him up, placing his friend's arm around his neck. "I got you."

"Is Chlo....is she..." He struggled to finish the sentence.

"She breathed in too much smoke. She needs a doctor. She needs Molly."

Wyatt looked up, his one good eye focused on Alex. "T-t-t-take...h-her."

Derek shook his head. "No, we're leaving together, brother..."

It took a second for Wyatt to form the words. "W-w-we...walk."

Alex glared at Derek with concerned eyes when she noticed both boys were crying. She couldn't help but hold back tears as well. She took one look at the injured, dying boy and knew he didn't have much longer. This was his last wish.

Alex nodded, then shuffled forward to give Wyatt a hug around his neck. She stifled a sob as she let go and started towards Derek's truck. She began bursting into tears as she backed the damaged vehicle out of the broken-down house, its structure slowly teetering on the foundation.

Derek looked at Wyatt as a cry came from behind them.

"Cowards! You would leave a boy defenseless?!? C-cowards!"

Derek turned his head slightly. He could see Robbie. His legs were missing, obliterated in the crash. Straw was sticking out of the bottom of his upper body that splayed out on the floor, his impossibly long arms clawing forward. His head split in half as he screamed in anger, his voice distorting into a garbled monster.

"He's coming!" The monster cackled. "Be afraid! Be afraid, children! He's coming!"

Derek brushed off the comments as they trotted out of the burning building. The air began to clear as they reached the road. Derek could hear the house collapsing in on itself, the wood crackling as thunder began to roll from a distant storm.

****

Ruttledge's guards stood in front of the women's locker room door, both boys standing in silence and sheer boredom. It had been some time since Molly had quieted down her yelling. She had been wanting desperately to go after the boy who had beaten Ruttledge, but they had strict orders to keep her inside.

One of the guards named Jobe had his right arm in a sling. He set his gun down, pulled out a lighter with his left arm, then a pack of cigarettes from his pockets.

"Heck of a morning, huh?"

He spoke as he opened the pack, then flicked the lighter on. The flame danced across the edge of one of the cigarettes as he held it in his mouth. He blew out a cloud of smoke through his nose nonchalantly.

"Yeah, I guess. None of this seems right in my eyes." The other guard said to him.

"How do you figure?"

"Well, the way I see it…people are just trying to survive. Ruttledge thinks his way is best, so does Wyatt. It's just sad to me that they couldn't come to terms before everything went down."

Jobe sat in silence, huffing on his cigarette. The other guard assumed he was contemplating on his own philosophy. "You want to know what I think? I think tha—"

A sudden, loud clang came from the lockers inside the room they were watching.

"Help! Something is in here with me!"

The calls echoed throughout the hallway. Molly was screaming from somewhere inside, her voice hoarse and filled with terror.

Jobe dropped the cigarette from his mouth and cursed, stomping it out as he reached down for his gun.

The other boy swung the door open, storming inside with his rifle ready with Jobe following in right after him.

The boys scanned the room but couldn't find Molly or any sort of hideous beast.

"I don't like this," Jobe exclaimed

The sound of the locker room door slamming behind them made both boys' eyes widen in realization.

One of them ran over to the handle and pulled on it. She had locked them inside.

The first boy cursed as Jobe sat down against the lockers. He pulled out another cigarette and his lighter once again.

"Clever girl."

****

Molly sprinted down the hallway, turning a corner sharply and plowing into another guard. He fell to the ground from the impact, dropping his shotgun. She quickly picked it up, then smacked him over the helmet with the stock of the gun. Another group came around the corner as she ran out the front door.

She took off at full speed, her eyes beginning to tear up, and the wind blowing through her hair, stinging the raw area beneath her eye.

470

"Molly!"

She recognized the voice calling out to her. She stopped and turned around. Alex was helping Chloe inside the building. She had not seen them in her hurry to leave.

"Molly, Chloe needs a doctor! She inhaled too much smoke! Please!"

"Where…Where is he? Where's Wyatt?" She stumbled on the words.

Alex shook her head. Molly noticed that her eyes were red from crying.

She turned back around and stared down the dirt road in the direction where she knew Wyatt had gone.

"Molly!"

Why do I care so much? Wyatt Richards was a narcissistic, sarcastic jerk. He annoyed her to death. Everything about him annoyed her. His personality. His comments. His little smirk when he said something snarky. The way he stood up for others. The little twinkle in his eyes when she smiled at him.

"Molly!" Alex yelled for her again. "Please!"

Molly didn't want to turn around. She wanted more than anything to go find him, to talk to him one more time. Tears began streaming down her cheeks as she tried to stifle her cries. Her chin trembled as she wiped her nose on her jacket sleeve. She winced, the sorrow and realization of her lost friend finally setting in. She felt the urge to keep running for him but was reminded of a conversation they had before.

Why have you been trying to keep me alive for this long? Wyatt had asked her.

Because I'm a decent human being, Richards.

Molly inhaled a shaky breath and turned around, dropping the gun to help her friends.

****

The two boys had made it all the way to the football field before Wyatt's legs gave out from underneath him. He had nothing left in him, so Derek just laid him down on the painted grass of the end zone he had been longing for just days ago during the playoff game. The oncoming storm from earlier had finally caught up with them as it began to sprinkle rain from the gray sky above them.

He turned to his best friend, whose eyes were closed. Fresh blood stained his white shirt, and his wild hair was sticking out in all different directions. His chest wasn't rising and falling, and his skin had turned pale. Wyatt Richards had passed away trying to avenge his friend and slay one of the beasts that haunted his town. Derek had a sneaking suspicion that this was only the beginning. Wyatt had simply chopped the head off, but two more would grow in its place.

He choked up at the sight of his friend, no longer fighting back the tears that blurred his vision. He let them fall as he sat next to Wyatt's lifeless body.

Thanks for everything, brother.

He laid down on the wet, green ground underneath them and stared at the sky. Only one thought entered his grief-stricken mind.

What do we do now?

A.P. JENNINGS

ABOUT THE AUTHOR

A.P. Jennings is the young, aspiring author behind Taken by the Night, a bold new entry in the Young Adult genre. He lives in Texas and is a fan of cinema, books, coffee, and classic rock. You can contact him at apjenningsbooks@gmail.com.

Made in the USA
Coppell, TX
18 March 2024

30274170R00275